The RIVERHAVEN YEARS

WHERE GRACE ABIDES

BJ HOFF

HARVEST HOUSE PUBLISHERS

EUGENE, OREGON

All Scripture quotations are taken from the King James Version of the Bible.

Cover by Koechel Peterson & Associates, Inc., Minneapolis, Minnesota

Cover photos © iStockphoto; Fotolia; Dreamstime; Photos.com

BJ Hoff: Published in association with the Books & Such Literary Agency, 52 Mission Circle, Suite 122, PMB 170, Santa Rosa, CA 95409-5370, www.booksandsuch.biz.

This is a work of fiction. Names, characters, places, and incidents are products of the author's imagination or are used fictitiously. Any resemblance to actual persons, living or dead, or to events or locales, is entirely coincidental.

ACKNOWLEDGMENTS

My ongoing thanks to the entire publishing community at Harvest House Publishers. It takes a surprising number of people to bring a book from its beginning to its release. These faithful folks apply their many and varied gifts to make every book they publish one of excellence and one that brings honor to the God they serve. To all of you and each of you, I am continually grateful for all your efforts to make every book I write the best it can be. If I tried to name each one of you, I'd be sure to leave someone out, but you know who you are—and I hope you know how much I appreciate you. Writing a book can be a long and stressful process. It can also be a lonely process were it not for all the help and encouragement I receive along the way.

Warmest thanks and appreciation to Nick Harrison, my infinitely patient and supportive editor. I couldn't begin to count the many contributions you make—and make so cheerfully—to my books. I genuinely wish my readers could somehow be aware of just how much an editor like Nick brings to a novel. I *am* aware of it on a continuing basis and extremely grateful for it all.

To Shane White, supreme motivator and tireless encourager—thank you for your unfailing optimism and your faith in your authors. You're our hero.

To Janet K. Grant, my patient and long-suffering agent who gives the song "Wind Beneath My Wings" new meaning. I am so grateful for you, and you know all the reasons.

To Kelly Standish and the geniuses at PulsePoint Design who pray for me, keep me centered, and do all the technical stuff that gives me brain freeze. You are an absolutely incredible team.

To my family—each precious one of you—for so many years you've made what I do not only possible but easier in every way. I am exceedingly blessed, and I never forget it.

And to my readers, let me say to you again what I've said many times before. For every note and email you've taken time to write, for every prayer you've offered on my behalf, for reading my stories and sharing my heart—God bless you.

FACING THE TRUTH

If we could push ajar the gates of life,
And stand within, and all God's workings see,
We could interpret all this doubt and strife,
And for each mystery could find a key.
But not today. Then be content, poor heart!
God's plans, like lilies pure and white, unfold:
We must not tear the close-shut leaves apart—
Time will reveal the calyxes of gold.

MARY RILEY SMITH

Amish settlement near Riverhaven, Ohio
Summer 1856

The truth weighed upon her heart, as heavy as a river rock.

Rachel stared out the window at the gloom of early evening drawing in on the meadow, bringing the long, dense shadows that held a hint of coming fall. A lonely quiet fell over the land every day now at this time, broken only by the sound of crickets sawing, an occasional barking of a dog, and in the distance the echo of the river running, always running its solitary way to other places she would never see.

He had pledged his love to her early in the spring. He meant to find a way to marry her, he'd said. He had asked her if she would be his wife, even going so far as to make her believe he would be willing to become Amish if she would have him as her husband.

"If you weren't Amish or if I weren't *Englisch*," he said, "would you marry me?"

And she had told him she would. Because she loved him. More than life itself, that's how much she loved Jeremiah Gant.

For two blissful months, she had actually believed it could happen. She had walked around like a dizzy schoolgirl with mush for brains, finding it nearly impossible to think a thought that didn't contain something of him in it, equally difficult to not speak of her ever deepening love for him even to her mother.

Of course, Mamma's own growing relationship with Dr. Sebastian made it easier than it might have been otherwise for Rachel to keep her silence. At any other time, her mother's sharp eye for the slightest change in her children almost certainly would have noticed the onset of an uncommon restlessness in her oldest daughter or the nearly giddy happiness that prompted her to smile when least expected.

And Susan Kanagy did have her ways of finding out what was going on in the lives of her young.

Oh, it had been so hard! At times Rachel had to stop herself from crying aloud that she loved Jeremiah Gant and he loved her. For the first time since Eli's death—going on four years now—she felt alive again, once more living in shining moments rather than in shadowed hours.

But the Plain People didn't discuss their courtships or romances, not even with their families, until after the banns were published two weeks before the wedding. Even a conventional courtship between two young Amish people was typically carried on in secret. The couple usually managed to be together only after dark. If their parents or other family members were aware of their trysts, they pretended not to notice.

Rachel and Jeremiah's love for each other was anything but "conventional." Truth be known, Rachel could be put out of the community for loving an *auslander*. Despite the fact that the People seemed to think highly of the former riverboat captain, if it were known that she had admitted her love for an outsider and allowed him to avow his affections for her—had even welcomed his embraces, chaste though they had been—she would be in deep trouble with the leadership of the church. She would almost certainly face the *Meidung*—the shunning.

Plain married Plain, and there were no exceptions.

Even Mamma and Dr. Sebastian never spoke openly about the near certainty that they would one day wed. Despite the fact that David Sebastian had been the physician to the entire Amish community for years and was treated with the utmost respect and friendship, until he had "proven himself" by living among them, learning their language, and in every way that mattered evidenced his sincere intention to convert to the Amish faith, the moments he and Mamma were able to spend together would be extremely rare and shared in secret.

But at least Dr. Sebastian's resolve to become Plain could be seen by all who knew him, and his pursuit of conversion met with the approval of the church leadership.

Jeremiah was another story.

Rachel had seen him only once in the past three weeks, at the carpenter shop he'd bought from Karl Webber. But her brother, who worked for Jeremiah, had also been there the entire time. No doubt Gideon believed Rachel had come solely to visit him, and of course she couldn't dare to tell him otherwise.

Not that she wasn't always glad to see her brother, especially since he'd left the Amish community to strike out on his own. Still, she'd been hoping for at least a few minutes alone with Jeremiah.

And just what did she think she could accomplish if she *had* managed to speak with him alone?

She could hardly come right out and ask him if his feelings for her had changed, even though that was exactly what she feared. Certainly he'd done nothing to make her think otherwise. He'd made no move to see her alone, and so far as she knew, he hadn't taken the first step toward becoming Amish himself—their only hope for ever being together as man and wife.

He knew she would never leave the People and had promised her he would never ask that of her, acknowledging that he would be the one to change. And yet as far as Rachel knew, he'd done nothing toward that end.

Was it possible that she was being unfair? After all, Jeremiah knew she was forbidden to be alone with him. Could it be that he was merely trying to protect her by keeping his distance?

And how could she be so sure that he *wasn't* talking with the leadership about the possibility of converting? Perhaps they simply hadn't given him their answer yet.

All her efforts to rationalize their situation brought little reassurance. Here it was, coming on to August, and so far nothing seemed to have changed. More than four months had passed, and their relationship remained the same as it had been back in April.

The questions, the doubts, and the seemingly endless waiting were quickly eroding her early happiness. Moreover, her faith in Jeremiah and his love was rapidly giving way to a sickness of the heart, a canker of discouragement and disappointment.

Rachel wanted to trust him, longed to believe in him. There had been a time when she'd been almost convinced that God had led him here to Riverhaven. Jeremiah, especially, had seemed so certain they could somehow overcome the obstacles to their being together that she'd found herself desperately wanting to share his belief.

Now she had to question if she'd simply fallen into the sin of believing that the Lord God's will was the same as *hers*. Had she been so eager for someone to fill her loneliness, so needy to love and be loved, that she'd only *assumed* Jeremiah to be God's answer to her prayers?

Shame and a bitter sense of humiliation swept over her. Might she have been so foolish, so naive, as to trap herself in a lie to her own spirit? It was a terrible thing to try to second-guess the Lord

God, even worse to assume that because she wanted something to be so, He willed it.

Would she ever be able to forgive herself if her love and her dreams had been based on nothing more than a flimsy cloud of self-deception?

More to the point, would *God* forgive her?

→ I ←

The Bishop's Response

Man's life is laid in the loom of time
To a pattern he does not see,
While the weavers work and the shuttles fly
Till the dawn of eternity…
Some shuttles are filled with silver threads
And some with threads of gold,
While often but the darker hues
Are all that they may hold…
God surely planned the pattern:
Each thread, the dark and fair,
Is chosen by His master skill
And placed in the web with care…
The dark threads were as needful
In the weaver's skillful hand
As the threads of gold and silver
For the pattern which He planned.

Author Unknown

Jeremiah Gant was in a sulk. A bad one.

In fact, he'd been in a black-water mood for two weeks now, and time, the proverbial healer of such things, had made no difference at all. Nor could he find any reason to believe it would.

So sour was his outlook this morning that he'd sent Gideon out on a delivery that just as easily could have waited another day or so. He liked Gideon Kanagy. The lad was a hard worker and good at his craft, and Gant had no regrets that he'd kept Rachel's brother as his employee upon taking over Karl Webber's carpenter shop. But this morning he needed to be alone. Something about working with wood, and working alone, usually helped him think.

And Gant needed to think.

When the bell clanged over the door, he ground his teeth, resenting the intrusion. He looked up from the table he was sanding to see David Sebastian. It was a sign of just how dark his mood really was that even the sight of his friend wasn't a particularly welcome one.

The doctor was wearing what Gant had come to think of as his "almost-Amish clothes." Doc had become a seeker—one in the process of converting to the Amish faith—and these days dressed accordingly in a dark shirt and trousers, suspenders, and a straw hat.

Normally Gant would be glad for such a visit. He and the physician had struck up a solid friendship over the past few months—albeit an unlikely one, Doc being British and Gant, Irish. But today, seeing the man in his Amish garb and knowing the direction their conversation would almost certainly take, Gant didn't feel up to feigning even the slightest cordiality.

Doc was well on his way to finally marrying the love of his life, once his conversion into the Amish church was final. Not only that, but his intended was Susan Kanagy—Rachel's mother.

And *Rachel* was the woman *Gant* wanted to marry but couldn't.

"Very nice," Doc said, coming to stand at the end of the table.

Gant shrugged. "It had better be. It's for Miss Marsh."

"Penelope Marsh?"

Gant nodded.

"She's fussy, all right. Obviously you've passed muster. Time was, no one but Karl Webber could please her."

"My being the only carpenter in town right now except for Gideon might have something to do with it."

"Where is Gideon?" Doc said glancing around.

Gant went on sanding. "Out on a delivery."

"Well, I just stopped by to say hello. But you seem busy."

Gant heard the tentative note in Doc's voice. "Not that busy," he said stilling his hand.

"I don't want to keep you—"

"I said I'm not that busy."

Doc regarded him with the eagle eye usually reserved for a patient. Gant recognized the look, having once *been* his patient.

"What's wrong?" said Doc.

"Nothing's wrong." Gant moved to change the subject. "You're looking pretty Amish these days. When do you grow the beard?"

"Not until we're closer to the wedding."

Gant pretended to study him closely. "It'll make you look older, you know."

"I don't care how I look so long as Susan will still marry me. And you can wipe that sneer off your face. You'll have to go through all this yourself once you hear from the bishop."

Gant glanced down at the table and started sanding again. "I heard from him."

Doc said nothing for a few seconds. Then, "*And?*"

Gant kept his head down. "He said, 'no.'"

He heard Doc draw a long breath. "No, *final*—or no, *maybe?*"

"Oh, it was final."

"So—what are you going to do?"

Again Gant stopped his work. "Not much I *can* do. The good bishop doesn't deem me a worthy prospect to join the People."

Doc caught a breath. "What, exactly, did he say?"

"Very little, in fact. Just that he has doubts as to the 'conviction' of my intentions. In so many words, he fears the only reason I want to convert is so I can marry Rachel, and that's hardly reason enough."

A long, heavy silence hung between them. When the doctor broke it, he seemed to choose his words carefully. "Well...that would be true enough if he's right."

Gant said nothing.

"You *have* thought this through, haven't you? I mean, you've told me more than once that you're convinced you can do this, that you *want* to do it—"

"What I want isn't actually the point now, is it?" Gant broke in. "It's what the Amish want. And clearly they don't want *me.*"

"So you're giving up?"

Short on patience and growing increasingly irritable with his friend's questions, Gant struggled to keep an even tone. "You know Bishop Graber better than I do. Am I missing something? His 'no' seemed pretty final to me."

"Surely he held out some hope for a later time."

"He held out nothing. He was civil, wished me well, and made it very clear I was to stay away from Rachel."

"Does she know about this yet?"

Gant shook his head.

"When did you find out?"

"Couple of weeks ago."

"A couple of *weeks* ago? And you still haven't told Rachel?"

By now Gant was grinding his teeth. "Just how am I to tell Rachel *anything*? I'm not supposed to go near her. I'm not supposed to talk to her or expose her to my *worldly influence.* How exactly am I supposed to let her know what's going on when I'm such bad business for her?"

"It's not like that, and you know it."

Doc shuffled his feet and made ready for one of his defenses of the Plain People, but Gant wasn't having any of it. Not today.

"But it *is* like that. It's manipulation, pure and simple."

"Oh, for goodness' sake. Put a lid on that Irish temper of yours and listen to me!"

Gant reared back in his chair staring at him. There wasn't another man this side of Ireland who could talk to him like that and get away with it. Only with an effort did he manage to hold his tongue.

Looking around, Doc pulled up a chair—a chair that Miss Penelope Marsh had already bought and paid for. He sat down, facing Gant across the table.

"You need to understand that the bishop isn't trying to shut you out because he's afraid you'll be a bad influence on Rachel."

"Is that so?" Gant made no attempt to soften the thick sarcasm of his tone.

"Yes, it *is* so. It's just that you represent the outside world to them, don't you see? It has nothing to do with your character or you as a person. You're simply an *auslander*. An outsider. It's a part of their faith to live separate from the world. They're committed to that."

Gant's face felt frozen in a scowl. "They've accepted you."

"But don't forget how long they've known me. I've been their physician for *years*. I've become their friend. They've finally grown to trust me, and—"

Gant waved off his explanations. "I know, I know," he said, finally managing to damp his irritation, albeit grudgingly. He met his friend's gaze straight on. "More to the point, you're their kind of person. I told you once before, it doesn't stretch the imagination to see you as Amish. You're already a lot like them. On the other hand, I'm not so blind that I can't see the distance between them and myself."

Doc regarded him with what appeared to be sympathy. His eyes were gentle—David Sebastian was a kind man—but his expression was solemn to the extreme. "Listen, my friend. I know you believe you can do this, but I have to ask: Is it possible that the bishop is right? Because if Rachel is your only motivation for wanting to join the Amish, it could well cause trouble for both of you eventually. And I know you care too much for her to hurt her."

Gant raked a hand down his neck. "Don't you think I've asked myself that a hundred times or more? I'm not stupid, Doc. Of course

I don't want to hurt her. I'd do anything *not* to hurt her. And to tell you the truth, I'm not sure but what Rachel *isn't* my only reason to wanting to convert."

He drew a long breath, then continued. "I thought there was more to it. I honestly did. But I'm beginning to wonder. Maybe I was wrong. Maybe if it weren't for Rachel, I would never have thought about turning. But right now, I'm more concerned about what it's going to do to Rachel if I *don't* turn. The last time we talked, it seemed to me she'd convinced herself that things were going to work out fine, that I'd be accepted, and other than maybe having to wait for a long time, everything would eventually fall into place."

He leaned forward a little. "How is she going to feel when she finds out I've been flat-out rejected? That we can't be together—not now, perhaps not ever?"

Doc sighed. "She'll be terribly hurt, of course. I hate to think how difficult this will be for her." He waited, then said, "There must be something to be done, some way to change the leadership's mind."

Gant wanted to believe his friend was right, yet didn't want to set himself up for another disappointment. "Well, you'd likely know more about that than I do. But right now, from where I stand, it looks pretty hopeless. And I have to tell you, I don't think this is right. No church ought to have this much control over their members, that they can tell them who they can talk to, who they can spend time with—who they can *marry*."

Doc was studying him as if trying to figure out what to say next.

"It's not a question of what's *right*," Doc said. "It's just the way it is, the way it's always been with the Plain People. At the heart of their faith and their culture is the belief that God wants them to separate themselves from the world, to live apart and be a community in and of themselves. For hundreds of years now, they've followed that belief, and they're not going to change."

He drummed his fingers on the table. "You already know the

Amish have been persecuted for their faith here in the States. But it was much worse for them in Europe. They were *martyred* there. Persecuted, jailed, driven out—and often killed—for their beliefs. If they didn't turn away from their faith in the midst of that sort of terror, then you can be sure they're not going to change now." He paused. "And if you've any thought of trying to persuade Rachel to leave the People for you, you'd best forget it."

"I wouldn't ask that of her," Gant said.

Wouldn't he?

More to the point, was his unwillingness to ask due to the unfairness of expecting such a sacrifice of her...or because he already knew her answer would be *no*?

"Don't take offense," Doc said. "You know, sometimes we're so convinced of a thing, so sure of it we can't help but believe it's God's will. Then when it doesn't work out, we get angry with Him. We even feel that He might have misled us. But God never misleads us. No matter how much it hurts, a disappointment is often simply His way of guiding us from the wrong path to the right."

He stopped, his gaze level but gentle. "This is a step of such importance, my friend, that you must be absolutely certain you take it for the right reasons."

"Well, apparently I'll not be taking it all," Gant muttered. He waited before going on. "But what about you? You're converting so you can marry Susan. Don't try to tell me it's anything else."

His charge didn't seem to faze Doc. "My desire to marry Susan is what finally gave me the shove I needed, that's true. But it's also what you said—I'm actually a lot like the Amish—at least I *want* to be like them. Being their physician and finally their friend after so many years has enabled me to get to know the people and their way of life well enough to realize that I want what they have. I want the peace, the simplicity, the abandonment to God in all things. I can live their way because I *want* to, not only because of Susan." He paused. "Is that how it is for you?"

Gant met his gaze for a long, silent moment before looking away. "I don't *know* how it is for me. That's as close to the truth as I can come right now."

"Well…I confess I wouldn't take you for a quitter. If and when you decide you're looking to make this change for the right reasons, I hope you won't take Bishop Graber's refusal as final. I don't know that you should."

"Is there something you're not saying?" Gant said, with a sour look.

Doc simply gave a half shrug. "No, I believe I've said enough. If you're in a better mood tonight, stop by for a game."

"You still allowed checkers, are you?" Gant grumbled.

"Oh, I'll still be beating you at checkers after I make my vows. As far as I know, checkers is approved as wholesome entertainment, even for the Amish."

With that, Doc said his goodbyes and headed toward the door, leaving Gant to nurture his bad mood by himself.

Thing was, Doc's words had left a mark on him. He'd have to think about what he'd said. Especially the part about not taking him as a "quitter." He *wasn't*. At least he never had been. Maybe… just maybe…Doc was right, that he shouldn't necessarily consider the bishop's decision as final.

He didn't want to, that much was certain.

For starters, though, he needed to shake this foul mood. Then he'd give Doc's little lecture some more thought.

2

WHEN HOPE FADES

Be strong, O Heart of mine,
Look toward the light!

ADELAIDE ANNE PROCTER

Rachel shook the last few drops out of the watering can. At the sound of a horse approaching, she turned and shaded her eyes, her hand trembling when she saw who was coming up the road.

Jeremiah.

The evening sun had begun to fade, but there was still enough light to frame his tall, erect form as he turned into the lane leading up to her house. He wore no coat—the day had been typically hot and humid for August—but what her sister, Fannie, called his "captain's cap" was pulled low over his forehead.

Rachel set the watering can on the garden bench but made no move to go and meet him. It had been nearly two weeks since she had last seen him, and even though she knew she shouldn't be seeing him at all—they had no business being together because he was an outsider and she, a widow alone—his absence had hurt and disturbed her.

The sight of him disturbed her even more.

She watched him ease off the horse he'd given the peculiar name of *Flann*, then reach for his cane before tethering the big ginger-red gelding to the fencepost. As he started up the path toward Rachel, his limp was obvious, though it had been several months since he'd been shot.

Doc Sebastian had warned him that he would always be lame but hinted that he might be able to do away with the cane eventually. The sight of his slow progress up the pathway tugged at Rachel's heart. He was so tall, so rugged in appearance and seemingly fit in all ways except for the stiffness and hesitancy of his gait. He still had pain too—she had seen him wince more than once at an awkward movement or unexpected stumble.

No matter how she tried to steel herself against feeling sorry for him—for Jeremiah was a proud man and would brook no pity if he were aware of it—she never failed to ache for what had been done to him.

His eyes locked with hers as he drew closer, his gaze steady but gentle when he reached her.

"Rachel," he said in the soft way he had of saying her name. Not quite a whisper but almost a sigh.

She couldn't find her voice, so she merely nodded.

For a moment he simply stood looking at her, his gaze as warm as a touch on her face, though his expression was unusually solemn. "We need to talk."

Instinctively Rachel glanced around.

His mouth tightened. "Surely you can't be faulted for standing outside with me. It's still daylight."

"I don't think—"

"It's important, Rachel."

He held her gaze, and Rachel knew with a sudden twist of dread that whatever he meant to tell her would not be anything she wanted to hear.

Surely it would be best to go inside so they wouldn't be seen together. But if anyone saw his horse, they would know who was here. No one else among the People owned such a brightly colored and fierce looking animal, so it was no secret who he belonged to.

"I know you'd rather not be seen with me—"

"It's not that—"

But it was *exactly* that. Jeremiah was forbidden to her. He was an *auslander*. An outsider. There was no acceptable reason for them to be together. Even standing here, in the golden light of evening, she would be risking her reputation, inviting censure or worse by keeping company with a stranger.

But Jeremiah was no stranger. She had cared for him in her home, helped nurse him back to health. He was her friend…No, much more than a friend. He was the man she had grown to love.

A love that could have her shunned, torn apart from her family, her friends, her church.

As if he could see the conflict of her emotions, he made the decision for her. "Let me just take Flann around back," he said, "and we'll talk inside."

Of course, anyone facing the rear of her property could still see the horse. Still, she decided it would be best to go inside. "All right," she said, her voice unsteady. "But you can't stay long."

There was no missing the irritation that crossed his strong features, but he said nothing, merely turned to go and get the horse.

Inside, the kitchen was already growing dim with the day's waning light, but Rachel made no effort to light the oil lamp, resolved to keep his visit to only a few moments at most.

He doffed his cap upon entering. When Rachel made no indication that he should sit down, he gestured to one of the chairs at the table. "May I?"

She hesitated but finally nodded. It went against everything she'd been taught not to offer him something to eat or at least a cup of coffee, but he seemed no more inclined toward a social visit than she did. To the contrary, she knew him well enough to recognize the drawn expression of his features. It occurred to her again that whatever he had to tell her wasn't going to be pleasant.

He waited until she sat down, then hooked his cane on the back of the chair across from her, and lowered himself to it.

She couldn't bring herself to meet his eyes. They sat not speaking until the silence became awkward.

"I've missed you, Rachel," he finally said, watching her, obviously waiting for a reply.

At last Rachel looked at him but said nothing.

"How are you keeping, then?"

By now she knew that this was his peculiar way—perhaps an Irish way—of asking how she had been. "I'm…well. And you?"

How foolish they sounded. How formal and stiff and—unfamiliar. Like strangers, they were.

He gave a thin smile and shrugged.

Although Jeremiah usually was one to come right to the point, he seemed to be having a difficult time of it today. "Have you seen Gideon lately? You might want to know that he's a fine worker, a real help to me at the shop."

"I'm glad," Rachel said. "He enjoys his work."

He gave an idle nod, lacing his hands together on top of the table.

Again silence overtook them.

Watching him, Rachel's throat felt as if she'd swallowed dust. "You said you wanted to talk with me." For some reason she couldn't manage to say his name. Perhaps because for so long she had loved saying it. It made her think of music. Even more it made her feel close to him.

At this moment, however, she sensed it would be foolish, even treacherous, to allow that feeling of closeness.

He looked up from his hands, his mouth bracketed by hard lines, his eyes shadowed. "I should have come sooner, I know."

Rachel felt his eyes on her, but she was unable to look at him, unwilling to hear what he had to say. Somehow she knew that his words would break her heart.

3

LEAVING RACHEL

Withered is the early flower…

GERALD GRIFFIN

She could at least *look* at him.

Clearly she wasn't about to help him through this. He hadn't expected such coldness from her. That she might be piqued with him or even hurt because he'd stayed away for so long—that wouldn't have surprised him. But he hadn't expected this *distance* from her. It was as if she scarcely knew him.

Gant wanted to reach for her, to take her hand, but he sensed that any such move on his part would meet only with rejection. So he swallowed, cleared his throat, and began.

"I met with Bishop Graber."

Still she kept her eyes averted. One hand rested in her lap, the other on top of the table. When he saw her fingers tremble, Gant's instinct to touch her was renewed.

"Rachel?"

Finally she looked at him. The pain that slipped past the guarded gaze warned him that she knew what he was about to say.

"He won't agree to my conversion."

Saying nothing, she stared at the table, then gave a small nod.

"He doesn't trust my motives. He thinks the only reason I want to join the church is so you and I can marry."

Her head came up, her eyes questioning.

"I wasn't able to convince him otherwise."

Now Gant found himself unable to meet *her* gaze. He knew the question that he would encounter in her eyes, and he couldn't bring himself to lie to her. As he'd told Doc, he no longer trusted his own conviction. Maybe Rachel *was* his only reason for wanting to convert. He couldn't be sure. But wasn't it enough that he *would* convert, that he would change his entire way of life to marry her? What if that *was* his only reason or, at least, the most important reason? Why couldn't that be enough?

"Then he also told you to stay away from me, didn't he?"

As always her voice was quiet, level, and controlled. But her eyes pierced his so intensely Gant felt as if she were cutting through to his very soul.

Even if he were tempted to lie to her—and he was, just for a moment—what good would it do? She would find out the truth soon enough. Besides, she deserved to hear it from him, not the bishop or someone else.

"Yes. He said we're not to see each other. At least not alone."

"Like this," she said quietly.

He made a gesture of frustration with one hand. "I don't accept his decision, Rachel. I can't. There has to be a way."

Something akin to alarm flared in her eyes. "No, Jeremiah. There *is* no way. There will never be a way."

"There has to be *something*—"

"There's not," she said sharply, her chair scraping the floor as she pushed back from the table and stood. "The only thing we can do is exactly what Bishop Graber said. We have to stay away from each other."

Gant also got to his feet. "You would do that, Rachel? You'd accept his decision without even trying to find a way to change his mind?"

"It's what I *have* to do! The bishop's decision is the last word in such matters. I can't go against him."

She turned away. Gant knotted his fists at his sides to keep from slamming them on the table. "Can't or *won't?*"

She came around slowly, and now her expression was one of sadness. "They're one and the same, Jeremiah. I can't go against my church. My faith. This is my life. It's all I have."

"You could have more, Rachel. We could have each other. A life together, children—"

"No." Her voice was little more than a whisper. "No, we can't. Not if it means giving up everything I know, everyone I love."

He stared at her long and hard. "But you're willing to give *me* up. What about *our* love?"

She blinked, and he thought he saw tears in her eyes. For one insane moment, Gant wanted to grab her and force her to admit that she couldn't face a life without him any more than *he* could her. He wanted to take her away from here, leave Riverhaven, go any place where they could be together.

Madness. The truth was that she *could* live her life without him. She had the support of an entire community and a family deeply devoted to her. If he were to leave, Rachel's life would go on, much the same as it always had.

Oh, she might miss him for a time—but probably not for long. Eventually she would get past whatever pain their parting might cause her and go on. One day she would marry another man and have a full life.

The very thought of that man, whoever he might be, blistered his heart with jealousy.

In this moment all he could see was a vast emptiness spread out in front of him. What kind of a wasteland would his life be without her, now that he had found her and grown to love her so fiercely? How could he just walk away, never see her again, never talk to her again, as if he'd never known her?

He couldn't. He *wouldn't*.

"Rachel—"

He took a step toward her, but she raised a hand to stop him. "Don't. I...want you to leave now, Jeremiah. Please."

He stopped, his eyes locked on her even though she wouldn't look at him. "You can do this, then? You can dismiss me, just like that, simply put me out of your life? Is it really so easy for you, Rachel?"

Slowly she raised her eyes to his, and the look she turned on him stunned Gant into silence.

"Is that what you think? That this is *easy* for me?"

He saw the tremor in her hands as she faced him.

"That's not what I meant—"

She shook her head as if to shake off his words. "When you first said that...you loved me, I told you then it was hopeless, that the only way we could ever be together was if I were to give up being Amish, leave my family, my life. But you wouldn't listen. No, you said we were meant to be together, that somehow we *would* be together, that you would find a way for us to marry—that you would make it happen."

He nodded. "I know what I said. And I meant it, Rachel. I believed it."

She dropped her gaze. "And in my foolishness, I believed it too. So when you hinted that you might be willing to become Amish, I suppose I believed that as well."

"Rachel, I tried, and I'm going to keep on trying—"

Again she shook off his attempted protest. "No. This is my fault, not yours. I surely knew that night when you—when you told me how you felt—I must have known then it couldn't happen. But I let you convince me, or rather, I convinced myself. I let myself imagine that it might be possible after all. That was my mistake— believing it could come about...just because I wanted it. I see now that I was wrong in letting *you* believe it and wrong in allowing *myself* to believe it."

She stopped. Her gaze searched his eyes. "Don't you see, Jeremiah? Truth be known, Bishop Graber has done us a kindness in refusing to allow your conversion. He understands that it would be wrong—so very wrong—for you to join us, to become Amish, only to marry me. Sooner or later you'd come to resent me. At the least, you'd resent your decision. To live Amish isn't simply a decision you make. It's a way of life. It *is* your life. It's everything you are, everything you do."

A sick heaviness settled itself over Gant's chest. She was giving him no room for argument, no opportunity to convince her that this wasn't yet finished, that he meant to fight for her, whatever it took. Yet at the same time, a whisper of uneasiness insinuated itself at the edge of his mind, that his determination to somehow win over the bishop's consent might actually confirm the old man's accusation—that his only reason for wanting to convert was so he could marry Rachel.

The pain in her eyes, the look of dejection clouding her loveliness nearly undid him. "Rachel—give me time. Let's think this through together. Somehow we'll find a way—"

"No, Jeremiah." In spite of the sadness that seemed to have settled over her, her voice was surprisingly firm. "The bishop's decision is God's will, and we have to accept it. I can't…" She let her thought drift off, unfinished, for a long moment. Then, "I can't deceive myself any longer. I want you to go now, and I'm asking you to not come back."

Gant clenched his fists at his sides until pain shot up his arms. "The bishop isn't God, Rachel!"

Her eyes widened as if he'd committed blasphemy. "Of course, he's not! But he's our bishop, and I can't go against him."

Again he accused her. "You mean you *won't* go against him."

A look of impatience flicked across her features, but her voice held that same maddening calm when she replied. "You don't understand, Jeremiah. I don't expect you to. Unless you're Amish, you *can't* understand."

Gant knew he was dangerously close to losing his temper. But at this point he was too afraid that he was losing *Rachel* to be careful. "I expect you're right. If being Amish means letting yourself be ordered about as if you have no mind of your own, then I definitely do not understand!"

She reacted to the harshness of his words by passing a hand over her face in a gesture of weariness. Her shoulders slumped slightly, and Gant immediately felt a sting of regret. The last thing he wanted was to hurt her, yet he was doing just that.

He studied her, waiting. When she said nothing, he expelled a long breath saying, "Do you really want me to go, Rachel?"

She bowed her head and gave a small nod.

Heaviness overwhelmed Gant, as he crushed his cap between his hands. "All right, then. I'll go, but, Rachel—"

She didn't look up.

"If you're determined to give up on us, I can't stop you. But don't you think for a moment that *I'm* giving up." He stopped, hoping for a word from her. When it didn't come, he added, "If you should change your mind, if you ever want to talk, or if you should need me for any reason—any reason at all—you've only to ask. You know where to find me. I'm not going anywhere."

He started for the door, then turned back only to find her exactly as she'd been, standing in silence, her gaze locked on the floor.

He left her there, forcing himself not to leave his hope behind as well.

⇢ 4 ⇠

A SECRET WANDERLUST

For we are the same things our fathers have been;
We see the same sights our fathers have seen;
We drink the same stream, and feel the same sun,
And run the same course our fathers have run.

WILLIAM KNOX

Gideon Kanagy was on his way back to the shop when he met up with Emma Knepp. As was her way, she walked with purpose, head down, her steps brisk, hands clasped at her waist.

Emma always seemed to know exactly where she was going, as if she'd plotted her destination well in advance and knew precisely what route would take her there. Gideon wasn't surprised to see that, though the day was warm, she wore a black shawl, pinned in front, and a black bonnet.

Emma lived the way of the Plain People, with great attention to the rules.

She was pretty though. The fair hair, just barely peeking out from under her bonnet, glistened in the afternoon light, and her complexion seemed touched year-round with an apricot blush.

It was a wonder she was still unmarried. From what Gideon had heard, it wasn't for lack of trying by some of the single fellows in the Riverhaven area. So far as he knew, though, she'd not yet allowed any one of them to court her.

He was almost in her face, before she looked up and recognized him.

"Emma," he said, planting himself in front of her so she had to stop.

Her face flamed. "Oh—Gideon! Hello. I didn't see you."

"Where are you headed in such a hurry?"

She looked confused. "I...was supposed to meet Dat and my brothers back at the buggy, but I ran into Sally Lape, and we got to talking. Now I'm afraid I'm late."

Emma was the only daughter in a family with three sons, all older than she. Her father, Levi Knepp, was known to be plenty strict with all his children—but especially with his only daughter. Gideon wasn't surprised that she seemed a little flustered by the thought of showing up late.

Even so, he made no effort to move out of her way. "How's your family?"

Without really looking at him—for whatever reason, Emma *never* quite looked at him but always just past him somewhere— she replied, "Everyone is *gut*. And yours? Your mamma and Rachel and Fannie?"

"Far as I know, they're just fine," he said watching her.

He hadn't been up close to Emma for several months and was caught unawares by just how attractive she actually was. She didn't have the dramatic good looks of his latest interest, Abby Frey, who was *Englisch* and prettied herself up by curling her hair some and using a little rouge. Emma, being Plain, wouldn't resort to such worldly adornments.

But then Emma didn't *need* such worldly adornments.

Even though she wouldn't meet his gaze, he knew those eyes. They were a color of a blue that held a touch of smoke and sky, with long, ink-heavy lashes that looked to brush her cheeks when she blinked. He remembered that she blinked often. In fact, more than once Gideon had wondered if Emma needed to wear eyeglasses.

He realized now that he always thought of Emma Knepp as a *girl*. A child. He was older than she by at least two years and had watched her grow up. For the first time, it struck him that she was no longer a girl but a young woman. A young woman lovely enough to steal a fellow's breath away and, unless she'd changed a lot, with a sweetness of spirit to equal her comeliness, though she'd always been reserved to the point of an awkward shyness.

"I should go," she said abruptly, looking past him as if in search of an escape route.

Gideon hesitated, reluctant to let her pass. Finally, though, he stepped aside, saying, "Give my best to your family."

She glanced at him, then quickly looked away. "Yes—all right," she stammered.

"And stop by the shop next time you're in town and say hello," he added, knowing full well she would do no such thing.

He would no longer be in the Knepp family's good graces—if he ever had been. Though he hadn't been shunned, having never joined church in the first place, he was living outside the community and working for an *Englischer*. Levi Knepp would not want him associating with his only daughter.

More to the point, Levi's *daughter* didn't seem overly eager to associate with him.

He watched her hurry up the boardwalk. From time to time, some of his Amish friends had teased him about Emma being "sweet" on him. Now he found himself wondering if she *had* been. Truth be known, he'd never thought of Emma that way. She had always been just Levi Knepp's shy daughter who lived up the road.

For a moment he entertained the idea of Emma liking him and found it oddly pleasing. Just as quickly he shook it off. There was no way he'd be courting Emma Knepp as long as he lived outside the Plain community.

Besides, he already had a girl, and a pretty one in her own right. Abby had the reputation of being a little wild, but that was all right.

He wasn't of a mind to settle down, not for a long time. An *Englisch* girlfriend who wasn't all tied up in a bunch of rules and restrictions suited him just fine for now, though when it came time to marry, she wasn't the sort he'd turn to.

He watched Emma until she was out of sight, then turned and started off again for the shop.

He saw the wagon at the same time he reached Edgar Folsom's leather shop.

The day was dry and hot, and the big draft horse kicked up a thick cloud of dust and stones in spite of its slow pace. The heat and the dirt burned Gideon's throat, and he put his hand up to cover his mouth.

It took him a moment to recognize the driver of the rattling farm wagon. He stopped where he was, struggling to remember the man's name. When it finally registered, he raised an arm to hail him.

"*Asa!*"

The big black dog stood up on the driver's bench and barked, and the driver shot a puzzled look in Gideon's direction. Then, as recognition lighted his eyes, he slowed the horse and pulled up to the rail beside the boardwalk, where Gideon met him.

Asa gave a nod. "Mr. Gideon."

"You remember me, then," Gideon said. "Well, I expect you're looking for the captain."

"I am." The dog barked again, and Asa shushed him. "Miss Rachel—your sister—told me I'd find him at the carpenter's shop here in town."

"You went to Rachel's first? Oh, that's right—you wouldn't have known where to come otherwise."

Asa looked past Gideon to the buildings behind him. "The captain—"

"The shop is just three doors down," Gideon said, hauling himself up on the side of the wagon. "You can pull around back. Come on, I'll show you."

The dog—"Mac," as he recalled—looked Gideon over with those eerie eyes that seemed almost human in their piercing intelligence, but he remained quiet.

Gideon pointed the way up the street to the narrow lane that ran between the shop and Hudson's dry goods store. "Turn down there. Captain Gant sure will be glad you're back. He's been real worried about you."

"How is the captain?" Asa's expression left no doubt as to his concern for his friend. "Is he well?"

"He's doing all right. Of course, you know about his leg. I can tell it still bothers him some. But he never mentions it."

Asa nodded knowingly, turning off the lane and pulling around to the rear of the buildings.

"Here we are," Gideon said, gesturing to the back door of the shop. "You can pull your wagon right up there by the storage shed."

Gideon smiled to himself as he imagined the captain's surprise. Gant was a quiet man, never a big talker, but lately he'd been even more reserved than ever. He was an unhappy man these days, there was no missing it, and if Gideon were to guess the reason for his employer's grim disposition, he was fairly sure it had to do with Rachel.

In any event, he hoped Asa's return would cheer the captain up a little.

It caught him off-guard to realize that he actually cared about his employer's feelings. When Gant first showed up in Riverhaven, Gideon's attitude had ranged between curiosity about the mysterious stranger's past and resentment for the problems he brought upon Gideon's sister Rachel by turning up wounded on her doorstep.

After working for him for several months, though, he'd found the former riverboat captain an easy man to respect, even like, albeit not an easy sort to get close to. From the beginning, Gant had treated him like a man, not a boy, complimenting him on his work when warranted and teaching him more than Gideon had ever learned from the former owner of the shop, Karl Webber.

Gant had magic in his hands when it came to wood, and there seemed no project he wouldn't tackle, no problem he couldn't solve. He was also an interesting man. Gideon had no idea whether he had educated himself or gone to some fancy school, but he clearly knew a lot about a lot of other things besides carpentry.

Gideon liked to get him talking about his life on the river and some of the places he'd been. It seemed that Gant had been in several different states, even way up north. He didn't seem to mind answering Gideon's questions. And Gideon never ran out of questions for him to answer.

He had always wanted to travel and see faraway places. Rachel had once accused him of having a "wanderlust" in him. Was that such a bad thing? He had never been *anywhere*, after all, had never ventured farther away from Riverhaven than Marietta and once, when he was a boy too young to remember much about the trip, had gone with his family to visit relatives near Columbus. Gant's stories made it possible to imagine different places, even though Gideon might never see them for real.

He had never taken to farming. He liked the land well enough, liked to be outdoors and even liked to watch things grow and come to maturity. But the *process* of planting and tending and harvesting he found tedious.

Many times while he was still growing up and living at home, he would walk away from their property. He would walk for miles through the fields and into the woods or sometimes go down by the river and simply sit and watch the big boats, trying to imagine where they were going and what they would see along the way.

He glanced at Asa, as they started for the back door, Mac trotting along at their side. Could be he'd have a chance to hear even more stories now. The captain never talked about the business he and Asa carried on with the runaway slaves, but Gideon knew what they were up to. He'd overheard enough conversations between his mother and Rachel—and between Gant and Dr. Sebastian—to be pretty sure that the captain and Asa were involved with the mysterious Underground Railroad.

He also knew that even though Captain Gant had had to give up his traveling for the time being because of his bad leg, he *hadn't* given up helping a runaway slave every now and then. He'd seen things the captain didn't know he'd seen—at night—when he stood at the window of his upstairs room in the back of the shop and looked toward Gant's house on the hill.

Every now and then, the flickering light of a lantern could be seen, traveling back and forth between the house and the barn, and on more than one occasion, he had spied the shadowed form of someone moving around the side of Gant's house. That was particularly strange, seeing as how the captain lived alone.

He wasn't quite sure why the idea of the Underground Railroad fascinated him as it did. Maybe because it represented a way of escape from a life that held nothing but back-breaking work and drudgery and the dreary repetition of days without excitement or adventure or joy. Until he'd left home, that was how he'd sometimes felt about his own life.

Or maybe it was more because the very thought of slavery repelled him. He couldn't imagine what it must be like to be *owned* by another human being, for one man to belong to another as if he were of no more worth than a dog.

He and some of his friends had often talked about the subject of slavery, and what he'd heard left him shocked and sickened. He had resolved that if he ever had a chance, he'd gladly do his part to make a difference against such an ugly, ungodly system.

Of course, it was forbidden to the Amish to meddle in the affairs of the world, but he wasn't living Amish anymore. Besides, it didn't even seem Christian to ignore such a rampant evil as if it didn't exist.

Not for the first time, he wondered how he might go about making Gant realize that he could be of some use to him—and Asa—in their antislavery efforts.

As they reached the back door, his gaze went to Asa again, who stood watching him, clearly waiting for Gideon to enter the shop first. The thought struck him that perhaps he could enlist Asa's help in convincing Gant to make a place for him on that "railroad" of theirs.

≫5≪

New Arrivals
in Riverhaven

Man is dear to man; the poorest poor
Long for some moments in a weary life,
When they can feel and know that they have been
Themselves the fathers and the dealers-out
Of some small blessings; have been kind to such
As needed kindness, for the single cause
That we have all of us one common heart.

Author Unknown

G ant was hunched over his desk, sorting through orders, when the back door slammed.

Gideon, of course. The boy didn't seem to know how to close a door without shaking the walls.

He looked up just as Mac came thundering across the room, his tail wagging wildly in a circle as he hurled himself at Gant.

The big black dog hit him full-force with both enormous paws, slamming against Gant's chest, nearly tipping the chair over.

Gant laughed with delight. "Mac! Where have you *been,* you big oaf?"

He put both arms around the dog's thick, furry neck and gave him a proper hug, so happy and relieved to see him he could have sent up a shout.

Another glance toward the back door revealed Asa and Gideon, both smiling as they watched. Gant's heart lightened still more. He pushed back from the desk and hauled himself to his feet. "Well, about *time*," he said, with feigned sarcasm.

They met halfway across the room. Gant grasped his friend's hand in both of his. "You're all right, then?"

Asa nodded. "And you, Captain? Are you well?"

Gant waved off his question. "Fit as can be."

Asa's dark gaze went over his face with an unsettling skepticism. Gant was aware he'd lost a bit of weight and hadn't been sleeping all that well. Still, he was sure he looked a sight better than his friend. Asa's features were taut, his hair sprinkled with more gray than Gant remembered, his clothes dusty and rumpled. He wore the expression of a man exhausted.

"Gideon—bring some water. For both of these fellows."

At the sound of the word "water," the dog followed the boy, tail wagging as he went.

"You got word about the delay?" said Asa.

"I did. Twice. Even so, I never thought it would take you this long."

"Ah. You were worried about me." Asa's grin returned.

"I didn't say that, although it did occur to me you might have got yourself lost."

An old joke between them, the other's sense of direction being flawless, in truth, even keener than Gant's.

"No trouble on the way back?" he asked.

Asa shook his head. "Other than a sheriff who didn't like the idea of my being a free man. I was…a guest in his jail for a week."

Anger stabbed at Gant. "Didn't you have your papers on you?"

He had paid for Asa's freedom years before and continually reminded him to keep his papers on him at all times.

Asa's smile turned grim. "The sheriff, he suspected my papers might not be legitimate. He thought they might be forged."

"Jail," Gant said with disgust. "That's not right. I'm sorry that happened to you."

Asa shrugged. "It wasn't your doing, Captain. And as you can see, I'm no worse for wear. Even the food wasn't too bad."

Because Asa's island accent tended to thicken when he grew indignant or angry, Gant wasn't fooled. Such an incident would have been humiliating to the extreme.

"So what convinced him to let you go? Where was this, by the way?"

"Northern Ohio. A small town close to Cleveland. Somehow one of their vigilance committees in the area got word of my circumstances, and a party of those good people made bail for me." He paused. "The sheriff seemed reluctant to part with my company, but the bail money apparently made all the difference."

Gant waited as Gideon put a cup and a jug of water on the table, then poured some into a bowl for Mac. Gideon remained by the table, watching them, apparently intent on taking in the conservation. That wouldn't do, as there were things he and Asa needed to talk about that the boy shouldn't hear.

"Don't you have deliveries to make?" Gant said.

"Nope. Took care of them earlier this afternoon," Gideon replied.

Gant looked at him. "You can be done for the day, then."

The boy's direct, studying gaze clearly said he knew he was being dismissed. "I don't mind staying. In case you need me later."

"It's almost time to close up anyway. I won't have anything more for you today."

Gideon's reluctance to leave was obvious. "Don't you want me to sweep up first? I haven't unloaded the wagon from the lumber yard yet either."

"In the morning will be soon enough. Go on now," Gant said with a dismissing motion of his hand. "Go and do whatever it is you and the other lads do to amuse yourselves after—"

He broke off when a horse shrieked outside, followed by the sound of someone shouting and a woman's scream.

The three men headed for the front door. His jaws dripping water from his hasty drink, Mac reached it first. The big dog stood waiting, clearly agitated and anxious to get outside.

It took only a moment to spot a rickety-looking wagon, listing heavily to one side. The few onlookers drawn to the scene stood watching, but no one seemed to be offering any help. The black horse still hitched to the wagon stamped the ground, puffing and snorting, while a man in dusty clothes held his arms up to a young woman swollen with child.

Gideon jumped from the boardwalk and started toward them, parting the bystanders as he went. Gant followed, moving as quickly as he could while Asa went for the horse.

The rear wheel was clearly broken. Gideon trigged a wheel to keep the wagon from rolling, then joined Gant and put a shoulder to it to make sure it held steady, while the man lifted the woman free and helped her onto the boardwalk. In the meantime, Asa tried to soothe the nervous horse, talking low and level as he unhitched it and tethered it to a post. Mac trotted back and forth from Asa to the wagon, as if to oversee it all.

After taking the couple inside the shop, Gant motioned to a bench behind a table, then moved to stand across from them. Her husband—at least Gant assumed he was her husband, given her condition—stood behind her hovering.

She was a mere slip of a girl with a delicate, waiflike face and flaxen hair tumbling free of her bonnet. Dust smudged her features, and she appeared mute with shock and exhaustion.

Gideon quickly appeared just then with two cups of water from the pump in back, and the strangers drained them as thirstily as if that water was the best thing they'd ever tasted.

Gant studied the man, who didn't look much older than his

wife. He was a red-haired fellow with a lean, somber face, mottled with dirt from the road.

As if he sensed Gant's scrutiny, he said, "I'm Terrence Sawyer— 'Terry,' folks call me—and this is my wife, Ellie. We're real grateful to you for helping us." His voice was quiet with a soft, easy drawl.

Gant introduced himself, then Gideon and Asa. "Where are you folks from?" he said.

"Virginia, sir. Western Virginia. We're on our way to Indiana. Looking to farm out there. But we've had some trouble."

"What kind of trouble is that?" Gant nodded Sawyer to the space beside his wife. "Why don't you sit down, son? I expect you're tired from traveling."

With a grateful look, Terry Sawyer slipped in beside his wife. "We got robbed on the road just after we crossed over into Ohio. Two fellows lookin' for runaway slaves, they said. But they seemed more interested in stealing what we had than catching slaves."

He glanced at Asa, then turned quickly back to Gant.

"They took all the money we had and some of our food." His face hardened. "Said they'd been on the road a long time and needed it worse than we did. They didn't hurt us any, though—just robbed us."

"That's bad luck," Gant offered, sending Gideon for more water.

Sawyer nodded. "I'm not sure what we'll do now. We're too far from home to turn around and go back, even if we could. Besides, we don't really have anything to go back to. My folks pulled up stakes a few months ago and moved to Kentucky to stay with my older brother, and Ellie doesn't have any family. And with the wagon wheel busted, we can't go anywhere."

Gant watched as Gideon returned and set a full jug of fresh water on the table. Sawyer filled his wife's cup, then his own, drinking it all straight down again without a breath.

"I expect I can fix your wagon wheel," Gideon said, moving to stand near Asa. "I've fixed a lot of buggy wheels. Most likely it's the axle."

"I'd be grateful," said Sawyer, "but we don't have any money."

Gideon shrugged. "That's not a problem. It won't take me that long."

Gant looked at him, not all that surprised to hear the boy make such an offer.

Sawyer glanced down at the floor, then at Gideon. "That's real kind of you. But I *will* pay for your work just as soon as I can. Once we're settled and all, I'll send you whatever we owe."

Always quick on the uptake, Gideon studied him for a moment. Then, as if he realized he might insult the other by refusing, he said, "Sure, that's fine."

"In the meantime," Gant put in, "you folks will need a place to stay." He turned to Gideon. "Take them down to Mrs. Haining's boardinghouse. She's always got an extra room or two."

Sawyer frowned, and a crimson stain worked its way up his neck. "I can't pay for a room. We'll do all right in the back of the wagon."

Gant considered his words. "Son, even if you could make do in the back of a broken-down wagon, you don't want to put your wife through it. She needs a good rest. Don't worry about the money for now. It'll be taken care of."

Sawyer's wife spoke for the first time. "We're ever so grateful, Mr. Gant. And we will find a way to repay you." Her level blue gaze left little doubt that they would do just that.

Gant waved off her thanks. "That'll be fine," he said, then motioned to Gideon to follow him. "I have something in back you can deliver while you're out."

In the back room, he gave Gideon some money. "This should cover a room and meals for a couple of days. Give it to Mrs. Haining and tell her if they need to stay longer, I'll take care of it. Be sure she knows they'll be needing supper."

"If you can spare me some time tomorrow, I'll work on that wheel."

"I can spare you the time, but I have a feeling they may not be going anywhere too soon."

Gideon shot him a questioning look, but understanding almost instantly filled his eyes. "Mrs. Sawyer—you think it might be her time soon?"

Gant shrugged. "It's not for me to ask, but I wouldn't be a bit surprised."

Gant's thoughts were troubled as he watched the boy return to the front of the shop. It seemed things couldn't be much harder for the Sawyers. A broken wagon, not a cent to their names, and if he wasn't mistaken, a baby about to be born. They were going to need some help, all right. Most likely a *lot* of help.

Yet there was something about them, something that left no doubt but what they would be all right even without the help of anyone else. In spite of their youth, their hard luck, and difficult circumstances, a warm steadiness and quiet strength bespoke the love they shared and the bond that joined them, no matter what.

Gant suddenly recognized a feeling inside himself akin to envy. Envy of what the Sawyers had together. Though they appeared to have *nothing,* he sensed they had *everything.*

They had what he wanted, what he'd hoped for—and still longed for—with Rachel.

He was the one who had nothing. He had a house and a business and more money than he needed. He had enough to help the Sawyers and others like them who lacked material goods and even the most tenuous means of security, and for that he was truly grateful.

But wouldn't they be surprised if they knew how quickly he would trade places with them if he could have Rachel at his side.

GATHERING OF DARKNESS

Dear refuge of my weary soul,
On thee, when sorrows rise,
On thee, when waves of trouble roll,
My fainting hope relies.

ANNE STEELE

September

Even though the day had been warm and still summer-sweet, a chill came on the air when evening gathered.

Susan Kanagy stood staring out the kitchen window, her gaze settling for a moment on her youngest daughter still playing happily on her tree swing, then traveling to her oldest, sitting at the kitchen table as she iced the last sheet of cookies they'd baked earlier that afternoon. Rachel's movements were slow and distracted, her features drawn in the all too familiar expression of sadness she often wore these days. Obviously icing cookies was the last thing on her mind.

Susan thought she knew what was on her daughter's mind.

Jeremiah Gant.

Rachel wore that look most of the time now, had worn it ever since Bishop Graber refused to consent to the captain's conversion to their Amish faith. The bishop's refusal, of course, meant that Rachel and Gant couldn't marry. Moreover, it meant they were to stay completely away from each other.

Susan hadn't seen her daughter so broken since Eli died. Her young husband's death, so untimely, so brutal, had left Rachel drowning in years of pain and sadness before she'd finally found a measure of healing. Jeremiah Gant's arrival in Riverhaven and their growing affection for each other had helped to further that healing, but now here she was again, her heart grieving, her spirit struggling.

Oh, she put a good face on things, Rachel did. With Susan and with her little sister, Rachel managed to pretend her days were full, her life good. Never one to burden another, even her closest friends would not see Rachel weep.

But Susan had. She had held her sweet daughter when Rachel sobbed out her accounting of the attack that had left her husband dead and her life in shambles. And she had held her again after the bishop passed down his decision about Gant, along with his stern admonition that the two could not marry and must not see each other again.

Although a couple's relationship wasn't to be discussed, there had never been many secrets between her and Rachel. The Amish did keep such things private, even among family members. Truth be told, she wasn't even supposed to know about the affection her daughter and Captain Gant shared. But she and Rachel had always been close, friends as well as mother and daughter, and when Rachel had sought comfort from her, Susan would no more have turned her away than she would have refused to tend to her wounds if she'd been physically injured.

In her heart of hearts, there were some things about living Amish she found difficult to accept. To pretend no relationship had existed between Rachel and the man she loved and then to know her daughter was in pain and not offer solace—this, she could not do.

She went to her now. "Your thoughts seem far away, daughter," she said, putting a light hand on Rachel's shoulder.

Rachel turned, looked up, and gave a small quirk of her lips—a smile that wasn't really a smile. "Not all that far, Mamma. I was thinking that the fall will soon be upon us. Summer is almost gone, *ja?*"

Susan sighed. "It is. I don't much like seeing the cold settle in, but we take what God gives."

"Yes," Rachel said, her voice so soft Susan had to lean forward a little to hear. "We take what He gives."

Susan waited a moment, then sat down next to her and took her hand. "I wish I could take away your sadness, daughter. Is there anything I can do?"

Rachel caught a sharp breath, clearly surprised. "Oh—no, Mamma! I'm not…sad. I was just thinking."

Susan searched her daughter's dark eyes. "Thinking about Captain Gant, were you?"

A faint blush stained Rachel's face. "No, I—"

She stopped, quickly glancing away. Rachel never could lie.

Susan patted her hand. "It's all right, Rachel. I know this has been a very hard thing for you." She paused. "It will take time, daughter, but eventually the pain *will* erase. You will heal."

Still not looking at her, Rachel said, "I'm sorry, Mamma. I didn't realize my feelings showed so much."

Susan cupped her daughter's chin and gently turned her around to face her. "Your feelings don't show to everyone, Rachel. But is there really a need for you and I to pretend?"

Rachel squeezed her eyes shut a moment. When she opened them, the tears that glistened there tore at Susan's heart.

"It hurts so much, Mamma," she said, her voice choked. "I love Jeremiah. Really, I do."

"I know you do." Susan hated this helplessness, this awful frustration of not being able to console her own daughter. "I'm so sorry, *mei liewi* Rachel. I wish it could have worked out differently for you and the captain."

Even as she watched, Rachel's expression seemed to clear. She straightened and reached out to touch her mother's cheek lightly.

"I don't want to take away from your happiness, Mamma. I'll be all right. Really, I will."

"You're taking nothing away from me," Susan said, forcing a note of firmness into her tone.

Now Rachel smiled, this time a more natural smile. "I hope you know how happy I am for you, Mamma. Truly, I am. You and Dr. Sebastian are so right for each other. And we need to be making plans for your wedding soon. November isn't all that far away, you know."

At the thought of just how close her wedding day actually was, Susan felt jittery inside. "There's plenty of time," she said, unwilling to let her nervousness show. "After all, David still has to say his vows and join church."

"Are you working on your wedding dress?"

Suddenly Susan felt like a girl again. She nodded. "I've started it. Oh, Rachel, I'm going to need your help so much to get everything ready, but I don't want to make things any harder for you."

Rachel took her by both shoulders. "Please don't you think that way, Mamma! Not for a minute. Your happiness doesn't hurt me—it *helps* me! I love seeing you so happy, and to think it's all because of a man the entire community loves and respects. Dr. Sebastian is a *wonderful* person. You be happy, Mamma. You deserve it!"

Susan put a finger to her lips. "No, Rachel. No one *deserves* the blessings we receive from God's hand. Who can say why He chooses to grant us any happiness at all, sinners that we are?"

Rachel's scrutiny somehow made her uncomfortable. "Do you really believe that, Mamma?"

"Why, of course I believe it!" Susan stopped. "Don't you?"

Rachel dropped her hands away, but her gaze still searched Susan's face. "What about His grace, Mamma? What if the Lord God blesses us simply because He wants to? Not because we deserve it or because we've earned it but just because He loves us."

"We're not worthy of such love, daughter," Susan said sternly.

Rachel sat motionless. She didn't look at her mother, but sat staring at the kitchen window as if looking for an answer there.

"You and Eli," Susan went on, "you let Phoebe and Malachi's beliefs about such things influence you."

Rachel met her gaze directly. "It's not just Phoebe and Malachi, Mamma. Others among the People have been studying the Bible as well. Eli and I weren't the only ones with questions."

Uneasiness stirred in Susan. She wasn't comfortable with this talk about questions. She knew about Phoebe and Malachi's Bible studies in their home, knew that there were those in the community who questioned some of the old ways and teachings.

True, she'd had her own questions at times, though she tried not to dwell on them. And when David asked her about some of the things he was learning in his instructions for turning Amish, even as she gave him the traditional answers—the approved answers— once in a while, she was hard-pressed not to ask *herself* how a thing could be so. If it *was* so.

"It's best not to ask too many questions," she said now. "With some things, faith is the only answer."

Rachel studied her. "But that's the point, Mamma. The Bible seems to teach that there are some things that can be known only by faith. Yet it seems that in some matters, Bishop Graber teaches us that faith isn't enough."

Susan found it difficult to meet her daughter's gaze. "That's not so, Rachel. Faith is always the most important part of our beliefs—"

"No, Mamma. Not always. What about the assurance of our salvation? The bishop says we *can't* be sure, that we can have only the *hope* of salvation, depending on how we live. That doesn't sound to me like faith."

Susan got up and began collecting the cookies to put in a tin. "We've talked about this before, Rachel, and I'm not going to go into it again. It's *unsinnich,* senseless, this questioning of what we already know to be true."

Rachel, too, stood and began to help put the cookies away. "All right, Mamma. I didn't mean to upset you. But do you really think it's so wrong to have questions about God's will for us? Don't you think He would *want* us to understand His teachings?"

"Not if we're so foolish as to doubt what we already know is true," Susan said, her tone sharper than she'd intended. Even so, though Rachel was a woman grown, she was still her daughter, and if Susan could help it, she'd not have her led away from their beliefs. "It's not wise to get involved in these Bible studies at home, Rachel, when there's no preacher or deacon to guide what's taught. Malachi is a good man, but he's not equipped to teach. You need to listen to the bishop and our deacon."

"You mean Samuel?"

Rachel's tone was laced with contempt, and Susan knew why. Over these past months, Samuel Beiler had made no secret of the fact that he meant to wed Rachel, and he had pressed his suit long and hard. Too hard, to Susan's way of thinking. He had actually managed to turn Rachel away rather than attract her. Of course now, with her heart still soft for Jeremiah Gant, neither Samuel nor any other man had a chance to win her daughter's affection.

There were things about Samuel Beiler that Susan didn't appreciate any more than Rachel did. He was known to be stubborn—unyielding and even headstrong. He was several years older than Rachel, but for that matter, so was Gant. In his favor Samuel was a deacon, a hard worker—steady and well-intentioned. He would no doubt make a good husband, but Rachel had never given him a chance.

Perhaps in time Samuel could help her forget Jeremiah Gant. If that were possible, Susan could easily overlook the few things about the man that bothered her and simply wish him well in winning her daughter.

"You could do worse than Samuel, daughter," was all she said.

Rachel turned from the counter to look at her. "Please, Mamma— don't start about Samuel again."

Susan sighed but said nothing else. She knew from experience that trying to persuade Rachel to listen to reason about Samuel Beiler only seemed to make her more resistant to him.

If there was to be any change in her daughter's attitude toward Samuel, it would have to happen within Rachel's own heart, not from another's counsel.

Later that night Susan lay abed, sleepless and unsettled. Fannie had been asleep for hours, so the house was totally quiet except for the few creaks and groans that had grown comfortably familiar after years of living there.

She had become used to a quiet house at night. They went to bed early, she and Fannie, and with Gideon and Rachel now gone, there was little to disturb the silence. Even so, she seldom slept deeply. Most nights she tended to wake several times. She would get up and go to check on Fannie or go to the kitchen for a drink of water. Sometimes she would pull up her rocking chair by the bedroom window and sit looking out on the field between her house and Rachel's, if there was enough moonlight to allow a view.

Sometimes she thought she might be more suited to sleeping through the day and doing her chores at night. She smiled at the thought. No doubt such an idea would scandalize her neighbors.

So restless she was that at last she got up and went to the window to look out. There was nothing to see except an occasional glimpse of the moon through the thick clouds scudding across the night sky. She stood there thinking of Rachel, so sad and so withdrawn again; of Gideon, her prodigal, gone away from his home and family except for the times he came back to help with the more strenuous farm chores; and of her sweet youngest daughter, Fannie, who these days seemed to be more herself than she'd been ever since that awful attack last winter, when some *Englisch* boys had taunted her and knocked her down into the snow. Thanks to Captain Gant, she'd been rescued in time and finally recovered not only her health but her lively spirits, though it had taken months.

Susan couldn't bear to think of what might have happened to the child had Jeremiah Gant not seen her lying in a snow drift and gone to fetch her, despite his own recent leg injury that made it difficult for him to walk. She would be forever grateful to the former riverboat captain who surely had saved her sweet daughter's life.

If only he could have helped her other *daughter build a new life as well. A new life with him...*

She shook off the thought. No sense thinking such things now. The bishop had said no to Gant and Rachel, and that was that. Their love simply wasn't meant to be. Somehow the two of them must get on without each other.

Though Rachel would hate knowing it, Susan still couldn't dismiss an uneasy sense of guilt when she thought of her own happiness as her wedding to David approached. It seemed so unfair that she, a middle-aged widow and mother, should be granted a new love, a new life, when her young daughter continued to live with a broken heart.

She caught herself then, recognizing that her mind had taken a treacherous path. It was almost as if she were questioning the Lord God with these forbidden thoughts of what was fair and what wasn't.

She closed her eyes in a prayer for forgiveness, then turned and went back to bed before her mind could wander any farther down that troublesome path.

7

NIGHT SOUNDS

The silence of the night
mocks my fainting heart…
ANONYMOUS

Something jolted Susan from a fitful sleep. She sat up and listened. Outside something cracked. Then again.

A strong wind had blown up in the night, and at first she thought she'd merely heard tree branches snapping. But then came the jangle of a harness and a shout.

Footsteps pounded the ground. The sound of running.

Another shout.

A horse whinnied and snorted.

She ran to the window, pulling on her night robe as she went.

A thick, oppressive darkness hung so heavy over the meadow she could see nothing for a moment. She'd left the window cracked but now tugged it all the way up and stuck her head out to look.

Nothing but blackness.

She hurried across the room to light a lantern, then ran out into the hall, stopping only long enough to look into Fannie's room. The child stirred but didn't wake.

Susan ran down the steps, her heart pounding, her hands shaking as she unlocked the door. Time was when the Amish didn't lock their doors. But no longer, not with everything that had happened over the past couple of years.

Stepping out into the night, she held the lantern high. The night air, dank and raw, slapped her skin.

She lifted the lantern even higher.

The barn doors stood open, the darkness within vast and gaping as if frozen in shock.

The horses!

Barefoot, she stumbled as she ran, stubbing her toe on a rock. Pain shot up her foot, but she kept on running until she reached the barn.

Her bare feet smacked the planked floor as she came to a halt just inside and stood listening. Cold and utter silence greeted her. The quiet chilled her more than the cold. Her hands shook as she lifted the lantern, swinging it first to the left, then to the right.

The two buggies—the small one and the larger, sturdier one that her husband, Amos, had favored—sat parked side by side looking eerily abandoned and useless.

Smoke, the sleek black buggy horse, and the older Rosie were both gone. Missing too was Cecil, the honey-colored Percheron Amos had brought home some years before he died. Susan counted on the big, powerful draft horse for all the heaviest farm work.

She called their names almost like a plea. The sound of her trembling voice unnerved her, and she called out again, this time more forcefully.

The dark, empty silence of the barn mocked her.

She tried to take in the reality of the missing horses, tried to quiet the thunderous pounding of her heart, tried to think what to do. The lantern dangling from her hand flickered crazily, creating shadows that seemed to move and lick the walls, then rush toward her.

Something nagged at the fringes of her mind. She lifted the lantern a little higher and swept its beam around the barn.

The cats. The little black and white spotted female and the

all-black male—neither was anywhere in sight. The two always came running when someone entered the barn. She called for them, but she knew that they too had gone missing.

Shock threatened to paralyze her as the enormity of her loss began to settle in. Tears burned her eyes, not only for the horses now but for the barn cats as well.

Contrary to Amos's warnings about treating animals like pets, she had always harbored an affection for the horses, especially the dependable, sturdy Cecil, whose massive size belied his gentle nature. And Fannie loved the cats, was always begging to bring them inside, though she knew Susan wouldn't allow it.

It suddenly struck her then that she couldn't just stand here doing nothing. They were her responsibility, after all. They hadn't run away of their own accord, this much she knew. She had to find them.

She *would* find them.

She whipped around, then took off running to the house and began to tug on the bell rope that would summon help.

8

A Call for Help

Whatever the wealth of our treasure-trove,
The best we shall find is a friend.

John J. Moment

The clanging of a bell dragged David Sebastian from a deep sleep. He'd gone to bed early, already trying to accustom himself to Amish ways—one being their early-to-bed, early-to-rise routine. With his approaching conversion to the Amish church and his marriage to Susan, he wanted to be reasonably well-settled into all the Plain People's ways.

At first he thought he'd been dreaming, for the sound seemed a great distance off. He turned on his side, intending to go back to sleep, but when the ringing didn't go away, he sat up.

Years of being awakened in the middle of the night rendered him instantly alert. Four gongs, a pause, then two more. Four again and another two.

Susan!

That was the help signal Amos had set up when he'd first hung the bell at the back of their house. Susan would never ring that bell in the night unless she was in need of help.

He fumbled for his glasses and lit the lantern, throwing on his clothes over his nightwear before rushing from the bedroom. At the front door, he grabbed his medical case.

Susan's house was just up the road. He hurriedly hitched the bay to the buggy and drove off at breakneck speed, praying all the way that the Lord would keep Susan and Fannie safe until he and others arrived to help.

The first to respond to the bell was Fannie. She came charging into the yard, barefoot and in her nightdress, even while Susan was still yanking the bell rope.

"Mamma! Why are you ringing the bell?"

Susan continued to pull the rope, saying, "You need your coat, Fannie. Go back inside and get it. I'll explain later."

Before Fannie could reach the back door, however, Rachel came running around the side of the house from her own farm across the field. "Mamma! What's wrong?"

She had thrown a coat over her night clothes, but like Fannie she arrived with bare feet. Of course, most Amish women didn't bother with shoes in warm weather, but the nights were too cool now to go without them.

"Inside, both of you," Susan scolded, dropping the bell rope, taking each of her daughters by the hand and coaxing them indoors. "And Rachel, we'd best get our clothes on. Malachi and the boys will be here any moment now, I'm sure. We need to be dressed."

"But what is it?" Rachel pressed as soon as they stepped into the kitchen. "What's happened?"

Inside Susan did her best to keep her voice calm as she explained. "It's the horses. Someone let them out of the barn. They're gone. And—" she glanced at Fannie. "The barn cats. They're missing too."

Fannie went pale, a stricken look crossing her features. Rachel reached to put an arm around her little sister, her gaze locking with Susan's.

"Rachel, hurry and get some clothes on now," Susan said. "You have dresses here, and if you want shoes, you can wear mine. Fannie, you might just as well get dressed too. There won't be any more sleep for us this night."

Even as she spoke, footsteps came pounding up onto the porch. "That'll be Malachi and his boys," she said. "Run on now, while I tell them what's happened."

But when Susan opened the door, she found not Malachi Esch but Samuel Beiler and two of his sons.

Embarrassed to be caught in nightclothes, she pulled her robe more tightly around her.

"Susan—what's happened here?" Samuel spoke sharply in the language of the People, his stern features and gruff voice declaring him ready to take charge. His eyes, however, roamed the room behind Susan, no doubt looking for Rachel.

Susan fought to collect herself as she answered him. "Samuel, it's good of you to come."

She waited as he and his boys came inside, disliking herself for wishing it was Malachi Esch who stood in her hallway. Samuel Beiler was a good man, a man who could be depended on in an emergency. She should be ashamed of herself for not feeling more gratitude and warmth toward him.

But Samuel was such a *hard* man, so strict and unbending. A good many of the Plain People were, if not exactly intimidated by him, at least guarded around him. There was also his persistence in pursuing Rachel. He should have remarried years ago for the sake of his sons, yet as far as she knew, he had never courted another woman since his wife's passing. He wanted only Rachel.

But Rachel didn't want *him*. And even though Susan would like nothing better than to see her daughter again content and settled in a good marriage with a good man, she had to admit she could almost understand why Rachel might resist Samuel's attentions. In spite of the fact that she and Amos had considered him a friend, Susan had never been completely comfortable around the man.

As she was standing in the open doorway, David pulled up in his buggy, with Malachi Esch almost directly behind him in their farm wagon.

Susan hoped she could be forgiven for the wave of relief she felt that others besides Samuel Beiler had arrived to help.

A little after four o'clock in the morning, Gant and Asa sat drinking coffee in Gant's kitchen. Gant had risen before dawn every morning for over a week, having received word that there would be runaways coming any day now. So far there had been no sign of anyone, and he was beginning to worry that something might have gone wrong.

Suddenly Mac growled and shot to his feet from his place by the cookstove as someone pounded on the back door. Asa was already out of his chair as Gant pulled himself up.

"Finally," he said, limping to the door without his cane.

He opened the door only about halfway, quieting Mac with a short command at the sight of Gideon Kanagy.

"Sorry to wake you, Captain, but I needed to tell you—"

Gant threw the door the rest of the way open before the boy could finish. "I was up," he said, motioning Gideon inside. "But what's got you stirring about so early?"

He caught a glimpse of another boy—an Amish boy—waiting in a farm wagon at the edge of the road.

"Gideon? Don't stand out there in the cold. Come on in."

Even in the flickering glow from the kitchen lamp, he could see that the lad was in a lather about something or other.

"I'd best not take the time, thanks. Reuben's waiting for me—Reuben Esch. He came to get me, but I thought I should stop here first. I'd told you I'd open the shop again in the morning, but I won't be able to. Something's happened at the farm, and I need to get out there right away. Mamm will need me."

Gant's mind fumbled to make sense of the boy's words. "Slow down, son. *What* happened?"

"I'm not exactly sure. Reuben said the horses are gone, and the barn cats—they're gone, too."

Gant stared at him. "*Gone?*"

Gideon nodded. "Looks like someone stole the horses. The cats probably got scared and ran off."

Mac had squeezed himself in between Gant and Gideon, and the boy leaned to stroke his head.

"Your mother and Fannie—are they all right?" Gant ordered Mac back inside.

Again the boy nodded. "Reuben says no one's hurt, but they're pretty upset."

Gant drew a long breath. "Rachel?"

Gideon's gaze remained steady. If he knew anything of the situation between his sister and his employer, he gave no indication. "She'd be there with Mamm by now. She'd have heard the bell."

"The bell?"

"The dinner bell Dat put up. He meant it to be used in case of trouble too, so the neighbors would come if ever help was needed."

Gideon glanced back at the boy waiting for him by the road. "I should go now," he said.

Gant's decision was already made. "Mind if Mac and I go with you?"

Gideon shot him a look of surprise but didn't hesitate. "That'd be fine."

"Will your mother mind?"

The boy's reply was quick in coming. "You're always welcome at Mamm's house, Captain. She'd tell you so herself, were you to ask."

Gant gave a nod. "Just let me get a coat, and I'll be right there."

He watched for only a moment as Gideon hurried off to the wagon, then turned to Asa. "I don't like the sound of this. Can you take care of things here?"

"You've shown me what to do if anyone comes," Asa said. "What about the shop later this morning?"

"Just put the *Closed* sign up on the door. I'll get back as soon as I can. One of the people will bring me, but for now I need to see what's going on out there."

"Has there been trouble before?"

Gant looked at him, as he pulled his coat off the wall peg and shrugged into it. "As it happens, they've had more than their share. Some while you were gone. I'll fill you in later." He paused. "You're sure you don't mind taking care of things without me if need be?"

"I know what to do, Captain."

Gant nodded slowly, watching him. "Yes. You always do."

9

AMONG FRIENDS

This is the charge I keep as mine,
The goal of every hope and plan—
To cancel the dividing line
Between me and my fellow man.
And so for me all fear shall end
Save this—that I may fail to see
My neighbor as a needed friend
Or sense my neighbor's need of me.

LESLIE PINCKNEY HILL

It never ceased to intrigue Gant how quickly and efficiently the Amish community gathered round one of their own in times of crisis or need.

Not that his people, the Irish, didn't typically rally about each other when possible, but by the time he left Ireland to come to the States, the island was so impoverished, its people so weak and ill from starvation, it was all they could do to put one foot in front of the other. Charity and kindness could be offered only by the few who had not been struck down and were still strong enough to provide help to others.

That left few in a position to offer benevolence.

By the time the men arrived at the Kanagy farm, neighbors and friends were milling about the yard and on the porch. As he and

Gideon made their way among them, Gant was pleased and somewhat relieved to be greeted by many with respect, even, in some cases, with overt friendliness.

With time the People seemed to have come to trust him. According to Doc Sebastian, this was no small accomplishment, so he was grateful for the acceptance they offered him. The thing was, he genuinely *liked* the Riverhaven Amish.

Even though he hadn't been able to convince the bishop when Gant first talked with him, he was coming to realize that he'd spoken the truth when he insisted that his desire to marry Rachel wasn't the only reason he sought permission to convert. And as the weeks wore on, the bishop's refusal to allow his conversion seemed to cut even more deeply. Only after the enormity of what he had been refused finally began to sink in, did he recognize that he had been wounded almost as much by the reality that he would forever remain an "outsider" to the People as the grim awareness that he and Rachel would never be allowed to marry.

He saw her then, as she moved among some of the latecomers in the yard, explaining to those who hadn't heard what had happened this night. She was fully dressed, her glossy hair neatly parted and covered with the little cap she always wore, its strings dangling and stirring slightly in the night wind.

Her eyes met Gant's as he began to make his way toward her. She looked away once but only for a moment. When she turned back to him, he saw the weariness that lined her face, the pale tautness of her features, and knew that for whatever reason, tonight wasn't the only night she hadn't slept well.

It shouldn't have pleased her so much, his coming all the way from town in the dark hours of morning. She shouldn't feel this rush of pleasure at the sight of him after all this time—his gaze, as warm as a caress, his tentative smile, his curly dark hair falling over one eye, the strength of him. But, oh, it was good to see him!

He was coming directly toward her, his eyes on her face as if he saw no one else except her. And in that instant, despite her apprehension and distress about everything that had happened in the hours before, Rachel knew nothing, saw no one but him.

Jeremiah. The man she was forbidden to love yet loved all the same.

"Rachel," he said in that quiet way he had of making her name the most important sound she had ever heard. "I'm sorry for your trouble."

She managed to nod and tried to unlock her gaze from his but couldn't.

"Where's your mother?"

"She's—" Finally she was able to look away from him. She glanced around, saw her mother talking with Gideon and Doc Sebastian. "There," she said pointing. "On the porch." She paused, then added, "She'll be pleased that you've come."

"And you?" he said watching her closely.

She caught a breath. "What? I—yes, of course," she said, trying to keep her tone light.

"What can I do to help?" His expression changed now, becoming less intimate and more practical.

"Oh…I don't suppose there's anything. Not really. Some of the men are forming groups to go search for the horses, in case they're still close by somewhere."

"What time did this happen? Or do you know?"

Rachel tried to think. "Mamma said she heard noises about one thirty or thereabouts. That's what woke her."

"I don't suppose you have any idea who might be responsible."

"There's no telling. Maybe some fellows just wanting to play tricks on us. If so, we'll find the horses unharmed. If not—"

"Captain Gant!"

Fannie came running up and caught hold of Jeremiah's coat sleeve. "I'm mighty glad you're here! Why have you stayed away so long? Did you come to help find our animals?"

Rachel didn't miss the genuine affection in her little sister's face as she beamed up at Jeremiah—nor the warmth in his expression as he smiled down at Fannie.

"Ah, my favorite little miss," he said, running a hand lightly over the top of Fannie's *kapp*. "'Tis happy I am to see you too."

Fannie giggled. "You sound funny when you talk Irish."

"Fannie—"

But when Rachel would have reproached her sister, Jeremiah merely laughed.

"Well now, Miss Fannie, I'll do my best to not let my Irish get in the way of your Amish. How will that be?" he teased.

Again Fannie gave another delighted giggle, though after a moment her sunny expression faded. "My barn kitties are gone too."

"Gideon told me," said Jeremiah, his tone gentle. "We'll do our best to find them for you, lass. For now though, Mac's over by the wagon, if you'd like to say hello. I'm sure he'd like to see *you*."

For a few seconds more, Fannie continued to stare up at him with her young girl's heart shining in her eyes. Then she turned and ran off to find Gant's dog.

As Rachel watched her, she could only hope that her own heart wasn't nearly so obvious.

Later Gant stood talking with Doc on the porch, though his gaze continued to follow Rachel's every move.

"Do you think this might be the work of the same bunch who accosted Fannie last year?" he said.

Doc shrugged. "Hard to say. There's no lack of troublemakers who fancy making sport of the Amish."

"Why is that, do you think?"

Again Doc gave a shrug, his expression cynical. "I don't have to tell *you* there will always be some who can't tolerate the differences in others. The Irish could write a book of their own on persecution."

"True. To some we're mostly a gaggle of dirty and ignorant Papists. A bunch of sub-humans, as it were. But what accounts for the bullying of the Amish? They're honest, hard-working, family folks who mind their own business and just want to be left alone in turn to live their faith as best as they can."

Doc's steady scrutiny was a bit discomfiting. "You're not that naive, Gant. I know you better."

"What?"

"It's the *differences,* man, don't you see? The Amish don't fit in any more than the Irish do. They may be good, honest people and work hard and live a quiet life, but they're *different.* Not to mention the fact that they won't fight back when they're wronged, they won't go to war, and they won't compromise their faith. Not for anything. And to a certain kind of person, that makes them suspect and open targets for harassment and even violence. There are far too many people in this world who have no tolerance whatsoever for those who aren't like themselves."

Gant knew he was right, knew also that there were other reasons for the intolerance toward the Amish that Doc hadn't mentioned. He'd long observed that there was something in a certain kind of man that couldn't bear any sort of disagreement with what he valued. If he needed a thing or valued it, then surely others should need it and value it also. If they didn't—well then, for some might that be cause for resentment and even vengeance.

To one who prized the things of the world, the Amish avoidance of those things, indeed the very simplicity of the way they chose to live, just might engender hostility and, ultimately, aggression. From what Doc had told him and the little he'd already known about the Plain People, it seemed that everywhere they settled, they eventually encountered antagonism that all too often took the form of mistreatment or worse.

His gaze traveled back to Rachel, now standing with her arm around her mother's shoulders. The thought of anyone daring to hurt either of them made the blood roar in his veins.

So perhaps the bishop had been right in telling him he was not yet "ready" to live the Amish way, perhaps never would be. For one thing was certain: He found it difficult, if not impossible, to imagine standing by and not retaliating in the case of violence or harm wreaked upon someone he loved—or for that matter, on any one of these good people he had come to care about.

As he stood watching, Samuel Beiler walked up to Rachel and her mother and began talking with them. Gant's insides clenched. He did his best to conceal the jealousy that squeezed his chest like a vise.

Not only did he dislike the deacon for the proprietary way he routinely treated Rachel, but he resented the fact that Beiler had the right to spend time with her if she chose to allow it. This, while his own attentions, other than as a strictly platonic friend, were forbidden. The people might treat him with kindness and even respect, but just let him go against the bishop's admonition to avoid any hint of a romantic relationship with Rachel, and he would no longer be welcome among them.

He couldn't help but watch her reaction to the man and was relieved to see that same careful, somewhat distant response in her that he'd observed other times. So the deacon hadn't won her over in Gant's absence.

At least not yet.

"Giving Sam Beiler the evil eye is a wasted effort, I should think."

Doc's dry words snapped Gant back to his surroundings. "That obvious, eh?"

"Beiler isn't easily put off, but Rachel has a strong will of her own.

I don't think you need to worry about the deacon. He's no farther along with her than he's ever been, and I don't see that changing."

An uncharacteristically sour look crossed Doc's features. "I expect I should count it as good luck for me that he didn't decide to court *Susan*. He's a lot closer to her age than to Rachel's, after all."

"Somehow I don't think he'd pose a problem for you," Gant told him. "Your bride-to-be seems unaware entirely of any other man on the premises so long as you're around."

Doc's smile was nothing short of boyish. "I need to get going. Why don't you go along with our group to search for the horses? It's just Gideon, Reuben, Malachi, and myself. We're taking Malachi's wagon. If that big Percheron of Susan's happens to be hurt, it could take more than one or two men to bring him in."

Gant nodded, casting one more look in Rachel's direction and drawing a satisfied breath when he saw Beiler walk away from her. He hesitated only another instant before following Doc across the yard to where Malachi Esch and the others were climbing onto the wagon.

10

DARK MEMORIES

The heart that has truly loved never forgets.

THOMAS MOORE

They found the horses a few hours later in an abandoned barn about three miles from the Kanagy farm. The animals were anxious and unsettled but seemingly unharmed.

Before leaving Susan's place, Gant had given his dog, Mac, a chance to sniff around the stalls and the paddock. It was Mac who alerted them to the dilapidated barn where they found the horses.

They had no trouble taking the animals home. Gideon and Reuben Esch each rode one of the buggy horses bareback, leading the big Percheron along with them, while Mac trotted in front of them, as if to make certain they reached their destination.

In the wagon Doc turned to Gant and said, "Are you thinking what I'm thinking, given that no harm was done to those horses?"

Gant nodded. "It was nothing more than harassment. They had no intention of hurting those animals to begin with."

"That's how I see it," Doc agreed. "This was just another way to trouble some of the Amish."

Gant thought about that. "You don't believe they singled Susan out for any particular reason other than the fact that she's Amish?"

Doc rubbed his chin. "I don't, no. But then I don't *want* to think that way. What they did was cruel but not quite so threatening as if it were personal."

Again Gant gave a nod, but another thought distracted him. "You keep saying 'they.' So you're thinking there was more than one person involved?"

"Don't you? Running off three horses—especially given Cecil's size—seems like the work of more than one fellow."

"Probably. Though someone used to horses could likely get the job done without any help, don't you think?"

Doc looked at Gant. "You believe that's the case?"

"No, not really. Just considering the possibilities."

Doc was quiet for a moment. "I wonder if I don't tend to see this as the work of more than one because of what happened to Fannie."

"Because there were four of them, you mean?"

Doc nodded. "There's no reason to believe this was the work of those same boys, of course. Yet it's easy to suspect them."

"It is. If that's the case, though, you have to wonder why they didn't hurt the horses. What they did to Fannie was nothing short of assault."

Something about the apparent lack of any ill-treatment to the animals bothered Gant. There wasn't time to dwell on it, however. The Kanagy farm was well in sight by now, and no doubt everyone would be waiting for any news.

He was glad for Susan's sake—and Rachel's—that the news, at least for now, would be good.

Throughout the week ahead, when Rachel remembered that night she was almost ashamed to realize that the thought of what *could* have happened to Mamma's horses disturbed her less than the feelings Jeremiah's return to her life had evoked.

That's how she tended to think of seeing him again, that he had returned to her life. Not that he'd ever really been absent from it. Even though they hadn't seen each other for some time, he had never really been out of her thoughts. But seeing him had shaken her far more than she liked to admit.

Now he was real to her all over again, a larger presence than her memories recalled, a stronger force with his intense gaze and easy smile. And his absence after he'd gone away again that night had left her bereft, as if a cold wind of abandonment had swept through her heart, leaving it dark and desolate.

He was the last thought on her mind before she drifted off into an often uneasy sleep and her first thought when she awakened. In the days that followed, the memory of him gave her no rest. When she heard the clip-clop of a horse on the road, she instinctively went to the window to look out. And if someone stepped onto her porch, she caught her breath as she opened the door, halfway hoping she would find him standing there, yet at the same time, dismayed by the awareness that if it *were* him, the right thing to do—according to the bishop and the leaders of the church—would be to turn him away because he was *verboten*—forbidden—to her.

She knew she *must* stop thinking about him, stop wanting to see him so badly that at times it became an ache in her heart. And yet her thoughts were all she had left of him. How could she bear to give them up?

When the bishop refused to allow Jeremiah's conversion, thereby shutting the door to any possibility they could ever marry, it was as if a light had gone out in her heart. After Eli, her husband, died, she plodded through the days and weeks and months almost like a blind woman making her way through the thick darkness of night. But Jeremiah had changed all that. His understanding, his gentleness, his sense of humor—all that he was—had, little by little, managed to lift the fog of depression from her days. Their friendship, slow growing as it was, had become a sure and steady light that gradually warmed to love.

Now the darkness was back, and this time it was even worse. Not only had she lost the first man she'd ever loved, but she'd had to give up the second, and somehow—though she hated to admit it even to herself—it seemed harder than it had been with Eli. She thought that might be because Jeremiah was still alive, still nearby. At times, like the night the horses were stolen, she still saw him, still talked with him, felt his gaze on her face, his eyes looking into her soul.

He was too...*present*. Too close. Too real. There was no escaping him.

And yet if she were to keep her sanity—and at the same time remain true to her faith and the church—she *must* escape him. She had to put him out of her life, out of her thoughts, out of her heart.

The question was *how*.

CRAVING JUSTICE

Thy will—it bids the weak be strong,
It bids the strong be just.

JOHN HAY

Over the next few days, Gant noted young Gideon's obvious preoccupation. The boy was still clearly upset about the ordeal with his mother's stolen horses.

Not that his work in the shop suffered. Gideon had proven himself to be conscientious. He gave a good day's work, even showed promise as a potential carpenter, although Gant suspected his interests didn't particularly lie in that direction. His work was as good as ever, but there was a tension about him that almost hummed with anger—a subtle but steady kind of anger that never seemed far from the surface.

His hand was heavier and quicker than usual no matter what he was doing. A tight frown seldom went away—he hadn't smiled in days— and he was quieter than was usually his way. Almost every attempt to engage him in even the most casual conversation fell flat.

Of course, there hadn't been much opportunity for small talk of late, it being a particularly busy time in the shop. They'd had so much business that orders were beginning to pile up, an uncomfortable situation for Gant. He liked keeping the work moving without a lot of backlog.

On the other hand, he was grateful for the business. Asa had volunteered his help, and Gant didn't hesitate to take him up on the offer. But Asa wouldn't be around much longer. Two "passengers" for the Railroad were hiding right now in Gant's barn, and Asa would be leaving with them soon. He always liked to wait for a good cloudy night to increase the cover of darkness before starting out. But Gant could tell he was getting anxious and would be going soon, with or without clouds.

Like most other days, this morning had gone by quickly, with business brisk as usual. By afternoon lunchtime had gone by with none of them having stopped to eat. Finally Gant sent Gideon for food, and when he returned, the three of them took a break at the table in the back room.

Following his last few bites, Gant downed the rest of his milk, all the while watching Gideon, who had eaten little. "You heard anything from your mother this week?" he said.

"Not so far," the boy replied. "I suppose everything is all right, or I'd have had word."

"I heard the law is asking around, trying to find out who might have been behind the theft of the horses," said Gant.

Gideon sneered. "That won't come to anything."

Gant looked at him. "Why do you say that?"

"The *Englisch* don't much care what happens to the Amish."

"I don't suppose that's true for all of us," Gant said mildly. "Seems to me your people have some good friends among the outside world. How about Doc Sebastian?"

The boy gave a short nod, but his expression was grudging. "Doc's different. Besides, he's soon to be Amish himself."

"True enough, but he was a friend to the Amish long before now," Gant replied. "Speaking of Doc, if you see him before I do, how about asking him to stop by and have a visit with Mrs. Sawyer? Terry was around early this morning, when I was just opening up. He's worried about her. The baby is due anytime now, and their trip was a hard one. He said she's not feeling a bit well."

"Has he found a job yet?" Gideon asked.

"Nothing so far. Things are hard in Riverhaven right now, but besides that anyone who knows that Sawyer is only looking for something temporary, until he gets enough money together to move on to Indiana, isn't likely to want to hire him."

Gideon stood and began to gather his leftovers. "I'll talk to Doc. I'll probably go out to the farm over the weekend. No doubt he'll be around."

Gant watched him. "You're all right with his marrying your mother, aren't you?"

"Sure. Doc's a good man. He makes Mamm happy. Besides, I'll be glad to see she and Fannie aren't out there by themselves anymore, especially after this last trouble."

Gant turned to Asa to explain. "Doc Sebastian—you remember him? He's joining the Amish church, and he and Gideon's mother are getting married this November."

"I remember the doctor—and Mrs. Kanagy as well," Asa said. "They took good care of you when you were wounded."

"Aye, they did. And I'm properly grateful to the both of them."

Gideon left then, taking the remains of his lunch to the trash barrel outside.

"Young Gideon is troubled," Asa said.

Gant nodded. "He's torn. He's determined to find out who's harassing his people but doesn't really know where to start. Last winter four boys jumped his little sister, Fannie, and tormented her to the point of being hurt. She fell into a ditch and ended up with a head injury, not to mention being badly frightened. Now this latest thing with the horses. The Amish don't believe in fighting back, of course, but Gideon is no longer living Amish."

"Has he left his people for good?"

"I suppose that remains to be seen. He's got an English—that's how they call anyone who's not Amish—girlfriend, but he hardly ever mentions her, so I'm thinking it's not all that serious. It seems

to me that the main reason he left home is because he has a problem
with the Amish way of nonresistance. He wants to protect his people,
but he worries that they'll always be in danger unless at some point
they start to fight back." He paused. "What worries me is that he'll
end up getting hurt himself."

"He seems like a good boy, with a good head on his shoulders."

"Aye, though I suppose it's time I quit thinking of him as a boy.
He's soon to turn twenty years old, and can do a full day's work
as well as any man—better than some. Even so, he tends to be
a bit hotheaded at times, so I'm hoping he doesn't do anything
foolish."

Asa smiled a little.

"What?"

"Nothing," said Asa, with a small shake of his head.

"You're thinking I'm a hothead myself."

"Not at all, Captain."

"Yes, you were. And I won't argue the point. I can be."

Asa looked directly at him. "Perhaps at times. But I've never
known you to be foolish. We'll hope young Gideon learns to apply
wisdom to his quest for justice."

Gant arched an eyebrow. "Sometimes you talk like a poet."

The other's reply was a silent shrug and the same small smile.

→ ←

After he closed up the shop for the day, Gant rode out to Jonah
Weatherly's farm. Jonah had been in the day before and let drop a
tidbit of information that interested Gant, and he'd decided then
and there to pay Jonah a visit.

An hour later he left the Weatherly place and started for Riverhaven.

Up until the night Susan Kanagy's horses had been stolen, he'd
been uncertain as to just what kind of a reception he might receive

from Rachel's mother. That night, though, he'd found her response to him as kind and accepting as ever, so he felt reasonably comfortable that he wouldn't be entirely unwelcome should he drop in for a few minutes.

Besides, he had a perfectly legitimate reason for stopping by.

He glanced back at the basket behind him and gave it a tug to make sure it was secure.

Gideon Kanagy was saving his wages for a horse. He needed a good riding horse if he was ever going to be able to make a worthwhile search for the fellows who were tormenting the People—possibly the same ones who had hurt Fannie.

He stopped at the edge of the boardwalk, looking out across the road. It was a slow time of day, with scarcely anyone to be seen other than a couple of business owners standing in the doorways of their shops, looking around. A man and a woman in Amish apparel climbed out of a buggy and went into the dry goods store. Meanwhile, a farm wagon pulled by a tired-looking bay lumbered down the road, leaving a trail of dust in its wake.

It occurred to him that, for all he knew, the ones troubling the Amish might be right here in Riverhaven. On the other hand, they could just as easily come from Marietta or one of the farm communities nearby. Without a ride he was hobbled from getting around well enough to search them out, even if he knew where to start.

He'd managed to save a fair sum so far and still give Mamm a part of his wages to help out at the farm. But he needed more if he was to buy himself a good, dependable animal, and he'd worked around horses enough through the years that he wasn't willing to settle for just any old nag to get him here and there. He'd have himself a good mount or none at all.

Captain Gant paid him more than a fair wage. Even so, he

wished he could think of a way to add to it. He'd hoped to have a horse before winter, but it was beginning to look doubtful.

Meanwhile, the no-goods who were bent on causing grief to the Amish were still out there—and no doubt still hatching their mean-spirited schemes to wreak even more trouble on the People. He had never been one for harboring anger—that much of the Amish way had stayed with him. Even though Dat had admonished him about his temper more than once during his growing-up years, he was quick to let things go and not allow them to fester.

But every time he thought of the attack on his little sister last year and now this recent bad business with Mamm's horses—not to mention the other troubles like the burning of Abe Gingerich's barn and the vandalism on Jacob Lape's buggies—he got almost sick with a kind of rage. Every instinct in him cried out for justice and the means to put an end to the harassment of his people.

He despised his own helplessness.

He started walking again, hating this feeling of being at odds with himself. He needed activity, needed something to do, yet there was nothing he really *wanted* to do.

Abby, his *Englisch* girlfriend, would be expecting him to come see her tonight, but he wasn't much in the mood for her company. Abby was all right, when he was in the right frame of mind. But really, they had little in common except a physical attraction for each other. And he was coming to realize that that might not be enough to sustain their relationship much longer.

Sometimes Gideon craved conversation with someone who liked to talk about more than the heat of summer or the latest dress she was sewing for herself. Abby—well, she didn't think much, so she couldn't talk much either, not about anything except herself.

One of the reasons he liked the captain's company was that the man was so *interesting*. Gant had been a lot of places and didn't mind answering questions about his travels.

He also read books—almost all the time, it seemed—at least when he wasn't working and sometimes even then when business was slow, not that there were many of those slow times anymore. Gideon had never been much for books. Neither Mamm nor Dat had encouraged them to read except for certain passages in the Scriptures or an occasional newspaper. He'd been more than ready to leave his schooling behind when he came of age. But the captain had given him free pick of all his many books, and Gideon had discovered that the more he read, the more he *wanted* to read. He actually liked learning when left to himself to read what he wanted, when he wanted.

As luck had it, Gant had invited him to share his and Asa's supper this evening. Gideon thought he just might take him up on it. He turned around and started back the way he'd come. He'd go to his room upstairs over the shop and clean up a bit, then go on up to the captain's house a little later.

He liked being around Gant and Asa just fine. Not only did they have some interesting tales to tell, but at times they could be pretty funny. This would also give him the chance to pick out a new book from the captain's shelves.

He stopped to pet Mac, who lay dozing in the shade, before climbing the outside steps up to his room. It struck him that he might be behaving a little strange, choosing the company of his employer and an older black man over the pert and pretty Abby Frey.

He felt a little surprised at himself, but it wasn't as if he had any kind of understanding with Abby—even though lately she'd been hinting more and more that she'd like to get married. He wasn't nearly ready to think about marriage yet, and even if he were, he wasn't sure he'd want to be married to Abby.

For one thing, he couldn't afford her. Abby was an only child, and she'd been spoiled by her fairly well-to-do folks. Abby liked pretty clothes and lots of other fancy things that Gideon would never be able to pay for by working as a carpenter's helper. It would take a banker or a lawyer to keep Abby happy.

She wasn't some Amish girl like, say, Emma Knepp, who would

→ 12 ←

GANT'S GIFT

And I spoke tripping Gaelic, and merry songs I've sung,
But now my wits are crazy and leaden is my tongue.

PATRICK BROWNE

G ant knocked on Susan Kanagy's door, then again. It stood open, a screened door revealing no sign of anyone's approach.

He would have thought that, given the troubles going on in their community, the Amish would have taken to keeping their doors closed and locked by now. But that didn't seem to be the case.

He waited another moment, then stepped off the porch, steadying the basket that hung over his arm. He started toward the side of the house but stopped when Susan Kanagy called out from behind him.

"Captain Gant!"

He turned and saw her coming around the house from the other side, carrying a pan of what appeared to be cheese and other food. Her smile was warm, her greeting friendly, as she approached him. "Have you been here long?"

"No, ma'am, I just got here. I hope I'm not bothering you."

"Not at all," she said, stopping at the porch steps. "Won't you come inside and have some coffee?"

Gant closed the distance between them. "That sounds good,

but I'd best explain why I'm here first. I've brought something for Fannie. Is she about?"

"Yes, she and Rachel are in back in the springhouse, helping me gather some food to deliver. We have widows and a few families who need help, so we're going to pack up some things for them later."

She glanced at the basket slung over Gant's arm. "That's a mighty big basket you're carrying around, Captain."

"Yes, ma'am. And I need to get your permission to give it to Fannie, if you could just spare me a minute."

Her gaze traveled from Gant's face to the basket on his arm, then back to him. "Why don't we go inside?"

"Ah...it might be better to stay out here," said Gant.

She looked at him. "All right. But come up on the porch and let me set these things down."

Gant followed her up the steps to the porch and waited until she turned back to him. "Now then, Captain, you've got my curiosity mighty sharp. What is it you need my permission for?"

Carefully Gant set the basket down on the top step and took off the lid, motioning that she should look inside.

She stooped over and looked. Her eyes widened and snapped to his. Then she looked again.

"You understand why I'd like Fannie to have this, Mrs. Kanagy?" he said.

"*Susan*," she corrected him distractedly, still studying the contents of the basket. "Yes, Captain," she said quietly. "I believe I understand. And you have my permission."

"You truly don't mind?"

"No, Captain Gant. I don't mind at all," she said straightening. Her voice was little more than a whisper when she added, "This is very kind of you."

At that moment Fannie came running around the side of the house. "Captain Gant! Did you come to visit?"

The girl charged directly up to him, her smile wide and bright enough to break through a storm cloud. "Is it all right if I go talk to Flann? He likes me, you know. And I'm not a bit afraid of him, even though he's so big. Cecil is still bigger, and I'm not afraid of him either."

"Fannie! Don't be so *bapplich*! So much chatter!" her mother cautioned. "Give Captain Gant a chance to catch his breath."

Gant laughed, happy to see the girl's high spirits had returned after the recent trouble they'd had with the horses.

He saw Rachel then, coming from the side of the house, walking slowly, a sack of food in each hand, her eyes fastened on him. He swallowed, trying to keep his expression impassive, yet feeling as though his heart must be bleeding through his eyes.

He nodded as she drew closer. "Rachel."

"Captain," she said, her tone even.

He hated that, the way she called him as she had at the beginning, before they knew each other. So, then, he would no longer be "Jeremiah" to her?

He was aware that Susan Kanagy had fixed her eyes on some distant spot across the road, as if reluctant to observe their response to each other.

It was Fannie who broke the tension. "What's in that basket, Captain Gant?"

"Fannie—" said Rachel, a note of rebuke in her tone.

"It's all right," Gant said. "Actually what's in the basket is a present for you, Miss Fannie."

She giggled. For some reason the girl never failed to giggle when he called her *Miss Fannie*.

"For me?" She looked at him, as if to see if he was merely teasing her.

"Indeed. Would you like a look?"

Fannie nodded so forcefully a few strands of hair escaped the little white cap she wore.

Gant gestured toward the steps. "You might want to sit down first."

Again she studied his expression, but only for a few seconds before hurrying over to plop down on the top step of the porch. Balancing his cane with one hand and the basket in the other, Gant went to sit down beside her, while Rachel set her things down and watched from the bottom of the steps.

"Here you are, then," he said, placing the basket in Fannie's lap.

She placed her hand on the lid, then hesitated. "It really is for me?"

"Just for you," Gant said.

With that Fannie undid the catch on the lid and lifted it off. She stared down into the basket, drawing a sharp breath and holding it so long Gant wondered if the girl was going to pass out. He lowered his head a bit so he could also peek inside.

A wiry little pup lifted a fuzzy black head and stared up at them both, his eyes nearly as wide as Fannie's, his nose testing the air.

"A *hundli!*" she cried. "It's a puppy! Oh! Oh! A puppy!"

Gant grinned at her excitement.

She turned to him with an expression of pure joy on her face. "Is he really mine, Captain Gant? For sure and for certain?"

Gant tugged gently at one of the strings of her cap. "He's all yours, Fannie. But understand now—he's going to need a lot of care. This is the first time he's been away from his mother, you see, so you'll have to give him a great deal of attention. Oh—and he needs a name as well."

Both Rachel and Susan Kanagy drew close enough to have a look at Fannie's "gift," offering a generous amount of admiration and interest as Fannie lifted him carefully out of the basket and put him to her shoulder. The puppy immediately snuggled against her and began to lick her face.

Rachel met Gant's gaze for an instant, her eyes moist and intent with what appeared to be gratitude. He managed a smile, but fearing his emotions might betray him, he forced himself to turn his attention back to Fannie. "I should tell you that he won't be this small for very long. I've seen his sire, and if he takes after him, he's going to grow up to be quite a large fellow. So you'll need to train him well."

Susan Kanagy lifted an eyebrow in his direction.

Fannie saw her mother's expression. "Don't worry, Mamma," she said. "I'll make good and sure he learns to mind. I'll do *everything* for him, you'll see."

"That you will, daughter," Susan said, her tone dry as she again cast a look at Gant. "Just how big *is* his sire, Captain?"

"Pretty big," Gant replied.

Another eyebrow went up, but she didn't look all that fussed with him.

The sky had been darkening while they talked, and now a low roll of thunder sounded. Gant stood, bracing himself on the step with his cane as he leaned to stroke the pup's ears. "I should be getting along before it storms," he said. "Flann doesn't much like thunder and lightning."

"I think we all need to get indoors," Susan Kanagy said. "You're welcome to stay and have supper with us, Captain."

Gant wanted to stay. But he figured Rachel would be more comfortable if he left. "Thank you, Mrs.—*Susan*. But Asa would have my hide. He's cooking tonight, and I told him I'd be back in plenty of time."

"Oh, please, Captain Gant! Please stay!" Fannie begged.

Gant smiled at her. "I'd best not, Fannie. Another time. I'll want to drop by again soon, so I can find out what you decide to name your new friend there."

"Oh, I already know his name."

"Do you now?" said Gant.

Fannie nodded. "I'm going to call him 'Thunder.' That way I'll always remember the day you gave him to me."

"Well, now, it seems to me that's a perfect name for him."

With the pup already dozing against her shoulder, she moved closer to Gant and looked up at him. "*Danki,* Captain Gant," she said, her face all seriousness. "I'll take real good care of Thunder. He's going to be my best friend."

"I wouldn't be a bit surprised if that's not the case, Fannie. He's already taken quite a liking to you, it seems."

"He's a wonderful-*gut* present, Captain! The best gift I've ever had."

Another clap of thunder broke the quiet of the evening, and Susan Kanagy tried to hurry Fannie and Rachel inside. But when Fannie started for the porch, the pup in her arms, her mother stopped her. "Oh, no, Fannie. We can't have the puppy indoors—"

"Mamma! We can't leave Thunder outside! Not his first night away from his mother—and in a storm! He won't be any trouble, Mamma! I'll make sure he doesn't bother you."

"Fannie, we've never kept our animals indoors—"

"But, Mamma, Thunder isn't just an animal. He's *special*! He's a special present. Please, Mamma! Please, don't make him stay outside by himself! He'll be scared!"

Susan looked at her, then at Rachel, who smiled and nodded slightly. "Well, I suppose it can't hurt for now, since he's still so small."

Gant watched, not surprised to see Fannie win her mother over. The girl then hurried inside, clearly anxious to make her move before her mamma could change her mind. Just inside the screened door, she turned and waved, flashing Gant an enormous smile.

Gant turned to Rachel, pleased to see that her smile didn't fade when she looked at him. "How you've blessed my little sister, Jeremiah. I haven't seen her this happy since—I can't even remember when."

He was relieved to hear her use his name again.

"I first thought I'd find her a kitten," he said, "to help make up for the ones that went missing. But I know there's no replacing something you've loved once it's lost to you."

She looked at him, then quickly glanced away.

Not wanting any more awkwardness between them than already existed, he hurried to add, "As I told Fannie, he's going to grow up to be a very big dog. And I understand from Jonah Weatherly that his sire is quite the fine watchdog. I thought—with everything that's been going on—it might be good to have a watchdog on hand. A big one."

To his surprise her lips again curved in a faint smile. "I think it might take him a while to grow into his father's reputation, though, don't you?"

Gant relaxed a little and returned her smile. "Aye. From the looks of him, he does have a bit of growing to do."

They stood looking at each other in silence for a few seconds more. But when thunder again rumbled in the distance, she said, "You should go before the storm settles in."

He nodded. "I expect so. So—it was good to see you again, Rachel."

She turned her face slightly away. "And you," she said softly.

He didn't want to leave her. He wanted more than anything else to stay. He wanted to drink in the sight of her, to touch her. "Rachel—"

Still not looking at him, she lifted a hand as if to stop him from saying anything more. "I—should get inside."

Gant drew a long breath. "Aye," he said. "I'll just be going, then."

Rachel stood just inside the door and watched him go, her heart aching to go with him. She pressed the palm of her hand against the screen, as if she could touch him and call him back.

Would it be easier to keep her heart from tripping over itself, to keep separate from him, if he were a different kind of man? His gentleness, the kindness that flowed through him like a steadily flowing current only made it that much more difficult not to care about him. It was the very thing that never failed to warm her to him, that called to the deepest part of her and drew her to him.

If only he were a different kind of man...

But then he wouldn't be Jeremiah. And she might not have come to love him.

No, she wouldn't want him to be anything other than what he was, even though it meant that the knife in her heart was permanently embedded there. She would rather live with the pain of a love that could never be anything more than a careful friendship than to have him be less than the man he was.

But she must be always careful—very careful—to keep her feelings for him tightly capped and unseen by those piercing, intense eyes of his. If he should ever recognize how treacherously weak she was, how fragile her emotions really were where he was concerned, he might again attempt to convince her that there was hope for them—hope for a future together.

When in truth the only hope she dared to hold was that she could survive the future without him.

MORE THAN ONE SURPRISE

God's own arm hath need of thine.

ARTHUR CLEVELAND COXE

Once Gant got back to Riverhaven, he had no time to savor Fannie's excited reaction to the pup. Fortunately there was also no time for the melancholy that had been brewing in him since his brief encounter with Rachel.

To his surprise Gideon showed up for supper. He'd invited the lad to eat with them a number of times, but he seldom accepted. This evening, though, he turned up, looking scrubbed and polished and in seeming high spirits.

The boy could be good company when he had a mind to, although of late that hadn't been the case. This evening, however, he seemed more himself, given to joining in the conversation as well as soaking up Gant's and Asa's tales of their travels.

"Don't you miss it, Captain?" he said now, having wolfed down the last bite of Asa's beef stew and biscuits. "Your life on the river?"

"Sometimes," Gant said honestly. "It hasn't been my way to stay in one place for any length of time. But like most anything else, you get used to what you have to do, and eventually it becomes as natural as everything that went before."

"I think it would be a swell life, living like that," said Gideon, a faraway look in his eyes.

"No kind of life is without its problems," Gant pointed out. "Most things usually look better from a distance."

"Maybe so, but I wouldn't mind an adventure now and again."

"That's your young blood," Gant teased. "Even an adventurous life loses some of its luster after a time."

They lingered at the kitchen table for a long time, Gideon plying them with questions about one thing or another and Asa clearly enjoying the boy's company. More than once, Gant sensed that the youth wanted to hear about their work with the runaway slaves, but he stopped just short of a direct question.

Gant was fairly certain the boy already knew more about their involvement with the Railroad than he let on, but he also figured that the less he actually did know, the safer it was for him. Thus, neither he nor Asa volunteered any information.

It was well after dark when Asa got up and started to wash the dishes. Gant pushed back from the table as well. "You cooked," he told the other. "I'll do the dishes."

Asa waved him off only to have Gideon stand and go to the sink. "I'll help," he said.

Gant couldn't resist needling him a bit. "An Amish fellow doing dishes? Now there's a surprise."

Gideon turned around with a grin. "Have to admit the first few times I cleaned up my own plates it felt mighty strange. I'm used to it now, but Mamm would probably faint if she could see me."

"Amish men don't do dishes?" Asa said.

"Woman's work," Gideon said, still grinning. "Men work outside the house. Women inside." He paused. "*And* outside sometimes—in their gardens, taking care of the animals—that kind of thing."

"So, your mamma probably would never expect to see you with your hands in dishwater?" said Asa.

Gideon started to reply, but a knock at the back door stopped him.

From his place behind the stove, Mac shot to his feet and barked.

Gant quieted him with a single command. When Asa cast a questioning look in his direction, Gant lifted a hand to indicate he would get the door.

It was late enough that he wasn't inclined to simply open up without knowing who might be there. "Who is it?"

At first his question met nothing but silence, so he asked the second time. "Who's there?"

A reply finally came. "A friend of friends." Then a pause. "Captain Gant?"

Gant glanced at Gideon, not comfortable with the boy being privy to this, but there was nothing for it but to open the door.

The fellow standing just outside was a small, aging black man clad in dusty clothes that hung loosely on his nearly emaciated frame. He clutched a knit cap close to his chest, his eyes betraying a numbing fear that Gant had seen all too many times before.

"You the captain, suh?"

Gant nodded. "And you are?"

"William Bond is my name." He hesitated, then went on. "Folks in Marietta told us to come here to you."

The man's voice trembled. In truth his entire body appeared to be shaking.

Gant looked past him. Even in the cover of darkness, he was overwhelmed by the sight that met his eyes.

"How many *are* you?" he asked.

Bond lowered his gaze. "Thirteen of us, suh. Only three full-grown men. Mostly women and children. A few young boys not quite grown."

He lifted his face then, and Gant saw clearly that he was expecting rejection.

"Can you help us, Captain? I know we's a lot of folks, but the women and the children, they is plain wore out. We need a place to rest and some directions on where to go next."

Thirteen! Did he dare to crowd that many into his barn along with the others already out there?

Children could be noisy. He'd be risking detection for certain. But what choice did he have? If the others were in as poor shape as the man standing at his door, they'd not get much farther before they collapsed.

He turned to look at Asa, who met his gaze straight-on but with an expression that revealed nothing.

He could easily be endangering the others already hiding in the barn by adding so many to their numbers. But he didn't have the heart to turn them away. They had already been through Marietta. He knew of no other conductors in this area. Malachi and Phoebe Esch ran a safe station, of course, but they couldn't possibly harbor so many.

"All right," he said, not without a fair measure of reluctance. "You'll have to stay in the barn. No lanterns. And no talking—no noise of any kind. You follow Asa here—his lantern is all the light we can risk. I'll get some food together for you. Be sure you keep the children quiet."

"You'll help us get away, then? To the North?" said Bond.

"We'll do what we can."

Gant turned back to Asa. "Take them quickly and as quietly as possible. I'll keep watch."

Without looking at Gideon, he started out the door.

"Captain—"

He glanced over his shoulder to see Gideon heading toward him.

"Maybe you can use an extra pair of eyes."

Gant hesitated, then gave a nod.

The night was thick and black with no moon. It was the kind of night in which Asa liked to transport runaways, but obviously that was now out of the question. There were too many for one man. They would have to wait until they could get word to another conductor for help. Besides, if the rest of the runaways in William Bond's group were in as poor condition as he was, they were going to have to have food and rest before they'd be able to go *anywhere*.

Back inside the house, after getting the runaways settled in the barn with some food and blankets, Gant faced Gideon. "You weren't meant to see what you saw tonight. If you don't keep your silence about this, you could put Asa and me in jail—not to mention the trouble you'll bring on those people out there."

The lad's gaze never wavered. "Captain, I've known for a long time that you and Asa are helping runaway slaves. I've never said a word. I won't start now."

Something about Gideon Kanagy allowed Gant to believe he could trust him. Still, he took nothing for granted. "You say you've known. How so?"

The boy shrugged. "I overheard some things said between Mamm and Rachel—and between yourself and Dr. Sebastian." He paused. "Besides, more than once I've seen the light from a lantern up here late at night. I might be young, Captain, but I'm not stupid."

Gant knew that well enough. "And you've said nothing? Not to anyone?"

"I've not. And I won't."

"Your hand on it? Your word?"

"You have my word."

Gant searched his eyes for another moment. "That's good enough, I expect."

Asa walked in just then. "You got any more hot coffee or tea ready, Captain? There wasn't quite enough to go around."

"There's more on the stove. Should be plenty."

"I'll take it out," Gideon said before Asa could cross the room.

Asa looked at Gant, who gave a short nod. "It's all right. Let him go. You and I need to figure out a couple of things anyway."

As soon as Gideon went out the door, Gant sat down at the table. Pain was shooting streaks of fire up his leg. He'd been on it more than usual throughout the day and was paying for it now.

Asa poured them each a cup of coffee and then sat down across from him. "So the boy knows what we're doing?"

"He does now," Gant said dryly. "He claims he already knew. And he probably did. That one doesn't miss much."

They talked for a time about their now precarious situation. Trying to hide even three or four runaways was always treacherous. Hiding fifteen of them—the new arrivals plus the two already waiting to leave—was beyond dangerous. It was downright foolhardy.

They bounced a few ideas back and forth but came up with no good solution. There seemed nothing for it but to wait.

"I'll send for help tomorrow," said Gant. "At best, though, it will probably take a couple of days. We can't send just anyone with you. We need someone we can trust—and someone willing to take the risk."

"Captain, we can't wait. There are too many. It could be two or three days—or even longer—before we can get someone here. We need to get food and supplies together as soon as possible, so I can take them out of here by tomorrow night. I can manage. I've traveled with as many as eight or nine before."

"There's no way you'll do this alone! For one thing, you're going to need two wagons. You can't pack fifteen slaves into one wagon without asking for trouble."

"Yes, we can. Most of them are women and young'uns. They won't take up that much room. Captain, we both know the longer we wait, the more chance of getting found out. All those people out there in the barn—you think you're going to be able to keep the children and the babies quiet?"

This was one of those times when Gant detested the shape he was in—hated being tied down, not only by his lame leg but by the business that had to be managed. If he ever needed the freedom to just pick up and go, it was such a time as this.

"Maybe I could go," he said, more to himself than to Asa. "Maybe I could leave Gideon to look after things here at the shop, and I could go with you."

"No offense, Captain, but you wouldn't be much help if we have to travel on foot for any distance. And you know that's a possibility— wouldn't be the first time we've had to leave the wagon and make a run for it."

"There's no reason *I* can't go."

Both Gant and Asa snapped around to see Gideon standing just inside the door. So preoccupied had they been on trying to come up with a solution to their problem, they hadn't heard the boy come back inside.

He stood there now, his chin lifted slightly, his jaw hard. "Asa's right, Captain," he said. "You ought not even to think of going." He looked at Asa. "I'll go."

Asa turned back to Gant with a questioning look.

"Impossible," Gant snapped.

"Why?" Gideon's expression held steady.

"You don't know anything about this. You have no idea of the risk involved."

"I probably know more than you think. And as for the risk—I know you still think of me as a boy, Captain. But I'm not. I'm a man, and I can handle myself just fine."

Gant studied him, knowing that at least in part he was right. The boy had become a man—a strapping, stalwart, clearly self-assured man.

A thought struck him. "Your mother and your sister," he said, "would have my head if I let you get involved in this."

The lad's mouth curved ever so slightly. "No, I don't suppose they *would* be too happy about it. But it would be *my* doing, not yours. I can settle Rachel and Mamm down well enough."

Gant went on sizing him up, admitting, albeit reluctantly, that the boy—the young man—standing just inside his kitchen might indeed be the answer to their problem. But if anything should happen to him, Rachel and her mother would never forgive him. Nor would he ever forgive *himself.*

"This is no game, lad," he said quietly. "There's no fun in it, and if it's an adventure you're looking for, you'd do just as well to take your chances with half a dozen water moccasins as with a gaggle of slave catchers. You don't know what you'd be letting yourself in for."

Gideon's gaze traveled from Asa to Gant. "Is it worth the risk?"

Gant frowned. "What?"

"You've been doing this for a long time—the two of you—haven't you, Captain?"

Gant said nothing.

Gideon pressed. "You must think it's important."

Gant drew a long breath. "It's different for me, son. The Irish understand all too well about the need for freedom. I come from a place where there's precious little to be had. I know what it's like to be under another man's boot."

A grim smile spread over Gideon's face, and Gant suddenly saw a glint in the lad's eyes that he hadn't seen before tonight.

"The Amish know something about oppression and the lack of freedom too, Captain. And you may be right about my looking for an adventure. But that's not *all* I'm looking for." He stopped, plainly searching for the right words. "For months now I've felt—useless. I haven't been able to find out *anything* about who's making trouble for the People, not even a hint. I don't know where to start. This, at least, is something I could do to make a difference for some folks who know what it's like to be ill-treated."

Again he paused before saying, "Asa? I believe in what you're doing. I want to help. And I *can* help."

"How am I supposed to get along without you in the shop?" Gant said, still not convinced.

Gideon hesitated, frowning, but it took only a few seconds before his features cleared. "What about Sawyer? Terry Sawyer. Didn't you say the man is looking for a job?"

"I need a woodworker, boy, not a farmer!"

"He's bright enough to learn," Gideon insisted. "Besides, you need someone to make deliveries and clean up and help with odd jobs more than you need another carpenter." His mouth quirked as he stopped for a breath. "No one can please you when it comes to the woodworking itself, anyway. And Sawyer needs a job. I expect he'd jump at the chance to work for you."

Gant leaned back in his chair, crossed his arms over his chest, and regarded the boy with no small measure of annoyance. "Well now, and don't you have an answer for everything, Gideon Kanagy?"

The lad's guileless expression didn't come off as altogether sincere when he replied. "No, sir. Not for everything. But I do think I'm the answer you need to help Asa get those runaways out of your barn."

It was entirely possible he was making a mistake that he would woefully regret later, but something at the fringes of Gant's mind urged him to take the boy up on his offer. "Asa? What do you think?"

Asa answered Gant, while watching Gideon Kanagy with a slight smile. "Why, I'd look forward to young Gideon's company," he said.

Gant feigned a sound of disgust.

"All right," he finally said. "If it's all right with Asa, I suppose it will have to be all right with me. But—" he raised a hand to ward off the boy's attempt to speak—"you'll be the one to tell your mother and sister. I'm not about to bring down their wrath on me when they find out what you're up to."

He didn't like himself for agreeing to this. Even if the lad got back safe and sound, Gant figured Rachel and her mother quite possibly would never forgive him for letting him go. But there was no way he was going to send Asa off alone with the responsibility for fifteen runaways. That would be inviting disaster. And if they stayed here in the barn even a day too long—well, that could also bring trouble to them all.

He expelled a long breath. This was one of those times when it seemed a man could do nothing right, no matter which way he turned. All things considered, he supposed he could only take what appeared to be the right way and hope God was in the decision.

✧ 14 ✧

AN UNEASY NIGHT

*For the dark places of the earth are full
of the habitations of cruelty.*

PSALM 74:20

I can't believe you're defending the man!"

Until recently David Sebastian had never seen his intended
in such a dither. Susan was generally of a calm, even temperament.
But ever since she'd learned that Gideon had gone off to places
unknown with Gant's somewhat enigmatic partner, Asa, she'd been
quick to fuss at David.

As if he could have stopped Gideon from leaving Riverhaven.
Susan's son had had a will of his own—and a strong will at that—
ever since he was a boy. But Susan seemed fixated on the idea that
David was simply taking up for Gant—"who no doubt was the one
who'd sent Gideon off with that Asa fellow in the first place."

"I'm *not* defending Gant, Susan," he insisted again. "Indeed, I
don't know of any reason I *should*. So far as I can tell, he's done
nothing that *requires* defending."

David had coaxed her into a buggy ride, hoping that an outing
would be good for both of them. The day's light was quickly fading.
It was a nice, quiet evening with a mild breeze, and he had hoped
that at least for a short time they could avoid the subject of Gideon
and Gant or anything else of an upsetting nature. There had been

so little time for them to be alone together lately that the prospect of an hour or so in each other's company felt absolutely golden to him.

It wasn't to be. They had no more than reached the crossroads just down the road from Susan's house when she started in again. "You can't tell me Captain Gant didn't have a hand in Gideon's leaving, David. No more does his friend Asa come back to Riverhaven than he takes off again, this time with my son in tow. Why would he do such a thing? And where did they *go*? Where are they?"

"I don't know, Susan. But at least the boy came to tell you he was going. He didn't simply leave without saying goodbye."

Exasperation—with *him* rather than with Gideon, David suspected—flushed her features and simmered in her eyes. "Oh, *ja*! Came to tell me he was going out of town on *business* with that fellow, Asa. Of course, he didn't mention *where* he was going or what kind of business was taking him away."

David gave a feeble shrug. Susan almost never employed sarcasm, so he was surprised to hear it creep into her tone of voice now. "Perhaps he didn't know exactly where they were going—"

"Oh, don't you tell me that, David Sebastian! And don't try to tell me *you* don't know where they went! You and Gant, the two of you are thick like thieves. They're on one of those trips to take runaway slaves to the North, aren't they? Tell me the truth now!"

So she did know. Or at least suspected. He'd been afraid of that. After all, Susan had helped Rachel care for Gant the night he first arrived at the farm, injured so badly from a gunshot wound he'd nearly died. She had spent a great deal of time, she and Rachel, nursing him back to health. There was no telling how much she might have learned about Gant's work with the fugitive slaves during that time.

She wouldn't reveal anything she'd heard, of course, not even to him. She'd be afraid of somehow implicating Rachel. When it came to her children, Susan could be a mother bear. He did wonder, though, if she knew that there were actually rumors that some of the Amish had also been involved in helping with the Underground Railroad, as it had come to be called. If there was any truth to the tales, he wouldn't be at all surprised to learn that Susan's closest friends, Phoebe and Malachi Esch, were among them.

"David? That *is* where they've gone, isn't it?"

"Susan—"

"Ach, don't say something just to make me feel better! I've been pondering this ever since the day they left. Oh, why would Gideon do such a foolish thing? *Unsinnich!* It's senseless! And dangerous as well. Don't try to tell me it's not. He knows he's needed here. He has a job. He helps with the farm. He's a man now—he should behave like one!"

David took her hand. "But don't you see, dear—that's just it. Gideon *is* a man. And as such, he needs to be free to do what he believes is right for him. If this wasn't important to him, he wouldn't have gone. There's a good reason behind his actions, you'll see."

To his dismay she began to weep. This had never happened before. Oh, when Amos, her husband, had died, of course she'd been distressed. But even then she had mourned in private, never breaking down in front of him. The Amish weren't ones to let their feelings show. It was only now, because they were to be married, that she apparently felt close enough to him to weep in his presence.

As soon as he could, he pulled the buggy off the road and stopped well into a half-hidden glen surrounded by aging maples and oaks. He turned to her and took her into his arms. "Here now, dear, don't fret yourself so," he said gently. "Gideon's smart and strong. He can take care of himself. And Asa—there's a good man for you, I'm convinced. He'll look after Gideon should he *need* any looking after. They'll be fine wherever they're going. And as for the farm, you know I'll help."

She eased away just far enough to look at him. "Oh, David— you're not a farmer! You're a doctor! I know you'll do all you can, but you've so little time. Gideon was just such a help. And I *miss* him! Even though he still came around two or three times a week to help out, it hasn't been the same since he started living *Englisch*. And now—now I won't be seeing him at all!"

Feeling more awkward than ever, he patted her back and uttered small sounds of reassurance. It had been a long time since he'd tried to comfort a woman, and he'd never thought himself very good at it. Even during his wife, Lydia's, illness, though he'd trusted his medical skills, he'd always felt somewhat at a loss when he tried to soothe her.

Still, Susan had quieted, her weeping gradually diminishing to small sobs.

David pulled her a little closer, hating the sadness weighing her down but, at the same time, loving her nearness.

"If you're right, dear," he said, "if Gideon *has* gone with Asa on a trip to the North, then I'm confident you can feel secure in his safety. Gant has told me a great deal about his friend Asa. I've come to believe he's a courageous, intelligent, and dependable man. He'll be a good influence on Gideon—and he'll keep him safe. Why, they'll most likely be back before you know it."

She made no move to free herself from his embrace. "The last time this Asa was gone, it was months before he came back," she pointed out.

"But I don't believe that's typical. As I understand it, the same people don't always take them the entire way. At some point they usually meet up with someone else who takes over and completes the trip."

She studied him. "You seem to know an awful lot about how this is done, David Sebastian."

Truth was he *did* know more than he let on, and definitely more than he wanted her to know. "I've read about this Underground Railroad business at some length," he said.

"Oh, I'm sure you have," she said, her tone wry.

He made no reply. She seemed content to let him hold her for a few moments more before she finally stirred. "David, we should go now. We still need to stop at Rachel's and pick up Fannie."

He nodded, albeit reluctantly, first seeking her lips for a kiss.

"We shouldn't, David…" But she clung to him for another moment, and his heart went spinning as if caught in a whirlwind.

"David…"

He sighed, wishing they could stay here exactly as they were. But the night air was growing cool, and he didn't want her to take a chill. There wasn't much danger that he would be getting cold. At least not at the moment.

Gently he released her and took up the reins, thinking not for the first time that November could not come soon enough.

In her kitchen Rachel tried to convince her friend, Phoebe, not to leave yet. "It's already dark. You mustn't walk home alone. I'm sure Mamma and Dr. Sebastian will be here any minute to get Fannie, and they'll be happy to take you home."

"*Danki,* Rachel, but that'd be silly! Don't I always walk home?"

Rachel stopped her at the door. "*Ja,* Phoebe. You always *used* to walk home. But things are different now. Please wait for Mamma and Dr. Sebastian."

Phoebe reached to pat her hand. "You're a dear to worry, but I'll be fine. I don't want to put Susan and the doctor out of their way." She tied her bonnet. "Tell your mamma I'll be by her place sometime in the morning with that gingerbread I promised."

Fannie came charging into the kitchen just then, hot on the heels of her puppy, who skidded up to the door and stopped right in front of Phoebe.

"Fannie, I told you to quit chasing Thunder in the house," Rachel warned. "You can run all you want outside but not in my kitchen!"

"Sorry, Rachel," her little sister said. "I forgot." Clearly, though, her mind wasn't on Rachel's rebuke. She was too busy watching the puppy's antics as he whirled in a circle around Phoebe's feet.

"Ach, I'm sorry, Phoebe," said Rachel. "Fannie, you settle him down or else! And settle yourself down while you're at it."

Phoebe laughed. "Tall order, that is. Must be something blowing in the wind. Both our dogs, Jasper and Tiny, have been wild today too."

Rachel shot a look at Fannie as she scooped up the puppy and carried him out of the kitchen. "I'm not sure who's worse, Fannie or the dog."

With reluctance she opened the door for Phoebe and stood on the porch, watching as she made her way down through the yard. "You be careful."

Phoebe waved a hand and started her brisk walk home.

Rachel waited until she was out of sight, then stepped back inside.

She hesitated only a moment before going in search of Fannie and the puppy, knowing their foolish play would help take her mind off the dull weight of worry pressing in on her.

The days saw darkness settling in earlier now. There was a definite promise of fall in the air, with the nights turning sharply cooler and the spicy scent of wood smoke coming from nearly every chimney.

Phoebe Esch had never been one to be frightened of the dark. She was used to being outside after the sun went down, especially on those nights when she had to traipse back and forth to the barn. Ordinarily she would enjoy the quiet that settled over the land when darkness drew in. For some reason tonight, though, she found herself walking uncommonly fast, anxious to get home.

The sense of peace and contentment that normally bathed the

fields along the way seemed different. The night held an oppressive stillness. Even the smallest sounds, sounds to which she seldom paid any heed, insinuated themselves into her mind and clung there, as if demanding her attention. The crack of a tree branch, the rustle of fallen leaves, the creak of a gate, and the whisper of the wind tracking along a fence rail seemed swollen and strangely ominous.

The few farmhouses out this way were set so far back from the road that any light glowing from their windows was faint and of no real help in easing the darkness all around her. Phoebe was glad for her lantern and lifted it a little higher, holding it farther out to illumine her way.

It had to be her imagination, but it sounded for all the world like voices coming from the dense woods on her left. Probably just some of the young people, out having their fun or even courting, such a mild night it was.

The thought made her feel better. She could have laughed at her own foolishness, letting spooky ideas and dark thoughts trouble her so. Still, it was only natural, wasn't it, to be a little jumpy, what with the bad things that had been going on lately?

Even so, she couldn't help but wish now that she'd done as Rachel had suggested and waited for Susan and Dr. Sebastian—especially since the mild breeze of early evening had blown up into a harder wind. Phoebe felt the first few drops of rain pelt her face.

Again she chided herself for being such a *dummkopf*. In another five minutes, she'd be home. She began to walk a little faster, a touch of lightheadedness setting her pulse to racing, her legs to trembling.

Not for anything would she tell Malachi about her foolishness. He wouldn't like to know she'd been scared, of course, but neither would he understand the reason for it.

For that matter, *she* didn't understand why she was so *naerfich* either. She was hardly ever nervous. Those things she couldn't take care of on her own, God would, so why should she be anxious?

15

LONGING FOR HELP

There is a night that builds a prison round the soul.

ANONYMOUS

Feeling better now?" David asked as they pulled up in front of Rachel's big white farmhouse.

Susan nodded. "I always feel better after talking with you. You always make such good sense."

David laughed a little. "I know some folks who would argue that point. But it *does* help to talk things through, don't you think?"

"*Ja.* I know that, but sometimes I forget. I also know I've been too hard on Captain Gant. No doubt Gideon didn't need any coaxing to make this trip. Unless my son has changed a lot, he has a real hard head all of his own. If he wants to do a thing, he does it, whether it's wise or not. I'll not pick on Captain Gant again. I promise."

"Oh, I don't think you're picking on Gant, dear. It's only natural you'd be worried about your son, especially if you don't understand why he acted a certain way. But I *do* think Gideon must have felt this was the right thing to do. He's a fine young man, Susan. It's just that he's still trying to find the right way for him."

"I know he is. But I can't keep from hoping that the right way for Gideon will turn out to be the *Amish* way."

"And it may well be. But even if he doesn't choose to live Plain, Susan, you've raised a good, dependable son—one you can trust to do what's right. There are other ways to live a life of faith and serve God besides being Amish."

Susan studied him, this good man who would soon become her husband. It still made her wonder why a man like David Sebastian had actually chosen to spend the rest of his life with her. She was only a simple Amish woman who had never lived any way other than Plain, who had little education, and absolutely no knowledge of the world except for the small corner in which she lived.

David, on the other hand, was a man of great learning and skill, a man of dignity and fine appearance. *British,* he was, using that term to express his heritage rather than *English,* to avoid any confusion since the Amish referred to everyone but the Plain People as *Englisch.*

She would never understand what he saw in her, why he had come to love her and want to marry her. But once she accepted the reality of his love and his insistence that he was willing to convert to the Amish faith so they could be married, she had mostly stopped questioning. Instead, she gave thanks daily that God had blessed her for the second time with a good man who truly loved her.

When Amos, her husband and father of her children, died, she had assumed there would never be another man in her life. She accepted the idea of spending the rest of her days growing old alone except for her family. How God had surprised her! A friend and physician to the Plain People for years, she had grown fond of David Sebastian and learned to trust him. But her love for him—and his for her—had been an unexpected but wonderful-*gut* gift.

"For the LORD hath done great things…"

"Well," he said now, "I suppose we should go inside and visit for a few minutes. Then I need to be getting you and Fannie home, though I confess I always hate saying 'good night' to you. It will be so good when we no longer have to separate at the front door at night."

Susan felt the heat rise to her face at the thought.

Like a schoolgirl, I am.

She loved their brief moments of closeness, and the very idea of sharing every part of life with David as his wife made her almost dizzy with anticipation. Not for the world would she say it aloud to him, but she was just as anxious for November to come as he claimed to be.

Half an hour later, Rachel's mother and Dr. Sebastian stood just inside the front door of Rachel's house, waiting for Fannie to gather her doll, the puppy, and the cookies Rachel was sending home with her.

Finally Fannie appeared, the puppy tucked securely in her arms, while her mother took her other things from her.

"*Danki* for the cookies, Rachel, and for letting me bring Thunder."

Rachel leaned to give her sister a hug. "You're welcome. And Thunder can come anytime. But you'd best start teaching him to obey, Fannie. Remember what Captain Gant told you—he's going to be a big dog someday. You want to make sure he grows up to mind you well."

"I know. I'll start training him right away."

"And I'll see that you do," their mamma said firmly. "You can already see him getting bigger. The sooner he learns obedience, the better."

It was raining when Rachel opened the door and they all stepped out onto the porch. They hesitated when they saw Malachi Esch pull up in his buggy.

Surprised, Rachel watched as he climbed down and hurried toward them.

"I thought I'd come get Phoebe," he said, holding onto his hat when a gust of wind blew up just as he reached the porch. "She catches cold mighty easy anymore and I didn't want her walking in the rain."

Confusion tugged at Rachel. "But Phoebe's already gone, Malachi," she said. "She left nearly an hour ago. You mean she hasn't been home yet?"

The big man stood looking at her. "*Nee.* Gone an hour, you say?"

"At least that."

Rachel exchanged a look with her mother, a cold ribbon of uneasiness coiling down her spine. The Esch farmstead was no more than a ten or fifteen minute walk from Rachel's house.

Malachi's face clouded with concern. "Why, then, she should have been home long ago. I didn't see anything of her on the way here."

"Maybe she took shelter from the rain somewhere." Rachel's mother no doubt meant to reassure him, but his expression was highly skeptical.

"But where? There's nowhere to go between here and our place."

"Well—there's the Gingerich farm," Mamma offered.

"By the time she went that far off the road, she could have made it home." Malachi shook his head. "No, she wouldn't have gone out of her way like that."

With a troubled look, he waved a hand. "Sorry for bothering you, I am," he said, turning and starting back for the buggy. "She must have taken a fall or something. Could be lying in the road somewhere, out in the rain. I'd best be going to find her."

"We'll both go, Malachi." Dr. Sebastian started toward the steps, then turned back. "Susan, you and Fannie stay here with Rachel, just in case Phoebe is on her way back here for some reason."

"I'm going with you," Rachel said. "Fannie, you stay inside with Mamma where it's warm."

"Rachel, I don't think you should—"

"I'll be fine, Mamma," Rachel said, grabbing her coat from the hook by the door and hurrying down the steps to join Malachi and the doctor.

→ ←

The rain was coming down hard as they drove away, beating a frantic rhythm against the top of the buggy. Rachel hugged her arms to herself, staring into the night, straining for the sight of her oldest and dearest friend.

A hand seemed to close around her throat as they splashed steadily through the rain, their eyes scanning the road and the trees and fields alongside it. The farther they went with no sign of Phoebe, the darker the dread that seized her heart. In spite of her best attempts not to borrow trouble, a sick certainty rose in her that trouble had already come.

After an hour of driving in the rain and stopping every few minutes to survey their surroundings, Rachel had grown nearly numb with apprehension.

Where is Phoebe? What could have happened during her short walk home? And why, oh why, didn't I try harder to make her wait for the ride that Dr. Sebastian would have gladly given?

The oppressive night seemed to engulf her and hold her captive as if she were trapped in a nightmare. But this was no bad dream. It was all too real.

Rachel couldn't help but wonder if whatever had happened to Phoebe was related to the other *baremlich* things happening to the Amish—those terrible mean things meant to frighten or, even worse, bring actual harm to the Plain People.

A night like this brought back the awful memories of the night she and Eli, her deceased husband, had been attacked. The night Eli had been *killed.*

In trying to save her from harm, he had gone against the non-violent beliefs of the Amish faith and fought against their attackers. His courage had saved Rachel's life. But Eli's life had ended, there on a road close to home, in the middle of the night when three unknown men beat him to death.

And why? What could prompt such evil, such hatred in one man for another?

For years now, there had been fires and thefts and other malicious occurrences, such as last year's attack on Fannie. But through it all, there had been only one death—her beloved Eli's.

Most of the time Rachel tried not to think of what might be yet to come, what other trouble or tragedy might lie in wait for the Plain People. But on a night such as this—how could she *not* give in to her fears?

A sudden longing for Jeremiah took hold of her. He would know what to do. Oh, how she wished he were here right now to help! And Gideon, her brother—if only he hadn't gone off with Asa!

Rachel knew the bitterness and resentment that suddenly swept through her held an irrational sense of betrayal. Gideon was already gone and might be gone for months. And Jeremiah certainly wasn't physically fit enough to go traipsing through a rainstorm in the dark of night. What else could either of them do that she and Dr. Sebastian and Malachi weren't doing?

Even so, it seemed that at some point her little *bruder* had become her "*big* brother." The boy who had once depended on *her* had become a man, and with all her heart, she wished she could go to him for help. He loved both Phoebe and Malachi. He would want to be here.

As for Jeremiah—the desire for his presence, his strength and wisdom, was never stronger than when something was wrong.

And at this moment, every instinct within Rachel screamed that something was wrong. Perhaps *very* wrong.

Phoebe Esch lay in a cold and wet place.

Her bed was rain-soaked and hard. It felt rough and scratchy, like an old wooden floor. Something scraped and scurried in the darkness as the wind whispered through the walls.

The voices she thought she heard a moment before were gone now, and the quiet was unrelenting. Something silent but threatening seemed to surround her, in front and behind and all around. The only thing she could hear was her own breathing, a heavy, wheezing sound. Her head pounded with pain, as though she'd been struck by one of the big river rocks.

She heard the rain hammering overhead. The darkness was thick and unrelieved. She could see nothing. And she was cold. So cold she couldn't stop shaking. Her body ached all over, as if she'd been thrown from a high place.

She stared into the blackness, listening, not wanting to know what the rustling sound nearby might be. Fear propelled her to push herself up with her hands, to wait, suspended there until the dizziness passed and she was able to clamber the rest of the way to her knees and wait again.

A wave of nausea flooded her. She gasped for breath, reached to yank the binding from her mouth.

Finally she managed to stand. She swayed but didn't fall, waited for her head to clear, all the while trying to ignore the pounding at the back of her skull.

Gradually the pain ebbed a little. Trembling as much from fear as the cold, she rubbed her arms and discovered that her coat was gone. She lifted a hand, only to realize that her *kapp* was also missing, her hair unbound and falling free.

Even terrified as she was, she cringed inwardly at the burden of this disgrace.

Inconceivably she felt the cold, wet boards under her feet. Where were her shoes? She'd worn them when she left for Rachel's earlier in the evening. She knew she had!

And where was she? How did she *get* here?

Slowly her eyes focused but not enough that she could make out any real shapes, nothing but shadows.

She started to creep across the floor, carefully putting one foot in front of the other, shaking so violently she lost her balance and nearly fell. She did stumble but put a hand out in front and touched a wall, regaining her balance.

The same rough wood as that of the floor scraped her hand. She felt her way along the wall, not able to see it but relying on her sense of touch to guide her.

Finally she came to what she thought was a door. She found a crossbar and tried to slide it. It moved easily, but when she pushed on the door, it didn't give.

She pushed again. It still didn't move. Desperate now, she began to pound on the wood with her fists.

Nothing.

She threw herself against the door with the full weight of her body, sending a hot arrow of pain blasting up her shoulder. But the door held firm, unmoving.

Like a prisoner, she was locked in a dark, unknown place that reeked of mold and animal droppings and rot.

Panicked, desperately fighting to keep her mind from snapping, she hammered on the door with both fists over and over again.

Finally she began to scream.

16

WHEN DARKNESS CAME DOWN

Tick-tick tick-tick! Not a sound save Time's,
And the windgust as it drives the rain…

JAMES CLARENCE MANGAN

David Sebastian wasn't given to nerves, but at the moment an oppressive sense of dread was crawling up his spine.

It was partly the night, he supposed. The unyielding darkness, the drumming rain, the silence that enveloped their surroundings.

He thought it might also be the product of these past months of harassment endured by the entire Amish community. These good people, who wanted only to keep to themselves and mind their own business, who wished no harm to anyone and wouldn't even retaliate when treachery of the worst sort was inflicted upon them, seemed caught in the grip of a strange and relentless malevolence.

Phoebe Esch was one of the finest women imaginable. Salt of the earth type and all that, for whom kindness and goodness were the only way of life she knew. Phoebe would give her last loaf of bread to a stranger even if she knew it would mean hunger for herself. She would never turn down one in need, whether the person was Amish or *Englisch*. She could no more refuse to lend a helping hand than she could walk away from a fire in her own house without trying to extinguish it.

That something might have happened to her—something harmful, perhaps yet another act of violence by the same mean-spirited, irresponsible ones behind the other trouble that had been visited on the Amish—was unthinkable. If that should be the case, however, it was time to make the authorities take notice and finally respond.

As far as David was concerned, the law had failed the Amish time and again in this matter, and now the danger was obviously escalating. Something had to be done on behalf of these nonviolent people. He knew there was a certain amount of resentment toward them because they lived a life of pacifism and refused to defend themselves—or others among them. There was always quite a lot of bitterness, even outrage, about the Amish refusal to take up arms, no matter the situation.

But David believed—and had always believed long before he made the decision to convert to the Amish faith himself—that the Plain People should be allowed to live the nonviolent life their faith prescribed. He had seen no evidence in his lifetime that violence or war or conflict served any purpose or brought any long-lasting solution to the problems of individuals, communities, or nations. Mostly it maimed and destroyed.

That there was a certain measure of apathy on the part of some when it came to investigation and the pursuit of justice for attacks against the Amish he didn't question. Throughout his years as a physician to the Amish as well as the *Englisch,* he'd seen more than enough evidence of it. It wasn't widespread—but it existed, and indifference did seem to be showing itself in the total lack of progress that had been made in finding the perpetrators of these hateful crimes against the Plain folk of Riverhaven.

Before he took his vows and became a full-fledged member of the Amish church—in other words, while there might still be hope that the authorities would listen to him more closely—he was resolved to push and push hard to get something done on behalf of the Amish.

Two officials and their families were patients of his. Perhaps he'd be able to get their attention.

He swallowed against the knot in his throat as he acknowledged the futility of his resolve being any help with the problem at hand—finding Phoebe Esch.

Beside him, her obviously worried husband drew a long, ragged breath and cracked his knuckles.

David turned toward him, forcing a firm note into his voice. "We'll find her, Malachi. We'll find Phoebe."

He noted that Malachi didn't look any more convinced than David felt.

Phoebe Esch finally gave up screaming for help. On such a night as this, who would be out in the weather to hear her cries?

She turned, standing with her back toward the door. Until now she had tried to ignore the strange sensation that every time she moved, something behind her made a rustling sound. But there it was again—the soft, whispering sound of something at her back.

There *was* something behind her. Slowly, carefully she twisted her arm and fumbled for her back, but she was stiff and sore and couldn't reach far enough around to feel anything.

Suddenly the terrifying thought seized her that something was *on* her back, clinging to her. She felt sick, dizzy with weakness and fear, and strangely weightless. Her head began to swim.

Mustn't panic…Wherever I am, the Lord God is with me. I'm not alone…Never alone.

She tried to pray, but the words in her mind were little more than rambling spurts of desperation making little sense.

She jumped when something moved in a corner across from her, a short, scraping sound. Overhead, rain continued to pound the roof.

So cold she could scarcely get her breath, Phoebe hugged her arms tightly around herself.

Malachi—he would come looking for her when she didn't come home. 'Course he would. She tried to think how long she might have been here, but she had no sense of time.

But Malachi wouldn't come right away. He'd simply think she and Rachel had got to talking and lost track of time, the way they did sometimes.

But if it was late, if it was bedtime, he'd come. He'd know she wouldn't stay out as late as that.

In her mind she willed him to come.

She was shaking so hard now it hurt, as if every bone in her body was bruised. The wind whistled down the side of the building as though looking for a place to gain entrance. Again came the scraping from the corner. It sounded closer now. Was it coming toward her?

She whipped around and again began to pummel the door with her fists, trying to ignore the rustling at her back, the scratching sound that was definitely closer, the stench that seemed to seep into the pores of her skin.

She screamed and pounded, crying now as panic flooded her. Her vision blurred, her fists raw and burning, she continued to cry out and hammer at the door as hard as she could.

A sudden blast of pain shot down her arm, shoulder to hand, stealing her breath.

Fire exploded in her chest.

Phoebe fought for breath as darkness came down and claimed her.

17

SEARCHING THE NIGHT

The storm was blowing wild…

When they still hadn't found Phoebe by midnight, they returned to Rachel's house, gathering in the kitchen to discuss their options, knowing very well they had only one.

"I know everyone's been in bed for hours by now," David said, "but we need to gather the People. We simply can't cover enough area by ourselves." He turned to Rachel. "You have a bell in the yard—like your mother has at her place?"

Rachel nodded. "Yes, and it doesn't matter about the time or the weather. The People will come."

"Yes, I know they will. Rachel, I'm sure you're chilled. You'll need to change into some dry clothes and get something hot to drink. And Susan, in the meantime, would you see if you can get Malachi to drink something as well. I know there's no point in trying to talk him out of going with us again, but we need to get him home so he can at least change into some dry clothes."

Phoebe's husband was a pitiful sight, seated on a chair at the table, staring at his hands as if unaware of where he was or those gathered at the other side of the room.

"There's already coffee, fresh-made. You must have some too, David. You're drenched."

"The bell first," he said, heading toward the door.

David *was* drenched and achingly cold as well. But with every minute that Phoebe Esch remained missing, the shadows of dread that had been building all evening deepened. By now the sense of urgency that they *must* find her, and find her soon, pressed so heavily upon him that he felt almost ill with the weight of it.

He no longer feared that something bad had happened to Phoebe. No, by now every instinct in him virtually shouted the fact that something *had* happened, that she was indeed in trouble somehow, somewhere. He could only hope and pray they would manage to find her before the *worst* happened.

He was so cold he trembled. But when he began to pull on the bell rope, he knew it wasn't the chill in the night air that had set his hands to shaking.

Standing in her bedroom as she finished changing clothes, Rachel fretted over her mother's insistence that this time *she* would accompany the others on the search for Phoebe, while Rachel stayed here with Fannie. She knew from experience, though, that when Mamma took on that tone, there was no arguing with her.

She hated the idea of her neighbors being called out again and at such a late hour. This was the second time in less than three weeks a bell had clanged in the night, summoning the People for help.

But even as she worried over the need that demanded the community's help again so soon, she knew there would be no impatience or resentment among those good friends who seemed never to think of themselves before others. They were a family, these Riverhaven Amish, a family who would unfailingly shy away from *causing* trouble but would never shy away from helping their neighbors when trouble came *upon* them.

What a comfort it was, this quickness of like-minded friends and family to come when needed, to offer assistance almost before it could be asked.

Yet in the midst of her warm thoughts about her good-hearted neighbors, Rachel couldn't shake the creeping sensation of fear that whispered at the fringes of her mind. She wasn't fooled by this brief respite in the haven of her bedroom. Outside something dark and sinister was at large.

If Phoebe had simply fallen along the road somewhere between Rachel's home and her own, they would have found her. They had covered the area thoroughly and more than once.

The reality was that her dear and closest friend was missing. Somewhere between here and Phoebe's, something had happened, and it could only be something bad.

She shuddered as she secured her hair under a clean *kapp*.

If only Jeremiah were here. What a difference his presence would make. The thought startled her. There it was again, that same longing and need for Jeremiah she had felt earlier.

It wasn't as if he could do anything to change the situation. His being here wouldn't make any difference in whatever had happened to Phoebe, nor was it likely that he would know any more about where to search for her than Rachel herself or anyone else would.

Even so, she craved his strength, his cool head, his way of looking at all sides of a situation without judging. Most of all she longed for the special way he had of infusing calm into most everyone around him.

With Jeremiah the People had come as close as they had ever come to trusting an *auslander*—an outsider. Only Doc Sebastian had been more completely respected and accepted in spite of being *Englisch*.

If only the bishop hadn't refused to allow Jeremiah's conversion, he might have been on the way toward becoming one of them by now. He could have been studying their ways and the language and the other many aspects of living Amish. And Rachel wouldn't be forbidden to at least be his friend. Or even his wife.

Things being what they were, Jeremiah wouldn't even know something had happened to Phoebe. They had trusted each other, those two, what with Phoebe being a part of Jeremiah and Asa's work with the runaway slaves.

No one knew, other than Rachel and her mother, of the Esches' involvement in helping the poor fugitive slaves trying to make their way to freedom in the North. But Jeremiah knew, and he would want to help however he could.

Caught up short by the direction her thoughts had again taken, she determined to stop them. She couldn't take on so in her mind every time there was trouble, always wishing Jeremiah were here. There was nothing he could do. Nothing.

Her reasons for wanting him close were selfish ones, that's all. She had to ignore the troublesome thoughts that defied what the bishop had ordered.

She offered another prayer—one of the many she had sent up this night—for Phoebe's safekeeping. Then, hearing voices downstairs that told her the People were starting to arrive, she pulled in a long, steadying breath and reluctantly left the room to see her friends and neighbors off on the second search of the night.

When David stepped outside again, he was relieved to see that the worst of the storm had weakened to a steady but easier rain, without the thunder and lightning and strong winds. The fanciful thought whisked through his mind that perhaps the gentling of the night would also herald something good for their search.

His heart swelled—not in surprise but in a mix of relief and thankfulness—to see the buggies lined up along the road near the house. Some were still driving up, while others came on foot, in spite of the rain. As he'd known they would, the Amish were rallying.

Faces were solemn as they gathered round, with no time wasted on greetings. As soon as David filled them in on Phoebe's disappearance, they divided themselves up into groups and briskly filed off, going back to their buggies or taking to the road on foot once again.

At nearly three in the morning, David knew they needed to stop, at least until daylight. The People were cold, wet, and exhausted. He was mindful of his own weariness, and he was beginning to feel unwell. But most of all, he worried over Susan. She couldn't be otherwise than chilled and damp from the rain, though he'd managed to convince her to stay in the buggy during those times he got out to scout an area.

More than her physical well-being, however, her emotional state concerned him. The longer they searched, the more tense and distraught she became, until he suspected she was on the verge of being ill with anxiety. She loved Phoebe Esch like a sister. They had shared a devoted friendship for years, and Susan's own tender heart would surely be shattered if Phoebe should come to any serious harm.

He decided to cross the covered bridge again. This time he would investigate the old abandoned mill house. If he found nothing, they simply had to turn back.

But when he said as much to Susan, she protested vigorously and clutched his arm. "We can't stop looking, David! She has to be out here somewhere!"

This time out, Malachi had gone with his son Reuben, who had come on foot but now drove the buggy for his father and himself.

David was somewhat relieved that he could speak more openly to Susan than he might have, had Malachi been privy to their conversation.

"Susan—dear, I'm afraid we've done all we can for tonight. We need to go to the authorities first thing in the morning and report Phoebe missing."

A stricken look crossed her face. "Oh, David, she'd hate that so! Phoebe wouldn't want anyone but the People involved in this. You know how private she is."

David considered just how to say what he felt needed to be said. "Susan, I hate this as much as you do, but I can't see that we can do anything more than what we've already done. I honestly believe we have to consider the possibility that Phoebe has been abducted."

"Oh, David! Surely not! Who would do such a thing? Phoebe has no enemies!"

"I know how unlikely it seems, but nothing else makes any sense. If she'd been injured on the way home, someone would have found her by now. I don't know what else to think."

They started over the bridge, and not for the first time, David felt a vague uneasiness about using it. He had to wonder just how stable the rickety old wooden structure really was. Apparently it had been here forever, even long before the mill had even been built. One could almost feel it swaying in the slightest wind, and every creak and groan caused David to hold his breath.

Once across he headed to the mill house. The place had been unused and abandoned for well over two years now, after Haden Rider left to build a new mill upriver. He'd never been able to sell the place because of the unpredictable and frequent flooding, not to mention the outrageous price he'd placed upon it.

He pulled off and sat studying the weathered, unpainted building. The place was almost entirely hemmed in by woodland, thick and dark. Veiled by the steadily falling rain, it looked much like a listing ship on an empty sea, built as it was on a slight slope of ground. The pathway that once led to the door was nearly obscured now by the heavy growth of brambles and weeds

A sudden sense of isolation swept over David. Whether it was the storm-driven night or the forbidding aspect of the building, he felt oppressed by the menacing appearance of the place. Ever susceptible to the mood or ambiance of a landscape or a dwelling, he could almost imagine a hovering malevolence about the setting before him. It was as if he could actually smell the rotting wood and the mold and the decay festering all around him. He cringed at the thought of what he knew he had to do.

"I'm going to have a look inside the place," he told Susan.

She looked at him, then at the mill house. "I'll go with you," she said, pulling her coat snugly around her.

"No," said David, putting a hand to her arm. "I want you to stay here."

"But, David—"

He looked at her, still restraining her with his hand. "I'll just be a moment. Wait for me here."

Just in case, he told himself as he lit the extra lantern he'd brought with them. *Just in case this dread closing in on me isn't merely a trick of my imagination.*

The haphazardly hung door was barred by a simple wooden plank that David easily turned to allow entrance.

The stench hit him full force the moment he stepped inside, a vile mix of putrefaction, dampness, and animal waste. He lifted the lantern out in front of him and stood surveying his surroundings. The place was filthy, with piles of dirt and debris, clumps of animal fur and droppings, grain dust, and scattered leavings that spoke of young people who might have used the building for idle mischief or even assignations.

He took a few more steps, extending the lantern even higher and farther out in front of him. Even with the lantern light, the place was so dark he could see little.

His gaze came to rest on another door, directly across from him. And at the foot of the door, he saw her.

Face down, her clothes in disarray, without so much as a wrap or a bonnet to protect her from the dank cold, lay Phoebe Esch, unmoving.

18

Finding Phoebe

But, oh, when gloomy doubts prevail,
I fear to call thee mine;
The springs of comfort seem to fail,
And all my hopes decline.
Yet, gracious God, where shall I flee?
Thou art my only trust;
And still my soul would cleave to thee,
Though prostrate in the dust.

Anne Steele

A dozen drums beat an agony in David Sebastian's head as he stood staring down at Phoebe Esch.

Finally he knelt beside her. Misery flowed a bitter stream through his soul. Though his eyes were dry, his heart wept, and his spirit cried for mercy as he checked for what he already knew he would find.

As a doctor he had met with death too many times throughout the years not to recognize it instantly. Even so something deep within him cried out that just this once he might be mistaken.

Please, Lord.

When he realized it was not to be, he clenched his fist against the reality of it and forced down the knife of pain that threatened to rend his chest. After a moment he studied the thing on her back for the second time, his blood thundering in his ears as he struggled with a rage forbidden by his newly adopted church.

Then he rose, whispered a prayer over Phoebe's lifeless body, and forced himself to return to Susan, still waiting outside.

The moment Susan saw David step out of the building and look toward her, she knew.

She put a fist to her mouth, her gaze locked on him, following every step he took. When he reached the buggy, their eyes met, and she choked on the well of tears she'd been struggling to hold back all night.

Still, perhaps she had misread him...perhaps Phoebe was hurt but yet within reach of help...perhaps she had been wrong about the terrible look on his face.

But when he climbed heavily into the buggy, set the lantern down, and reached for her, Susan felt her last thread of hope slip away and slowly unravel, releasing her fear and shock and pain into a churning well of despair.

"I have to go to her."

"No, Susan. There's nothing you can do now."

"I need to see her, David!"

But he held her even more closely. "Please trust me, Susan. It's not what Phoebe would want for you."

Her soft weeping broke his already aching heart. He felt weakness descend upon him, but he held her firmly, resolved that she not see the ugliness inflicted upon her closest friend.

Finally he felt her go slack in his arms. "Like a sister, she was to me," Susan murmured. "Who would hurt our gentle Phoebe? She knew nothing but good, nothing but living her faith and following the Lord God."

David remained silent, unwilling to tell her that Phoebe's goodness had almost certainly been her undoing.

19

A GRIEF SHARED

Fret not thyself because of evildoers.

PSALM 37:1

G ant was down on one knee, showing Terry Sawyer how to replace a front stretcher on a broken rocking chair.

Over the past few days, Gant had found the younger man to be just as Gideon predicted: a quick learner and grateful for a job, albeit a temporary one. He was turning out to be a good helper, though no real replacement for Gideon, who had developed into a surprisingly good carpenter in his own right.

Gant looked up when the bell chimed and Doc Sebastian walked in. One look at his friend's face told him there was trouble.

"That'll do it," he told Sawyer, as he hauled himself to his feet. "We'll let it dry and finish up tomorrow. You'd best see to the deliveries now."

As soon as Sawyer exited the back of the shop, Gant turned to Doc. "That's the fellow Gideon may have mentioned to you, the one whose wife is going to have a baby. I was hoping you could pay her a visit."

Doc gave a distracted nod but said nothing.

"What's wrong?"

Gray-faced, his eyes deeply shadowed, Doc looked as if he hadn't slept for days. He stood in silence, his hat in hand, his tall, lean form slightly stooped. From exhaustion Gant surmised.

"Doc?"

"It's Phoebe Esch. She's gone."

"Gone?"

"She died last night."

Doc expelled a long breath, as though the effort of those few words had depleted him.

Gant stared wordlessly at him, his body going rigid with surprise. "*Phoebe?* What happened?"

As he watched, a wintry expression spread over the other's face. "It seems she was abducted."

"*Abducted—*"

Again Gant sensed the fatigue wearing on his friend. "Let's go in the back," he said. "I'll get us some water."

In the back room, Gant pulled out a chair from behind the table. "Here. Sit down."

After pumping them each a cup of water, he sat down across from Doc.

He waited until the other took a long drink before asking, "What happened?"

Doc shook his head. "We don't know. Apparently she left Rachel's to walk home after a visit. She never got there. We searched for hours, just Rachel, Malachi, and I at first. Finally a little after midnight, we called out the People to help."

He sat in silence for another moment, staring at the cup in front of him. Tension built up in Gant, and he caught himself holding his breath, dreading what he would hear next.

Doc went on, his voice sounding hoarse and unsteady. "We found her, Susan and I, at the old mill house. You know the place?"

Gant nodded.

Doc sucked in his breath. "She had been…badly treated. Not beaten, exactly, but knocked about. And dragged, I think. She was wet—it rained most of the night, you know. And she was barefoot, her legs scratched and bruised. Her prayer cap was missing, and so was her coat. There was a bad cut and a lump on the back of her head. Clearly she'd had some rough treatment."

"Rough enough to *kill* her?"

The thought of someone hurting a woman like Phoebe Esch, mistreating her, bullying her, scalded Gant's blood. For a moment his mind lost touch with what Doc was saying.

But the other's next words called him back. "No, her injuries weren't that severe. I examined her more thoroughly this morning, and I'm fairly certain she died from a heart attack."

He paused. "The people who did this to her probably had no intention of causing her death, but as far as I'm concerned, they murdered her just as surely as if they'd put a gun to her head."

A storm blew up in Gant's mind. Phoebe Esch had always struck him as goodness itself. From the first time they'd met, she had shown him nothing but kindness. With her gentle features and clear, honest gaze, the Amish woman had the kind of saintly presence that inspired a man to speak softly and tread quietly when near her.

"How could anyone hurt that good woman?" he bit out. "*Why* would anyone hurt her?"

Doc rubbed a hand down the side of his face. "There's more."

Gant looked at him.

"They had pinned a piece of paper with some writing on it to her back."

Sickness welled up in Gant. He clenched and unclenched his hands once, then again.

"'*Slave Lover.*' That's what it said. Just those two words."

Gant's rage froze to shock. "Somebody knows about her and Malachi helping the runaways."

Doc nodded. "Obviously that's the case."

Gant tried to think. "And it's someone nearby, close enough to have seen something. How else would they know?"

"Not necessarily. There have been rumors over the past year or so about some among the Amish harboring refugee slaves. No names were ever mentioned, but where did the stories come from in the first place?"

Gant could make no sense of it. His mind felt fragmented, his thoughts scrambled with questions and confusion. "Do you have *any* idea who might be behind this?"

"It could be anyone," Doc said. "I've already been to the authorities—and not for the first time. They said what they always say; 'We'll look into it.' And I suppose they will. I suppose they'll give it another cursory investigation, but they won't spend much time on it."

Gant had heard this before. Like Doc he found the lack of action on the part of the law highly frustrating. On the other hand, what exactly could they do? Where would they even start?

Another thought struck him. "This has to be hard on Rachel and Susan. They were so close with Phoebe."

Again Doc gave a weary nod. "They're having a difficult time of it. But the Amish accept death with a great deal of grace. They see it as a part of life itself, as God's will. And as you know, their acceptance of His will is total. It's not that they don't grieve. But for the most part, it's a shared grief. The People face any kind of loss as a community, and that somehow makes it a little easier to bear. Susan and Rachel—and Malachi and the boys, of course—are finding it difficult to cope right now, as you can imagine. Especially given the shock—and the cruelty—of Phoebe's death. But they'll be all right in time."

He stopped, his tone reflective as he added, "Through the years I've seen it time and time again. The Amish persevere. They grieve. They accept. They forgive. And they go on. It's their way."

Gant leaned back and studied his friend. "I suppose you understand how that can be possible, your being so much like them. But I confess I *don't* understand."

"No, I suppose you don't. But how I wish you could." Doc regarded him with a strange look, a look that seemed to hold a touch of both sadness and fondness. "Your first thought is most likely vengeance. You'd like to go after the ones who did this and exact justice. Am I right?"

Gant shrugged.

"The Lord says vengeance belongs to Him."

"I know that," Gant said, though more than once he had questioned if God never used one of His creation to exact His vengeance.

Doc was watching him with a thoughtful expression. "I pray for you, you know."

Gant made a grumbling sound of some embarrassment, and Doc actually smiled a little—the first time since he'd arrived. "Oh, yes, I do, my Irish friend. I pray that one day you'll find yourself a community—a *family*—to be a part of, so you can know the grace of burdens shared instead of always trying to bear them alone."

Gant quickly glanced away. Not that he wasn't grateful for his friend's concern and his prayers, but the painful truth was that he had already found that community, that *family*, only to realize that he would always be standing on the outside looking in.

He swallowed down the lump in his throat to ask Doc about the services for Phoebe Esch. He might not be a part of her family or the Amish community, but he definitely cared enough to share their grief.

20

VALLEY OF SHADOWS

Life with trials hard may press me;
Heaven will bring me sweeter rest.

HENRY F. LYTE

Gant didn't go to Phoebe Esch's funeral service, which in the Amish tradition was held at her home on the third day after her death. He chose not to view her body, wanting instead to remember her as the sweet, lively woman who had always been so kind to him.

He did, however, go to the cemetery, standing just outside the fringes of the crowd. Although Doc and Susan had invited him to be with them—and thereby with Rachel as well—he thought it more respectful to the People that he remain at a distance. To them he was still an *auslander,* and despite their respectful and even friendly demeanor toward him, they might prefer him to keep his distance on a sad and tragic day such as this.

Besides, he knew that if he were anywhere near Rachel, the desire to comfort her would be unbearable, for to do so was forbidden.

So he stood now, scanning the grounds where the most modest of gravestones marked the final resting places of the Riverhaven Amish. As best as he could tell, the stones stated only the deceased's name and what he took to be a birth date and date of death, carved in the German language of the Plain People. The markers all looked the same to him, and that would be just like the Amish—no one would want to show status or wealth with a more distinctive or elaborate gravestone than that of his neighbors.

It was an overcast, gloomy day with low-hanging clouds that only minutes before had begun to release a light drizzle. Phoebe's grave had already been dug and awaited the simple pine coffin in which she would be buried. From the looks of the crowd, it seemed that every Amish person in the community was in attendance. A significant number of "outsiders," like himself, also stood at a respectful distance.

Doc had explained to Gant the day before that the graveside service would be brief and extraordinarily quiet, with no singing, although the words to an Amish hymn would be read. The Lord's Prayer would also be prayed silently, after which the People would disperse, only to gather once again at the Esch farmhouse for the traditional funeral meal.

Gant's eyes came to rest on Rachel, who stood just behind Susan, Fannie, and Doc Sebastian. Jealousy stabbed at him, for it seemed that Rachel would not be without comfort during the service after all. Samuel Beiler and three boys Gant assumed to be the Amish deacon's sons hovered close to her.

Beiler's usually stern and somewhat cold countenance today was directed toward Rachel in a look of attentive concern that caused Gant to look away. Inexplicably the boys stood in a stiff and formal manner that very nearly duplicated a military stance—which, given their Amish heritage, would almost certainly scandalize them, were they aware of the resemblance.

Gant found it curious that the youngest—a lad of perhaps ten years or so—every so often would glance up at his father with a look that seemed to border on anxiety, while the oldest, almost a copy of Beiler himself in size and appearance, wore an expression that could only be described as barely concealed boredom.

For her part Rachel seemed nearly unaware of the foursome gathered around her. Gant winced as he took in the paleness of her skin, the smudged shadows under her eyes, the taut features that clearly indicated that only by the most deliberate effort was she maintaining her self-control.

He watched her for another long moment, his heart aching for the sadness engraved upon her features. At last he tore his gaze away lest his attention become too obvious.

When Gant glanced back toward Rachel only moments later, he was surprised to see the eldest Beiler boy glaring at him with open hostility. He had to wonder what the deacon might have told the lad about the *auslander* in their midst.

Or was the boy simply aware that Gant had once been a rival for Rachel's affection? No doubt he resented any interference with his father's interests.

❖

Rachel thought her heart might surely shatter before the graveside service for Phoebe ended. The past days of sorrow had wrung her dry and left her feeling like a fading shadow.

Her grief had been brutally sharpened by the awareness of the cruel treatment and physical pain that had been inflicted on her dearest friend before her death. Every time she thought of the awful fear and humiliation Phoebe must have suffered that terrible night, she felt overcome with despair and a forbidden rage. She knew her bitterness and anger were as wrong as could be, and she made every attempt to shut them out from her emotions, but then she would remember, and fury would seize her again.

She wished Samuel and his sons wouldn't hover about her so. Their nearness just made it that much more difficult to conceal her feelings. No doubt their intentions were the best. Even the boys had shown their concern for her sadness during this difficult time. But she found their nearness and protectiveness strangely suffocating, as well as embarrassing. It wasn't as if she and Samuel were betrothed or in any way committed to each other.

Why couldn't he realize that right now what she needed more than anything else was to be alone to grieve?

Not so, she admitted to herself. What she really needed more than anything else was to be with Jeremiah. Just to have him nearby, to know the strength of his presence would have comforted her. Instead, she had seen him standing at the edge of the crowd of mourners, alone because he was prohibited from being with her.

In this moment the bishop's order that they remain separate from each other seemed so terribly unfair.

Her thoughts might be rebellious, but truth was she was too exhausted and weak to exert much self-control. The days since Phoebe's death had been a nightmare. No matter how hard she tried not to think about what her dearest friend must have endured, she couldn't stop the terrible images from rushing in on her when she least expected it. Even when she finally dozed off for a blessed few moments of fitful sleep, such awful dreams plagued her that she would awaken in anguish.

And always there was the question of *why.* She had the distinct feeling that Mamma and Dr. Sebastian knew more about Phoebe's death than they were willing to tell, though why that should be she couldn't think.

She dared to look at Jeremiah only once more. When she did, the tender depth of concern she encountered in his gaze nearly undid her. She looked quickly away, blinking back the tears she didn't want him, or anyone else, to see.

At last the service was at an end. Samuel moved to take her arm as if to help her walk away, but she evaded his touch by stepping forward and gripping her mother's hand.

How she would endure the funeral meal that still awaited, she didn't know. But endure it she must for any chance to comfort Mamma...and out of respect for the precious life now lost to the People but surely received by the Lord, whom dear Phoebe had served all her life.

21

THE ROAD NORTH

The dictates of humanity came in opposition
To the law of the land
And we ignored the law.

LEVI COFFIN

They had been on the road only a few days, but that was long enough for Asa to observe that, with the exception of one stubborn, steely-eyed youth who had not quite attained manhood, young Gideon had a way with the slaves they were transporting. In spite of the vast differences between their worlds, he seemed to have won their trust early on.

There was nothing too surprising about that. The boy had an easy, agreeable way about him that wasn't in the least off-putting. Moreover, his genuine interest in folks as individuals and not merely as "cargo" to be transported probably warmed them to him.

Most of these folks weren't accustomed to being treated as human beings, but more as property—chattel to be used or abused at the whim of their owners. To have such an apparently decent young man committed to their safety and to helping them attain their dream of freedom must, in itself, hint of a self-worth previously unknown to them. But for understanding to gradually dawn that this same unlikely advocate actually *cared* about them—was even capable of developing a true *fondness* for them—well, Asa reckoned that could take awhile to grasp but, once realized, would surely go a long way in helping a fellow win their trust and respect.

That's how it had been for him with Captain Gant years before.

"You're deep in thought, Asa, *ja*?"

The question from Gideon, sitting beside him on the wagon bench, brought Asa back to his surroundings. "My mind does tend to wander on these long nights of travel, I suppose."

He didn't pull out the pocket watch the captain had given him to check, but he figured it must be going on ten o'clock or so by now. There was a little too much moonlight to suit him. Unlike some conductors, he preferred as much cover from darkness as possible. At least the rain they'd encountered over the past two days had finally let up.

Behind them, in the trough behind the bench, Mac stirred and sniffed the night air. Gideon twisted around to pet the dog. Tonight his appearance was that of a typical farm boy. Although the lad no longer lived among the Amish, on occasion he still donned the clothing of his people—especially if he was planning to pay a visit to his mamma. The captain had warned him against the practice for this journey, however, pointing out that if they should encounter any slave catchers, they would be immediately suspect. An Amish boy traveling with a man of color was no ordinary sight.

"So, how did you and Captain Gant meet?" Gideon asked when he turned back to Asa.

It was as if the boy were reading his thoughts, bringing up the captain all of a sudden, even as Asa's own thoughts had ventured in that direction.

"My owner hired me out to Captain Gant on a temporary work detail."

He felt the boy's eyes on him. "You were a slave, Asa?" The question came as a near whisper.

Asa nodded. "I was."

"I'm sorry." Again the words were little more than a murmur.

"Important thing is that I'm not a slave now, thanks to the captain. He eventually bought my freedom for me."

"Captain Gant is a good man."

Asa glanced at him. "He is indeed. A better man than most folks will ever know."

"How did that come about—the captain buying your freedom? Or maybe I shouldn't ask?"

Asa gave a twist of his hand to show he didn't mind the question. "I worked for him on his riverboat for quite some time—on a temporary basis, as I said. Eventually he decided he wanted to hire me full-time, so he talked to my owner about buying my papers. It took some doing, but the captain persisted, and they finally worked things out."

Asa went on, briefly explaining to young Gideon that Cottrill, his former owner, later changed his mind and tried to get Asa back. Ainsley Cottrill had a vicious temper, and when the captain refused to sell Asa back to him, Cottrill started hunting him down.

Indeed, the bullet that had so seriously wounded Captain Gant had come from a gun belonging to one of Cottrill's men. Asa had been right in the line of fire, but at the crucial moment, the captain jumped in front of him, risking his own life to save Asa's.

"So you've been together a long time then?"

Asa nodded. "Several years now."

"Where are you from originally? Before you came here to the States?"

Gideon stopped, then pulled a face. "Aw, I'm sorry. Seems like I'm asking too many questions. But I can't help noticing that you talk a little different from the rest of us."

Asa smiled. To be young was also to be curious, it seemed. "I'm from one of the islands in the Caribbean. I never knew its name. I was brought to this country as a boy."

"With your family?"

Asa delayed his answer, intending his reply to satisfy the boy's curiosity for now. They were nearing areas into which he wasn't willing to venture. "My parents and myself, yes."

He didn't speak of the beating that had killed his father in later years nor of his half-sister, sired by Ainsley Cottrill, their owner. Cottrill had sold Ariana into a brothel as punishment for trying to escape the plantation. After that she simply disappeared from Asa's life. He and the captain searched for her everywhere they went, but their efforts always proved futile. Asa had never entirely given up hope, though he knew that with the passing of the years it became more and more unlikely that he would ever see her again.

They drove along in silence for several minutes. As if the boy had sensed Asa's reluctance to field any further questions into his personal life, he changed the subject.

"What do we do if we're stopped? You know—by a slave catcher?"

"We need to pray hard that doesn't happen. With fifteen people in this wagon, the only thing we can do is hope we're close to a woods so they can scatter and run and hide."

"But you and I, we have to stay with the wagon, right?"

Asa nodded. "We don't dare give up the horse and wagon." He paused, then added, "You remember to let me do the talking if we're stopped."

"Don't worry none about that. I'd probably be too *naerfich* to say a word."

"*Naerfich?*"

"Nervous," Gideon explained.

Asa looked at him. "I need to trust you to keep your head, boy. If we're found out, it could mean jail for both of us and a lot worse for those folks in the back of the wagon."

Gideon's expression sobered. "I was just joking with you, Asa. I won't let you down."

After that the boy seemed to run out of questions and let the steady rolling rhythm of the wagon lull him until his head began to nod.

Sometime just past three o'clock in the morning, Asa was beginning to feel a touch of the nervousness Gideon had mentioned earlier. The folks at the Spencer station had turned them away because of lack of room. They were a small dwelling, with no barn and only the smallest of cellars, in which they were already hiding half a dozen runaways.

Joseph Spencer had been obviously reluctant and apologetic, but Asa understood his dilemma. Now he could only hope it would be different at the next station, just outside of Freeport, which they ought to reach within the next hour.

If they, too, were short on room, the best he could hope for was a nice dark forest. Trees were a poor substitute for a roof over their heads, but at least they provided a hiding place of sorts. And as long as they could evade discovery, he knew from experience there would be little complaining.

The concern of a runaway slave headed for the North wasn't comfort, but freedom.

22

BROKEN TRUST

Before I built a wall I'd ask to know
What I was walling in or walling out...

ROBERT FROST

From her kitchen window, Rachel could see Samuel Beiler pull his buggy off the road and step out, then start briskly up the path toward the house.

She drew a long breath, hoping this unexpected visit wasn't going to be another in his ongoing efforts to convince her that she ought to marry him. Her emotions were still raw from the shock and aftermath of her dear friend Phoebe's death. The last thing she felt like dealing with right now was the pressure of Samuel's persistence.

It would be all too easy to be impatient with him at a time like this. While his tireless attempts to court her might be pleasing, even flattering, to some of the other women in the community, for Rachel they had become awkward and wearisome.

Especially since the only man she would even consider marrying was forbidden to her.

Even so she made up her mind that she must strive for patience with Samuel. Although he often irritated her with his stringent judgments and overbearing manner, she supposed he meant well. Certainly she had no desire to antagonize him or hurt his feelings.

Quickly she ran her hands down the sides of her dress, then smoothed her *kapp*, waiting for his knock on the door.

"My sister Rebekah thought you might enjoy these with your supper."

Samuel stood just inside the kitchen as he handed Rachel a pan of fragrant honey buns.

"Oh, they smell wonderful, Samuel," Rachel said, taking the pan from him and setting it on the table. "Be sure to thank Rebekah for me."

"Well, we know how hard these past few days have been for you, what with Phoebe's passing and all. Just wanted to let you know we're praying for you and for Susan also."

This was a different Samuel from the one she was used to. In place of the stern expression and ramrod straight posture common to him, he actually seemed a softer, kinder man, more relaxed and genuinely concerned for her. Was the bad trouble that had come to the People having a softening effect on him? Maybe she had misjudged the intent of his visit after all.

"Thank you, Samuel. It's true that these days have been difficult— for all the People but especially for Malachi and his family."

"*Ja*, of course," he said. "But I know you and Phoebe were awful close. I just wanted to see how you're doing."

"That's kind of you, really. Keeping busy seems to help."

He pointed to one of the kitchen chairs at the table. "May I sit?"

"Oh, yes! I'm sorry, I wasn't thinking. Please, sit down. Would you like me to fix you a cup of tea?"

"No, no. We had dinner at Rebekah's house today. I must say her tea isn't so *gut* as yours, but I drank more than I should have anyway."

Rachel wished she didn't feel so awkward around this man, who had actually been a good friend to her and her family through the years. Most likely her uneasiness stemmed from the awareness of his interest in her. Whatever the reason, she was never altogether comfortable with Samuel, never totally accepting of what he said on the surface as opposed to what his unstated meaning might be. Sometimes it was an effort simply to be polite.

All the same, she *would* be polite.

"I haven't seen Malachi since the funeral service," Samuel said. "Is he getting along all right?"

"I took supper to him last evening. He's very sad, of course, and a little lost. He and Phoebe were so close."

Samuel nodded. "Such a good marriage they had. To lose our life's partner is a very hard thing." He gave a long, heavy sigh and stared down at his hands. Rachel almost got the feeling that his morose words and manner might be an attempt to play on her sympathy.

Now *that* really was unkind of her. She knew what it was like to lose a beloved spouse. Was she so hardhearted she couldn't offer him at least a little understanding?

"Yes, a very hard thing," she said gently. "How long has it been since Martha went to be with the Lord now?"

He raised his head and fastened a strange look on her. "A long time. As you know, she died giving birth to our Joe, and he's going on eight years now." He paused. "But of course we have no way of knowing that Martha *is* with the Lord God. We can only hope that she is."

"Oh, Samuel, surely you don't doubt that she is! Martha was such a fine Christian woman—a good person and a wonderful wife and mother."

He nodded still watching her. "She was all that, but it would be arrogant of me to assume that her goodness won her a place in heaven. Only the Lord God knows where each of us will spend eternity, based upon how we live our lives here on earth."

Rachel hadn't believed that particular view of heaven for a long time now, thanks, at least in part, to Phoebe and Malachi helping to open God's Word and the truth to her and Eli and others over the years—that it was God's grace that saved them, not any works on their part.

Samuel's gaze sharpened. "I suppose you know that there was talk about Phoebe and Malachi studying the Scriptures on their own, without guidance. You and Eli being such good friends with them, I hope they didn't change your belief in the Old Ways with their forbidden interpretations of the Holy Word."

There was no way Rachel was going to get into this discussion with him. She knew how extremely set in his opinions Samuel was, especially with his being a deacon and all.

"There's always talk," she said with a shrug. "I try not to listen to gossip."

He didn't reply right away. When he finally spoke, it was with what Rachel had come to think of as his *deacon's* tone of voice. "A good idea. But as a deacon, I have to be aware of what's going on among the People. It's no secret that some so-called 'Bible studies' are taking place without the approval of the leadership, indeed have been going on for some time. That kind of practice goes strictly against the *Ordnung*." He paused, then added, "As you know, Rachel."

She said nothing. When Samuel was speaking as a deacon, Rachel usually gave little input into a discussion. Sometimes it was a tricky balance as to when she could safely carry on a friendly conversation with him, as opposed to those times when she knew she'd only be inviting rancor if she tried to make him see her point of view. It seemed easier to let him have his say with no comment from her.

As quickly as he had assumed his stand as a church leader, he now returned to his former role as her friend and neighbor. "I hope Susan is getting along as well as can be expected."

Rachel nodded. "Mamma is strong. And she stays busy, keeping up with the farm and all—and what with the wedding not so far off now."

"Oh, *ja,* that's right. She and Dr. Sebastian." He ran a hand across his chin. "Ordinarily this could never have happened—a marriage between Plain and *Englisch.* But Bishop Graber thought an exception was in order for the doctor."

Rachel looked at him. "But Dr. Sebastian will no longer be *Englisch* when he and Mamma wed. Soon he'll be saying his vows and joining church. He'll be Amish then."

Was it a glint of disapproval that flicked in Samuel's eyes?

She wasn't about to carry this any farther. "So, how are your boys, Samuel?"

Again he let out a long breath. "It's hard for them, of course, with no mother."

Well, she'd walked right into that, hadn't she?

"It's especially difficult for Joe, his being the youngest," he went on. "Noah's twelve now, and a big help with the work around the farm. He's my quiet one. But Aaron," he said shaking his head, "he worries me. He's in his *rumspringa,* you know—a foolish idea and such a treacherous time for our young people. I wish we gave them far less freedom than we do. I can only hope he uses good sense and doesn't decide to join the *Englisch* world."

"I'm sure you don't have to worry about that, Samuel. You have good sons. They'll be all right."

He regarded her with a gaze of such intensity that Rachel felt suddenly ill at ease.

"They're good boys, *ja.* I've done my best with them. But even good children need a mother."

When Rachel made no reply, he cleared his throat, saying, "As you know, Rachel, I've always hoped that you would fill that role."

"Samuel…please, not now…"

"I'd be a good husband to you, Rachel. If you're worried about the years between us, we know each other well enough that age shouldn't matter. And I've always believed that a strong friendship

is the best foundation for a good marriage. And you and I, we're
friends, *ja?*"

"Of course, but—"

"Eli's been gone plenty long enough for you to take a husband,
Rachel, don't you think?"

"Time has nothing to do with it—"

"Then why do you hesitate? Why do you prefer to be alone instead
of becoming my wife?"

"Samuel—I've already explained this to you. More than once in
fact. I don't...feel that way about you. I can't marry a man simply
because I don't want to be alone."

Abruptly he stood, his chair scraping the floor. "It's because of
that *auslander,* isn't it?"

Startled by the sudden change in him, the roughness of his tone,
and the deep red stain that crossed his features, Rachel fumbled for
words but found none.

"Oh, I know about *Gant!*" He spat out the name like an obscenity.
"I know all about the two of you."

Rachel felt the blood rush to her head in an almost dizzying
wave. "What do you mean?"

"I know Gant went to the bishop and sought permission to convert
to our faith. Because of *you*—so he could marry you! And I know
you must have agreed to marry him, or he would never have gone
so far as to approach the bishop! Not to mention the times you've
been seen together."

His mouth twisted in disgust as he punched the palm of one
hand with his fist. "How could you take up with an outsider like
that, a man you scarcely know, when you won't so much as give
me the time of day?"

He glowered down at her, his expression so angry Rachel had
to fight against feeling intimidated. She got to her feet, somehow
managing to meet his gaze with a level look of her own.

"Bishop Graber told you this?"

"Of course, he *told* me. He was outraged at the nerve of the man, just as I was. Do you know how this makes me feel, Rachel? I've waited for you for years, putting up with your excuses and your delays, only to find out that you've indulged in a forbidden relationship with an *Englischer!*"

Caught totally off guard, shocked—and furious—at the idea that the bishop would divulge what was meant to be held in confidence, Rachel groped for control. Clenching her fists at her sides, she refused to back down, even though his angry tirade had badly thrown her off balance.

"The bishop had no right to break a confidence. And *you* have no right to accuse me of anything, Samuel! It wasn't *my* fault that you wouldn't accept 'no' as my answer to your attempts to coax me into marrying you. I told you—I told you repeatedly—why I wouldn't. Long before Jeremiah Gant ever stepped foot in Riverhaven, I refused to become your wife, and I explained why—more than once. My feelings for you weren't what they should be for us to marry."

"But your feelings for this man, this *Gant,* now that's a different thing entirely. Is that how it is, Rachel?"

"It doesn't matter what my feelings are now. And since you obviously know all about the situation, it seems I don't need to explain anything to you!"

Rachel stopped, her chest burning as she tried to swallow her anger. It was wrong, terribly wrong, to be so infuriated with Samuel—with *anyone.*

As though he sensed that he'd gone too far, that he'd actually made things worse for himself, Samuel seemed to make a visible attempt to subdue his outburst.

"I'm sorry, Rachel. I forget myself sometimes. You mean so much to me—"

"Is this why you came here today? To *accuse* me?"

"No! I had no intention of upsetting you. Honestly I didn't, Rachel. I meant only to look in on you and see if you're all right."

Watching him, Rachel could almost believe he was telling the truth about that much, at least. But his temper had flared at her rejection, again erecting a wall between them.

She had known that Samuel had a temper, had seen it on occasion, and had heard about it from Eli and a couple of Martha's friends. What she hadn't known was that he could flare so quickly and be so hurtful when he did. He had almost frightened her.

She felt suddenly weary. At the moment she wanted nothing more than for him to leave. And she told him so.

He looked anxious and even hurt at her dismissal, but he didn't argue. "*Ja,* I'll go, Rachel. But first I apologize for taking on so. I spoke truth, but I spoke it in anger, and that was wrong of me. For that I'm sorry. I hope…may I dare to hope…that you'll forgive me and not turn away from me? I *care* for you, Rachel. You must know that. I care too much to ever intentionally hurt you."

She forced her voice past the knot in her throat. "Please, Samuel— it's best for now that you go. Please."

He turned and left, walking with the familiar straight-backed precision and deliberate purpose that made him identifiable even from a distance.

For a long time after he had gone, Rachel struggled with the anger and indignation he had provoked in her. The fact that the bishop had broken Jeremiah's confidence, coupled with Samuel's insinuation that she had somehow indulged in a questionable relationship, churned inside her with a force that ground into her flesh and bone.

She tried to sort her thoughts out in an effort to get to the bottom of the anger that had left her reeling, but the gathering dismay and uneasiness crowded out any sense of clarity. She knew only that a man of God like Bishop Graber had no right to breach the Amish tenet of privacy and spill secrets to which he had been made privy, whether the individual involved was one of the People or an out-sider. And Samuel—whom she'd known for years and would have thought knew her better and respected her more than to believe his own accusations—that he would say the things he had. Why, she could scarcely comprehend what she had heard this day!

Her distress over the awful things Samuel had said burned like a vicious fire deep within her—especially because she was forced to admit that she wasn't entirely innocent of the accusations Samuel had hurled at her.

Truth was her feelings for Jeremiah *had* gone beyond the bounds of what was pure and acceptable for an unmarried Amish woman. Not only that, but she'd made assumptions. In her all too human arrogance, she had assumed that the Lord God would grant their desire to be together, that Jeremiah's conversion would be approved, that they would be married, that their love would be recognized and legalized in the eyes of the People and the church.

Even so, the bishop was wrong too. Oh, she felt like confronting him, throwing back his judgment of Jeremiah with an accusation of his own guilt. But of course she couldn't. There was no accusing a bishop. There was no telling *anyone* what he had done.

How, then, was she to calm the turbulence of her emotions and put to rest the wrong feelings sweeping through her?

She couldn't. But there was One who could—the One who could tame the storms at sea and still the wind could surely put to rest the turmoil in her spirit.

Rachel knew that at this moment she was in desperate need to commune with that One. Without hesitating, she dropped to her knees in the middle of her kitchen and sought His forgiveness and His peace.

23

SPECIAL REQUESTS

A good man grants favor to his enemies
As well as his friends.

ANONYMOUS

G ant had given Terry Sawyer the morning off because his wife
wasn't doing so well, so he was alone in the shop when Samuel
Beiler walked in.

He'd been caning a chair for Lucas Reilly. Caning wasn't a process he particularly enjoyed. He wouldn't do it for just anyone, but
Lucas had become a friend and had also sent a number of customers
to the shop, so it seemed a small enough favor.

It was the middle of the morning, and he had a dull headache
from lack of sleep. In truth he hadn't slept well since Phoebe Esch's
death. Not only had her loss touched him deeply, but he couldn't
help but wonder what might come next. No more would he drift
off into a restless sleep than he'd wake up and lie sleepless the rest
of the night, thinking about Rachel and worrying about her being
alone out there on the farm in the middle of nowhere.

Last night had been no different, so he was not in an especially
good mood. Beiler's entrance caught him completely unaware. In the
narrow gap between surprise and confusion, however, he somehow
groped and found enough composure to be civil.

"Mr. Beiler," he said straightening, "what can I do for you?"

The Amish deacon wore the typical work clothes of the Plain People, but he looked pretty starchy for a man who worked hard for a living. He doffed his black, broad-brimmed felt hat as he entered. A good indication that summer was over, the Amish straw hats were being put away now until warm weather returned.

His features were set in the solemn, fixed stare with which Gant was familiar. There was no mistaking the glacial edge of contempt in his eyes or the hard set of his mouth.

He stopped a few feet away.

"I am told you make good furniture, *ja?*"

Gant gave a guarded nod, wondering what this was about.

"I have a piece I wish you to make for me. It is to be a special gift to someone." As Beiler said the words, his eyes took on a curious glint.

His curiosity aroused and his instincts on the alert, Gant studied him. Why in the world would Beiler consider placing an order with a man he obviously didn't like?

"You want me to build a piece of furniture for you?"

Beiler's chin went up a little. "*Ja,* that's right."

"And what would that be?"

"A nice sideboard, about so big—like this." Beiler used his hands to demonstrate the size he wanted. "Something very fine." He paused. "It must be special. Can you do that?"

Gant felt the muscle beside his eye twitch. "I expect I can. But you said this was to be a gift. Does that mean you need it fairly soon? The reason I ask, I'm kind of backed up with orders right now."

Beiler seemed to consider Gant's question. "Not too soon, *nee.* Rachel's birthday does not come until the end of January."

The dull ache at the back of Gant's skull escalated to a hammering. Why was Beiler doing this? Clearly the man was trying to make a point of some kind, but what? And why?

Even as he struggled to control his anger, his mind raced. Then it struck him. Beiler was marking his territory. He was striking a claim, warning Gant off—trying to wall Rachel in and Gant out by making him believe that there was more to his and Rachel's relationship than just an alliance of friends.

If that was the case, it meant that somehow Beiler knew Gant was in love with her and, possibly, Rachel with him, or at least that she *had* been at one time. But if the man knew *that* much, did he also know that the bishop had closed the door on any possibility of a future for them? Or was he simply trying to make certain the door *stayed* closed? Was the sideboard nothing more than a ruse, an excuse to come here today to confront Gant?

Or had Rachel given him reason to do this? He didn't think an Amish man would give a special gift to a woman unless they were married or betrothed or at least had made a commitment to each other. Had Rachel finally given in and agreed to marry Beiler?

He felt sick with shock and disappointment. And yet he couldn't believe Rachel had changed that much. He'd seen the way she looked at Beiler at times—almost as if she didn't even *like* the man, much less would consider marrying him. He also had a sense that Beiler wasn't actually expecting him to accept an order from him, that in fact he'd assumed Gant would refuse out of hand to make the sideboard.

Well, guess again, deacon. Guess again. Because if you're prepared to spend the kind of money I'm going to charge you for this, I'm prepared to do the job. If for no other reason than because you thought I wouldn't.

In the meantime he refused to believe—not unless he heard it from Rachel herself—that she had changed her mind about marrying Beiler.

"That'll be a nice surprise for Rachel," he said, biting down on his pride and the bitter swell of anger lodged in his throat. "But it won't come cheap. I'm sure you don't want anything but the best, though, and by ordering this far ahead, I'll be able to take my time and give you a fine piece of furniture."

Clearly he'd caught Beiler off guard with his quick acceptance. The Amish man's eyes widened, and he turned a bit red in the face.

But after a few seconds, he nodded agreement. "Price is not a problem," he said stiffly, "so long as it is reasonable."

"I have to say, I'm a little surprised that you'd have an outsider undertake such an important project," Gant remarked. "It's been my observation that a number of you Amish fellows are handy with carpentry yourselves. Are you sure you want me to do this?"

Obviously flustered, Beiler seemed to collect himself quickly. "I've no time to waste on carving wood. My business is farming."

"I see. Well then, let me just get some information from you about your choice of wood and design. I'll fetch some drawings I have on file and be right with you."

Without so much as a glance in the other's direction, Gant headed for the back room, where he stood gritting his teeth and clenching his fists. Finally when the wave of anger stopped slamming against his chest and he could once more get his breath, he gathered up some design illustrations, broke a grim smile, and returned to write up Beiler's order.

He was just finishing his lunch in the back room when Terry Sawyer charged in. The younger man was clearly upset and out of breath, his hair falling in his eyes, his face flaming. He looked as if he'd run all the way from the boarding house.

"Captain Gant!"

"What's wrong, Sawyer?"

"It's my wife! The baby's coming! That Dr. Sebastian who looked in on Ellie before—do you think we can get him to come again and right quick?"

Gant pushed away from the table, his chair scraping the planked floor as he got to his feet. "I don't know how quick we can get him here, but I'll send someone to find him."

Upon a closer look at Sawyer's face, he added, "You go on back and stay with your wife, now. We'll find the doctor."

Sawyer turned and hurried out, calling his thanks over one shoulder.

Gant grabbed his cane and went in search of Harley Ware, a black youth who helped his family with the money he made doing odd jobs and running errands for the townspeople. After asking around, he found the boy at Loyal Frissom's mercantile, digging out the decaying wood around a window that was to be replaced.

Frissom agreed to let the boy delay the work on the window to go fetch Doc Sebastian, and Harley wasted no time. After wiping his hands on a paint rag, he brought the delivery wagon that Frissom offered around to the front of the store.

"Bring him back as fast as you can," Gant told him, recalling the look of panic frozen on Terry Sawyer's face.

Of course, most new fathers probably wore that same look when the birthing time came. All the same, he liked the young couple and wanted things to go well for them.

It would be nice if *something* went well around here for a change.

→ 24 ←

CONCERN FOR A FRIEND

Help us to help each other, Lord,
Each other's cross to bear;
Let each his friendly aid afford,
And feel his brother's care.

RALPH HARRISON

Gant was still working when Doc Sebastian and Susan Kanagy walked into the shop that evening.

They both looked pleased. In fact, Doc was all smiles, even if he did appear a little bedraggled.

"Well, I see Harley found you," said Gant. "And I must say, your new assistant is a real improvement to your practice, Doc."

Susan smiled at him, and Gant grinned back. The lady had one of those smiles you warmed to in an instant.

As did her daughter.

"I thought Mrs. Sawyer might appreciate having another woman at her side," Doc said. "She hasn't really been here long enough to get to know many women in town. Susan's helped deliver more than one baby over the years, so I brought her along."

"So—we *do* have a baby, then?" Gant said.

"We do," Doc replied. "A little girl. She's a tiny one, but she seems healthy enough."

"And Mrs. Sawyer? How's she doing?"

"Better than *Mr.* Sawyer," Doc said dryly. "She's worn out, of course, but considering all the trouble they had on their way here, I'd say she's none the worse for wear."

"Well, that's good. They name her yet?"

"Naomi Fay. After Mrs. Sawyer's mother, she said."

"Pretty name." Gant pointed to some chairs in the corner. "Sit down. I expect you're both tired."

"Actually we came to take you to supper," Doc said. "We *are* a bit tired, but we thought we'd get something to eat before starting home. Why don't we all go down to the boarding house and have some of Mrs. Haining's fried chicken and dumplings?"

Reluctant to intrude on the couple's time to be alone together, Gant hesitated.

"You've worked late enough," Doc said, going to the front of the shop and turning the *Closed* sign around on the door. "Besides, you have to eat."

Truth was Gant didn't feel he'd be very good company tonight. He'd run a gamut of emotions since his encounter with Samuel Beiler this morning, most of them dark. And Doc knew him too well to not recognize one of his sour moods.

Again he attempted to protest. "I'm actually way behind in my orders—"

"You're the only carpenter in town," Doc said. "Of course, you're behind on your orders. Folks will wait when they haven't a choice. Come on now—we're not leaving without you."

"Oh, all right," Gant grumbled. Bad mood or not, he didn't feel much like being alone right now. "Just let me wash the sawdust off my hands and face and lock up in back."

⇨ ⇦

"If you'd like to go upstairs and say hello to the newest member of the Sawyer family," said David, "I'm sure you'd be welcome."

Gant shook his head and pushed back from the table. "I'll wait till tomorrow. I expect all three of them could do with some rest right about now."

The proprietor, Mara Beth Haining, stopped at their table just then. "I hope you all enjoyed your meal tonight."

After her words brought a round of enthusiasm from each of them, she leveled a small frown in Gant's direction. "I haven't seen you in a spell, Captain. Does that mean you've been disappointed in my cooking or that you're simply not eating the way you should?"

"Mrs. Haining, only an absolute fool would be disappointed in your cooking," Gant assured her. "No, ma'am, I've just been busy, is all. You still make the best fried chicken in three counties, and your dumplings are enough to make a grown man weep."

"And aren't you the silver-tongued rascal, though?" she teased.

Turning to Doc she asked after the new baby and her parents. "Is there anything they need yet tonight? I'll have supper sent up to them in a bit. Is there anything else I can do?"

"I told them just to let you know if they need any help at all," Doc told her.

Mara Beth Haining was a genuine southern belle with a delightful Virginia accent. In David Sebastian's estimation, the lady possessed just the right mix of motherly attentiveness and the kind of warm, engaging informality that made her boardinghouse guests and dining room customers feel as though they had a home away from home.

She and her husband had moved to Riverhaven and opened the boardinghouse only two years before Emery Haining died of a stroke. Mara Beth, unwilling to give up what they had worked so hard to establish, had rolled up her sleeves and set herself to doing an admirable job of running one of the most successful combination inn and restaurants in southern Ohio.

Sweet-faced and matronly, she reigned as one of the few female entrepreneurs in the county. While childless, with hair as snowy white as the immaculate shirtwaists she always wore, she mothered and hovered over every soul who came under her roof.

David liked and admired her as much as anyone in town. He also liked the young couple upstairs with the new baby and thought them fortunate to have found shelter in Mara Beth's homey establishment. Of course, Gant was to thank for that.

After she moved on, David said, "Now there's a woman who would have made an extraordinary mother. A shame, really, that she never had children of her own."

"I think she makes up for it by taking half the town, in addition to her guests, under her wing," Gant said. "Folks around here can't say enough good things about her."

"Speaking of mothering," Susan said, "some of our neighbor women have been sewing and collecting clothing for the baby. I plan to bring everything into town tomorrow morning."

"Not alone—" David put in quickly.

"I won't be alone, David. I'll have Rachel and Fannie come with me. We'll bring some baked goods as well."

"I could come along," he said.

"There's no need. You're busy, and we'll manage just fine." She paused, arching an eyebrow. "Don't fuss, David."

Fuss? If she only knew. Truth was he didn't want to let her out of his sight. Not for a moment. If anything should happen to Susan...

He didn't allow himself to finish the thought.

"Feel free to come by the shop," Gant offered. "In fact, maybe I could go with you? I might not feel quite so awkward that way. I confess I don't know much about paying a visit to a new baby."

David saw the studying look Susan turned on Gant.

"Why, that's a good idea, Captain Gant," she said. "You can help us carry some of our things, and it will give Fannie a chance to say hello to you. She'll like that."

David was a little surprised at Susan's suggestion, but seeing the pleased expression on Gant's face, he was glad she'd offered it. Of course, it wasn't only Fannie the captain would be looking forward to seeing.

"Do we need to stop at Rachel's and pick up Fannie?" David asked as they drove away from town after supper.

"No," Susan said. "She's spending the night. She wanted to stay, and Rachel said she could use her help putting some finishing touches on a birdhouse or two in the morning. I want to do some more baking first thing, so I'll pick them up later. They can help me collect everything from the neighbors and get it packed up."

"It was kind of you to include Gant in your visit," he said. "I suppose you saw how pleased he was."

Susan nodded. "It will be good for Rachel to get out too. She's still grieving Phoebe. We both are, but I think Rachel tends to go too much inside herself when she's sad." She sighed. "I suppose we all have to grieve in our own ways."

"So Rachel's still building her birdhouses, is she?"

"Oh, she works hard at it, David. Always putting one together or painting another. She enjoys it."

He said nothing until they passed over the ravine near the Lape farm. "Too bad things are what they are between her and Gant. They'd so enjoy being together, I think—even working together, what with both of them having a liking for woodworking and building things."

"Too bad for a lot of reasons," Susan said quietly. "'Course the bishop doesn't approve of her building the birdhouses, you know."

"The bishop doesn't seem to approve of a lot of things," David said, his tone sounding unusually sharp. "Including Gant." He paused, then went on. "I beg to disagree with him there. I've always thought Rachel and Gant would be good for each other—and good *with* each other."

Susan turned to looked at him, admiring, as she always did, his lean profile, the gentle wave to his silvering hair, and the kindness engraved upon his features. How fortunate she was to be able to talk to David openly, knowing that whatever she told him would go no farther than his ears. Not only was he to be her husband—but he was also her dear friend, indeed had been a good friend long before they ever became engaged.

"Truth is," she said, "I don't understand why the bishop wasn't at least willing to give Captain Gant and Rachel a chance. It seems to me he closed the door on any hope for them awful quick-like."

When he didn't answer for a long moment, Susan knew him well enough to realize that he was mulling over what she'd said.

His eventual reply sounded thoughtful, even a little hesitant. "You don't suppose the bishop's attitude toward Gant has anything to do with Samuel Beiler, do you?"

"Why on earth would you think that?" she said, puzzled.

He shrugged. "Well, Samuel *is* a deacon, one of the leaders of the church. If the bishop is aware of his interest in Rachel, wouldn't it be possible that he might favor him over Gant? Even to the point of making sure he had a 'clear field,' so to speak? After all, Samuel was born and raised Amish, has established himself well as a deacon—it might be only natural the bishop would prefer Rachel to marry a Plain man instead of an outsider."

His words stunned her. "But—that wouldn't be *right*. He's the *bishop*. Surely he wouldn't want Rachel to marry a man she's repeatedly refused."

"I don't know that it's all that unlikely, Susan. Think about it. If you look at it from the bishop's point of view, Gant is an unknown, an outsider, a total stranger. Why, he's even originally from another country and entirely separate from the Plain community."

She stared at him. "But, David—you could be describing yourself."

He looked at her, smiling a little. "That's true, dear. But with a big difference: The People have accepted me as a friend and as their physician for years now." He stopped, then added, "More to the point, Samuel Beiler has never courted you, whereas he's wanted to marry Rachel for years now."

Susan looked away, staring at the road as she tried to take in the significance of his words. Surely David was wrong. Would a bishop even think in such a way, much less *act* in so callous a manner?

"Susan? I didn't mean to upset you."

She turned to him. "Oh, you didn't upset me. But really, David, I can't begin to believe such a thing about the bishop."

"I'm sure it wouldn't be anything malicious on his part. He'd simply want what's best for Rachel. In his mind Samuel would be the better husband for her."

Susan studied him. "But if you're right—why, it would be so unfair!"

"Yes, wouldn't it?" he said softly. After a moment he added, "Now don't you be troubling your pretty head the rest of the night with some silly notion of mine. I'm sure you're right. A bishop should be above that sort of behavior, and I'm sure Bishop Graber is. Forget I ever brought it up."

Susan found a deep breath and nodded. "You're right. Let's not give it another thought. Best to forget it altogether."

He reached to squeeze her hand. "Forgive me?"

"There's nothing to forgive. I can see how you might think such a thing, especially with us concerned for both Rachel and Captain Gant, what with things as they are. But truly I can't believe you're right."

"As I said, it was just a foolish thought. I confess that I do continue to wish that something could work out for the two of them, though. I suppose when a man's as happy as I am with you, it's only natural that he'd want his friend to have a measure of that same kind of happiness."

Now Susan squeezed *his* hand. "You and Captain Gant have become good friends, haven't you? You truly do care about his well-being."

He nodded. "He'd never admit it, of course, but I think he's a lonely man. I'd very much like to see something good happen in his life."

Susan didn't say so aloud, but she thought she well understood David's concern for his friend. In truth she, too, would be ever so pleased to see happiness come to Captain Gant.

Especially if it meant happiness for her Rachel as well.

25

A Moment of Wonder

Hopes, fears, prayers, longings, joys and woes—
All yours to hold, O little hands!

LAURENCE BINYON

Rachel hung back at the entrance to Jeremiah's carpentry shop, feeling out of place and awkward about going in, yet wanting to see him so much a permanent ache seemed to have moved into her heart.

Fannie, however, displayed no hesitation, tugging on Rachel's hand to hurry her inside. "I'm so glad Captain Gant is going with us to see the baby, aren't you, Rachel? Everything is more fun when he's around!"

Fun had nothing to do with the emotions rioting inside Rachel at the moment, but she managed a smile for her little sister as she followed her and her mother into the shop.

At first she kept her eyes downcast, looking up only when he spoke.

"Well now, this is a big event," he said, his deep, rich voice rolling over Rachel like a silken wave, shaking whatever calm she had thought to display.

"Three lovely ladies in my poor, humble shop and all at the same time. Keep an eye on the rafters there, Terry, lad—the building may fall at any moment."

At Fannie's giggle Rachel looked up. To her relief he didn't meet her eyes right away but stood, arms crossed over his chest, grinning at her sister.

Rachel hadn't seen him since Phoebe's funeral, and her throat went dry at the sight of him. She had all she could do not to gawk like a *dummkopf*. He wasn't in his work clothes but had obviously spruced himself up to go calling.

Jeremiah was a handsome man at his worst—and she had seen him at his worst, right after he'd been gunshot—but today he looked ever so appealing in a crisp white shirt and a dark silvery tie. He had even managed to tame his usually mussed curly hair into neatness. The question as to who might have laundered that nice white shirt to its state of starched perfection teased at her mind, but she dismissed it before she could speculate on the answer.

Thankfully her mother stepped up just then and handed him the applesauce cake she'd baked early this morning, still fragrant from the oven. "I thought we'd bring you and Mr. Sawyer something for yourselves, Captain."

Jeremiah's eyes widened as he took the cake from her and lifted a corner of the napkin covering the pan. "Oh, my! If that tastes even half as delicious as it looks and smells, Mrs. Kanagy—*Susan*—" he corrected, "I can't wait to dig in!"

Mamma turned to Mr. Sawyer then and asked about his wife and baby. In that moment Jeremiah met Rachel's gaze and held it. The warmth and tenderness that brimmed in his eyes caused her to look quickly away.

As if he'd seen her discomfort, Jeremiah turned his attention to Fannie. "And how might Thunder be doing these days, Miss Fannie?"

"Oh, you should see him, Captain Gant! Mamma says he's growing like a bear cub and that he's just as clumsy too! I've been training him some, though, and he's real smart. He catches on ever so fast!"

"Well, I'm glad to hear that." He straightened then and said, "Ladies, we can go anytime. Terry, here, is going to mind the shop while we pay a visit to his new daughter. It's a nice morning, if you'd like to walk."

"Oh, we have too much to deliver, Captain Gant," Mamma told him. "I don't think we could carry everything, not even with all three of us helping."

"Well then, why don't I drive your buggy for you? Will we all fit, do you think?"

"Well, if you don't mind, Captain, I'll just let you drive the buggy, and the rest of us will walk and enjoy the sunshine. Would that be all right with you?"

"That would be just fine. Whatever you like."

"I want to go with Captain Gant, Mamma," said Fannie.

"No, you'll walk with us, daughter. No sense crowding the captain."

An indefinable emotion sparked in his eyes, and Rachel wondered if he thought Mamma didn't want Fannie to ride with him because he was an *auslander*—an outsider.

Whatever Jeremiah thought, Rachel knew her mother trusted him. She wouldn't have meant to hurt his feelings. Her resistance to let Fannie go with him more than likely had to do with the way she had sheltered the girl—to a fault Rachel feared—ever since the attack on her sister last winter.

But when Fannie pleaded with her one more time, her mother seemed to change her mind. "Oh, all right. As long as Captain Gant doesn't mind. But don't you talk him to death on the way now."

"It would be my pleasure to have your company," he said, dipping his head a little to Fannie, whose smile broke wide enough to crack her face.

As Rachel followed her mother out of the store and watched Jeremiah help Fannie into the buggy, then go around to climb in and take the reins, she had all she could do not to wish she might take her little sister's place beside him.

The realization that even after all this time of separation she still wanted to be close to him hammered her with a fist of guilt. She was ashamed of her weakness, humiliated by her wrong feelings for a man forbidden to her, and disgusted with herself for holding onto even the slightest shred of hope that somehow, at some time, things might change so that they could still be together.

She knew that she should make every effort, do everything she could, to bury that hope once and for all. Yet she sensed that she clung to that last fragile remnant of hope because she knew that if it died, her heart would break beyond all chance of healing and the future that awaited her would be nothing more than a vast, dull wasteland of empty days and abandoned dreams.

To believe such a thing was probably wicked, a violation of her faith itself, and yet the thought of living the rest of her life without love—the love of Jeremiah—seemed to bring her to an impasse where faith and love found it difficult, if not impossible, to meet.

Rachel could feel Jeremiah watching her as she stood in front of the window holding the sweet baby girl, but for once his intense gaze didn't fluster her. She was too absorbed by the tiny Naomi Fay, the warm bundle in her arms with her soft baby fragrance, to pay much heed to anyone or anything else in the room.

What a wonderful gift a baby was! No matter what else might be wrong in the world, in spite of sadness that lingered and problems that plagued, a baby could bring light and gentle goodness and such peace!

Rachel had long regretted that the Lord God had not given her and Eli babies. It would have meant so much to have had his child to raise and love. She studied the tiny face nearly hidden by the blanket and carefully drew her even closer, breathing in her warm sweetness as she rocked her ever so gently in her arms.

She was the last to hold the precious bundle—except for Jeremiah—and on impulse she went to him now and held the baby out to him. He looked startled, then more than a little leery, as he hesitated. He shook his head, but Rachel could tell he was tempted.

"You'll hurt Mrs. Sawyer's feelings if you don't hold her, at least for a moment," she murmured, her voice low.

He looked at Rachel and then to the bundle in her arms, took a deep breath, and finally accepted the baby from her. Staring down at little Naomi Fay for a long moment, his startled expression changed to a smile as he walked to the window with her and stood where Rachel had been standing before.

Rachel was totally unprepared for the way the scene across the room affected her. Seeing the tiny girl nearly lost in the security of Jeremiah's sturdy arms, bundled so carefully against the broadness of his chest, she felt her heart leap.

But it was the expression on his face that was her undoing. The ever so strongly molded features had softened to a look of wonder. He seemed to behold the child in his arms in abject amazement, as if nothing in his world ever could have prepared him for such a miracle as this.

Whatever worries, frustrations, and concerns had creased his craggy features before were now gentled and bespoke an awe and fascination that shook her to the depths. All of a sudden, the solitary man was gone, and in his place stood a man who had glimpsed amazing love and perfection and was, at least for a moment, transformed.

A fierce longing rose up in Rachel, swelling her heart and throat and senses. She could have wept for what they would never have together, this miraculous gift, this blessing they would never share.

And she prayed right then, in that very moment, that somehow the Lord God's grace would one day fall on Jeremiah and end his loneliness, granting him this joy beyond all joy, this precious gift of incredible love and sweetness.

"Oh, Lord God, even if it cannot be with me, fill his arms and his heart and his life with the wondrous blessing of a family of his own to love and cherish."

Then she turned away, so neither he nor anyone else in the room would see the unshed tears scalding her eyes.

Too preoccupied to concentrate, Gant said his goodbyes at the boardinghouse, insisting that he would walk back to the shop.

The earlier brightness of the afternoon had faded, the sky darkening with a threat of rain and a rise in wind.

The promise of a rainstorm on the way matched his mood.

He'd seen the way she looked at the Sawyer baby when she held her—the unmistakable expression of longing, the almost holy wonder that settled over her lovely face. It had hit him like a hammer-blow, that look of yearning and the glow that seemed to radiate from somewhere deep within.

In that instant the awareness had washed over him like a tidal wave that Rachel hungered for the same things he did—an end to loneliness, a family, and a home to share with that family. She was meant for those things, meant to love a man and hold a baby in her arms. Not someone else's baby, but her own.

He wanted—he desperately ached—to be the one to give her those things.

But he *wasn't* the one. He'd been told he couldn't *be* the one.

He wondered—how many times a day did he wonder—was it God's will that had closed the door on any chance for them to be together, or was it solely an elderly *bishop's* will?

Had he given up too easily? Should he have fought harder, longer? Or by doing so, would he have only made things more difficult for Rachel, more difficult for them both?

He had tried to stay away from her, but every time he thought he was getting strong enough to finally free himself, something seemed to throw them together—and it took only a moment of being close to her to drive the knife of longing into his heart even more deeply than before.

So intent was he on the path his thoughts had taken that he almost tripped over the broken board in front of the mercantile. He caught himself just in time and went on, more slowly now, feeling the first few splatters of rain on his shoulders but only in the vaguest way and not really caring that the sky looked about to open and unleash a downpour at any moment.

Something pressed in on him, some urgency began to drive him. He had felt this kind of relentless pressure only a few times in recent years, but often enough to know what it meant. So he slowed his pace even more and silently breathed the words battering at his heart and in his mind, words that eventually took the form of an impassioned, albeit a reluctant, prayer.

"You know I don't want to give her up, that everything in me wants her as my wife, my friend, my lover for a lifetime. But it seems that, even more than I want her for myself, I want her to be happy. She's not meant to be alone—what a waste that would be, Lord. What a waste. She's meant for love and goodness and motherhood and joy. She's meant for all the finest things, the very best You can give her.

"So if she can't have all that with me—if it's truly Your will that we remain separate—then give me the strength to step aside and not in any way interfere with what You do *want for her. Give me the strength to walk away if that's what You want, not just for a little while, but for good. For Rachel's good."*

Only now did he become aware of the cold, wind-driven rain pelting his skin and drenching him through. Hunching his shoulders against its sting, he picked up his pace and hurried on.

26

CONTINUING GOD'S WORK

No matter what may be the test,
God will take care of you.

CIVILLA D. MARTIN

The week passed steadily in the brisk cadence of fall. With much help from good neighbors, the hay had been baled, the apple harvest brought in, cider and apple butter made.

Susan couldn't be more thankful for the way her friends—both Amish and *Englisch*—had pitched in to make up for Gideon's absence. Most of the heavy work of this time of year was now behind, and she could content herself with the last of her canning and other seasonal chores.

By midmorning she had set several loaves of bread to rise, thoroughly cleaned the wood stove, swept the kitchen floor, and baked what looked to be a mighty fine apple pie, if she did say so herself. She would spend the rest of the morning baking an assortment of cookies and other sugary treats for the common meal after tomorrow's preaching service at Abe Gingerich's farm.

Susan always looked forward to their every-other-week preaching services, conducted in private homes and barns rather than in a formal church building. Tradition had it that this practice began with the persecution of their ancestors in the old country. Supposedly, moving their preaching services from place to place had made them harder for the authorities to locate. That was no longer the case, of course, but the reason didn't really matter. The Plain People believed a home was also their church.

These days the Amish had other problems, some more fraught with danger than being apprehended during their church services.

A knock sounded at the front door, and Susan glanced down at her dress before going to answer. She was still in her choring dress, spotted with flour and pastry stains, when she started down the hallway.

Before she reached the door, however, Malachi Esch stepped inside and called out to her. Only then did she remember that she hadn't locked the door after sweeping the porch early this morning. There had been a time when she felt no need to bar entrance to anyone, but more often than not, these days the People took advantage of their locks.

"Oh, I'm glad it's you, Malachi," she said, wiping her hands down her apron as she went. "I'm so fuzzy brained I can't seem to remember to lock my doors."

"Best be minding the caution to do so," he said, his features still heavy with the burden of his loss.

"Come in, Malachi. Is everything all right?"

"Oh, *ja*," he said, removing his hat but still clutching the bag he'd brought inside with him. "You have a minute for a visit, do you, Susan?" As was usually his way, he spoke in the language of the People.

"I have plenty of time for a visit. It's ever so good to see you," she said, taking his hat from him and hooking it on the wall peg beside the door. "Let's go to the kitchen. I have coffee on the stove."

"Never knew a time when you didn't, Susan. So where is young Fannie this morning?"

"Oh, she and her puppy are already over at Rachel's. They're making sweet potato pies for the preaching service tomorrow."

"That sounds right good," he said. "I'll have to look for those pies."

In the kitchen, he didn't seem to know what to do with himself until Susan told him to sit. Only when she put a fresh cup of coffee in front of him and pulled up a chair to sit down did he release the bag he'd brought inside.

With any other minister, Susan might have felt a measure of awkwardness at an unexpected visit like this, but not so with Malachi Esch. She and Amos had enjoyed years of good friendship with him and Phoebe before the lot ever fell on Malachi.

Susan had never seen any sign that serving the community as one of their preaching ministers had changed him in any way. Malachi was just—Malachi. Yet she knew that if word ever got out that he and Phoebe had been studying *all* the Scriptures for years now, not only the ones approved by the bishop, it might bring trouble down on him.

Not to mention the other business about helping the runaway slaves. Susan still hadn't quite recovered from her surprise upon learning about *that*.

"Wanted to bring you this before any more time passed by," Malachi said now, pushing the bag he'd carried inside toward Susan.

Malachi had never been the talkative sort, except when he was preaching, and now he seemed to grope for words. "Phoebe said once that if something should ever happen to her, I was to give you this. There's something in there for Rachel as well. You know, Phoebe thought the world of both of you. I thought you might want something to remember her by. His voice caught on the last few words, and he glanced down at the table.

Susan looked from Malachi to the bag.

As if I would ever need anything to help me remember my dearest friend...

She peeked inside, then pulled out a Bible. Carefully, she opened it, realizing after a moment that it was *Phoebe's* Bible.

"Oh, Malachi—I can't possibly take this! Surely you want to keep it yourself."

He shook his head. "No, we each had our own *Biewel.* A long time ago, Phoebe said I must give it to you." He paused. "More than likely you'll find lots of marks in it. She liked to mark the passages that meant the most to her."

Susan hardly knew what to say. "What a precious gift this is, Malachi. I promise you, I'll cherish it always. Really I will."

Malachi, never a sentimental man, cleared his throat. "Well, that's good, then. There's a little book of poetry in there for Rachel. Phoebe liked to read it sometimes. Can't say that I remember her ever reading anything else besides her Bible and those poems. You give it to Rachel, then, will you?"

"Of course I will." Susan hesitated but finally asked, "How are you doing, Malachi? I know it's hard."

He nodded, passing one hand down the side of his beard. "Can't deny that I struggle sometimes. But you know how she was. She wouldn't want me sitting around looking all *schlimm*—all sad and long-faced. God is good—I know where *mei fraa* is—my wife is safe in the arms of the Lord Jesus. In only a little while, I'll be with her. She'd tell me to be patient, don't you know?"

There had been a time when Malachi's confidence of salvation would have made Susan uncomfortable, would have even shocked her. This belief wasn't a part of the Old Ways. But lately she had begun to wonder. According to Rachel—and Phoebe and Malachi and David too—the belief of a heaven for Christians didn't depend on doing all the right works throughout one's life. Phoebe herself had insisted more than once that if Susan would just study God's Word in its entirety, she would discover the assurance of salvation for herself.

Her hands smoothed the well-worn cover of her dear friend's Bible, and in that instant she decided that maybe now she would follow Phoebe's advice. Could be those marked passages Malachi had spoken of would lead her to the truth Phoebe had been so anxious for her to discover.

She looked up to find Malachi watching her. "I'm sorry," she said, embarrassed that she had let her mind go roaming during his visit. "I was just thinking of Phoebe."

He nodded. "What better thoughts to have?" He stood then. "I've taken enough time from your morning. And I have work to do. Best get to it."

Susan also got up from her chair. "Thank you again for coming by, Malachi, and for bringing me Phoebe's Bible."

For a moment he looked everywhere but at Susan. "You've been a good friend to us—to Phoebe and me—and our sons," he said lowering his voice. "I expect if she could, she would tell you to be careful, to look after yourself and those two girls of yours."

Puzzled Susan said, "Why yes. I'll do that."

He stood there another moment, a deep frown creasing his forehead. "I know she told you about what we do."

"What you do?"

"Helping the runaways. Phoebe said she told you." He actually glanced around, as if to make certain no one else was nearby.

"*Ja,*" Susan said, wary of what he was getting at. "She told me."

"That's why they went after her as they did, seems like." He hesitated, then went on. "It's no secret that our families have been friends for a long time. Could be some might think you're also involved with what we do, Susan. Maybe Rachel too. So you be careful, now. You keep your doors locked and take caution."

"Oh, Malachi, do you really think that's why they hurt Phoebe?"

"Don't think there's any doubt about it, given what they wrote on that paper," he said, his features going hard.

"Well—don't you worry about us," Susan said, hoping she sounded braver than she felt. She hesitated before asking. "I've wondered, though—do you plan to continue? After what happened—"

He shook his head slowly, not quite looking at her. "Best you not know too much about things," he said. "Let me ask you, though, if

I had been the one taken instead of our Phoebe, do you think she would have stopped doing God's work?"

Susan studied him closely. "You still believe that, then—that what you do is God's work? In spite of what happened to Phoebe?"

"I can't think otherwise. I believe like Phoebe did. She used to say we might be a touch of God's grace to those poor enslaved souls, that it would be a terrible sin not to help them if we could."

He paused, his gaze mournful but convicted. "Phoebe always said there should be no fear for us if we're doing God's will, that one way or another, He will defend us and rescue us. It wasn't that she didn't get nervous at times about what we were doing—but she believed we mustn't let evil get in the way of good."

Susan almost pointed out that God *hadn't* rescued Phoebe, but as if Malachi knew her thoughts, he said, "Our Phoebe would surely tell us that the Lord did indeed rescue her in the best way of all, by taking her to be with Him." He stopped, then added, "I'll pray that the Lord God will keep you and yours safe."

"Thank you, Malachi. And *da Herr sei mit du,*" Susan said quietly. The Lord be with you.

She stood on the porch watching him as he trudged down the path toward his buggy, his shoulders slightly hunched, his steps obviously heavy.

His caution to stay safe filled Susan's mind. She shivered—not from the cool of the day, but more because she couldn't help but wonder if staying safe was any longer a possibility for the River-haven Amish.

27

QUESTIONS AND ANSWERS

I hear that Queen Victoria says
If we will all forsake our land of chains and slavery
And come across the lake,
She will be standing on the shore
With arms extended wide.

FROM AN ABOLITIONIST BALLAD

Gideon was becoming so accustomed to this night travel by now that he scarcely felt the need of sleep before dawn. He half suspected that Asa sometimes wished he *would* grow drowsy so he wouldn't ply him with so many questions.

Still, the older man was usually nice as could be, replying as he chose, fixing a level look on Gideon if he deemed a particular question either not worth an answer or outside of some sort of boundary set by Asa himself.

For his part Gideon was learning where to venture and where not to go. He had discovered, for example, that Asa wasn't keen on providing information of a personal nature. Even though they'd been on the road together for more than three weeks now, he knew no more about Asa's life as a slave than he had when they left Riverhaven. That was all right, though. Gideon thought it likely that if *he* had lived the life of a slave, he wouldn't relish talking about it either.

He found it frustrating, though, that it was almost as difficult to pry information out of the other regarding the Underground Railroad as anything personal. Earlier tonight, for example, Asa had started to shut him down pretty hard when Gideon asked about the "stations" in and around southern Ohio.

"There's more than a few, not as many as needed," had been Asa's vague reply.

Gideon had been a little piqued with the man's shortness, especially considering that here he was taking a few risks of his own—according to Asa and Gant, anyhow—to help with the mysterious goings-on of the Railroad.

When a second attempt to extract information also failed, Gideon withdrew into a silence of his own making. After an hour or so of this, however, he was beginning to feel like an ill-tempered schoolboy and decided to apologize.

"Sorry for being so nosy, Asa," he said. "Seems I don't always know when to quit with the questions."

He saw a small twitch at the corner of Asa's mouth and recognized it as a sign that the other wasn't really all that annoyed with him.

"What's all this interest in runaway slaves, young Gideon? I do believe you're the most curious boy I've ever met. Seems you have a question for just about everything."

Gideon grinned. "Not everything. But since I'm involved now in this Underground Railroad doings, I *would* like to know as much as I can about it."

Asa turned and regarded him with a curious look of his own, as if considering Gideon's words. "I suppose I can understand that," he finally said. "But here's the thing—the more you know about how things work, the more danger you're in. Not telling you anything other than what you absolutely need to know is a way of protecting you."

Gideon chafed at the inference that he needed protection. "I'm not a boy to be coddled, Asa. I'm no longer a child, though you and the captain seem to think I need to be treated like one. And I'm not asking you to fill me in on all the secrets you and Captain Gant are privy to. But when I told you I wanted to help, I didn't mean just this one trip, don't you see? I meant doing something over the long haul." He paused. "I just want to know how things work, is all. Nothing you don't feel comfortable telling me."

Again Asa turned to study him. After a long moment, he drew a breath and nodded. "All right. I suppose if you're going to take such risks, then you have a right to know something more of what you're getting into. But you need to understand, the Railroad isn't some kind of organized, fixed system. It's always changing, sometimes so often that even some of us who have worked in it for years can't keep up with the changes.

"Basically it's just an operation spread over many states to help runaway slaves get to freedom, preferably to Canada—but at least as far north as possible."

"Why Canada?"

"It's safer. A black man can live free in one of the northern states for years, but if a slave hunter comes upon him and captures him, he can still be sent back to his owner. Canada's laws are different from ours. I believe we will see the day when all the states are truly 'free states,' but for now freedom isn't really guaranteed in most places, not even in the North. In Canada the law protects a freed slave. But even here in Ohio, the law works against him."

Eager to learn and fascinated by the tale Asa told in his deep, resonant voice, Gideon listened, seldom interrupting unless it was to clarify something too difficult to grasp at first hearing.

"You have to understand that a slave is not generally viewed by his owner as a *person*," Asa said. "A slave is *property*. Bought and paid for, owned and managed by the one who bought him. In the owner's way of thinking, he can treat that slave well or mistreat him, work him to death or sell him. He owns him completely, body and soul—if he happens to believe a slave actually *has* a soul.

He can kill him at will, though that's an expense and not a good investment of his money, so he's usually reluctant to do away with a 'good' slave.

"A slave has no education—it's against the law to teach a slave to read. He has no money, no law but white man's law, and no rights whatsoever, even where his own family is concerned.

"Time after time a slave's family members are sold without warning, and if he protests, he can be beaten for raising his voice to his 'master.' He can own nothing, go nowhere, can't even acquire a skill unless his master approves it. To his owner he's a beast of burden and little more."

Asa glanced quickly left and right, scanning their surroundings long enough to interrupt the flow of his account. When he again set his gaze straight ahead on the road, Gideon could almost feel the heaviness in the man's heart. He realized in that moment that Asa was giving him, indirectly, a painfully clear picture of what his own life as a slave must have been like.

"You can see, then, how difficult—how *impossible*—it is for a slave to escape to freedom without help," Asa went on. "Much of this help comes from the white man: abolitionists, preachers, farmers, merchants, doctors, teachers, housewives. But other blacks are also deeply involved in the work. All kinds of folks in all different places risk jail and even their own lives to help runaways succeed in their escape.

"Through the years routes to the North have become well-traveled. Safe places—'stations'—where good folks—'stationmasters'—are willing to provide shelter and provisions to the runaways dot the route. Others like myself—I'm called a 'conductor'—make it their business to transport them and give them what protection they can. I suppose it was only natural that the name 'Underground Railroad' and other railroad words sprang up because at the same time the *Underground* Railroad was being established, the *actual* railroads were being built across the country—and because of the secrecy of the operations the name 'underground' and 'railroad' and other railroad words came about.

"Lately there's been concern that some of those railroad terms are being bandied about too freely, that there's too much talk now about how things work, that some folks involved might be speaking out too much about the Railroad and their part in it. That not only endangers them and the slaves being transported to the North, but it also threatens the slaves still in bondage. Their owners have heard about all the successful escapes, and so they're becoming more careful and taking extra steps to stop those escapes."

He glanced at Gideon. "The more active the Railroad becomes, the more the need for secrecy increases, not only for the protection of the folks involved in the Railroad itself, but also for the slaves waiting for their chance to run. That's why Captain Gant is so strict about us keeping our silence."

Again he scanned both sides of the road and strained a little to look ahead.

"Where does the money come from for all this, Asa?" Gideon asked. "Sounds like an awful big operation."

"It's big all right and getting bigger," Asa replied. "And though it's always in a state of change, it's not without some organization. The funding may seem haphazard, but so far it's been enough. Lots of people donate to the cause. You'd be surprised at the sacrifices some folks are willing to make to help. Stationmasters are used to providing food and clothing with little or no warning, and I've seen good Christian women take blankets off their own beds and clothes out of their closets to keep some runaways warm in the winter."

When he turned to Gideon this time, Asa's dark eyes glowed with a compelling light. "God uses people who are *willing* to be used, young Gideon. We don't have to be saints or without fault. We just have to be available." He stopped. "Like yourself. You made yourself available to be used for God's work—and here you are."

Gideon hadn't thought about it that way. Truth be known, he

hadn't thought about it much one way or the other. He did detest the idea of slavery, and he did want to do something that had purpose—something with meaning. But he sure hadn't thought about being used by *God.*

He decided maybe he *should* think about it.

They had no more than another hour or so until dawn. Although some days they traveled short distances after daylight, Asa had warned that wouldn't be the case this morning. They were nearing a stretch of road near Canton, which was notorious for slave catchers, and so they would need to hide in a heavily wooded area until nightfall.

Gideon was driving, and Asa seemed to be dozing when something suddenly spooked the horses. Mac had been asleep in the trough behind the driver's bench but now came alert and started a low growl that threatened to grow louder until Gideon shushed him. Asa jerked wide awake and shot upright when one of the horses whinnied and pulled left. In the back of the canvas-covered wagon, a child whimpered and a man coughed.

Without warning a bearded man dressed in a hat and fine clothes stepped out of the trees and onto the road just ahead. Gideon hauled on the reins to bring the horses to a stop.

Mac again gave a threatening growl, and again Gideon silenced him. "Who's this?" he said under his breath to Asa, who shook his head.

"No idea."

The man raised a hand. "I'm a friend," he said, his voice so low Gideon could barely make out his words. "You're in danger! There's no time to explain. Pull your wagon over here, into the woods." He gestured toward the dense trees that flanked the road on the right.

"Go deep. Get completely out of sight! I'll show you where. Slave hunters are swarming all over the place! Get your people out of the wagon as quickly as possible," he urged, sounding slightly out of breath. "One of you take some of them with you. The other take the rest. Hide yourselves in separate places, not all together. I'll take care of your wagon. When it's safe, I'll come back for you. Don't move. Don't leave your hiding place until I come back. Go now—you *must* hurry!"

With that he climbed onto the sideboard of the wagon and rode with them, the wagon clattering and bumping treacherously over uneven ground and stones, stopping only when they reached a place so thick and dark with tree cover, it was almost like entering a cave.

Gideon handed over the reins then and leaped from the wagon, stopping only a moment to ask, "Your name, sir?" But the man shook his head and again raised a hand, saying, "I'm a friend."

Gideon hurried around to the back of the wagon. Mac watched as he and Asa hushed the runaways into silence and helped them to the ground. One woman with a little tyke clinging to her skirts looked so thin and sickly Gideon thought she'd pass out at any moment, so he grabbed the child, hoisted him to his shoulder, and continued to herd the others toward an even deeper section of woods.

There they parted company, with Asa's group going to the left, while Gideon took his folks farther into the trees at his right. When they finally stopped, the young runaway named Micah, who had been surly and disagreeable ever since they'd left Riverhaven, walked up to Gideon, splayed his hands on his hips, and said, "So what do we do now?"

Gideon regarded him warily. He would guess the fellow to be somewhere around sixteen or seventeen years, but he was big— bigger than Gideon or Asa—and seemingly all muscle. From the start of the trip, he had seemed to be itching for a confrontation of some sort.

Gideon had no inclination to oblige him. "We wait. And you

need to keep your voice down. According to the man who warned us off the road, there are slave catchers everywhere around here. You could help keep the children quiet too."

The youth uttered a sound in his throat much like a growl, and with that Mac pushed in between them and stood as if fixed in place. Micah shot the dog a look of disgust, but Gideon noted that he came no closer.

"Fine fix this is," he spat out. "We all gonna be caught—you wait and see."

Gideon set the toddler he had been carrying to the ground and sent him off to his mother.

"We won't be caught if we stay here, stay quiet, and wait—like the man said." Irked at the boy's insolent glare, Gideon added, "You think you could help with the little ones instead of complaining for a change?"

Clad in a pair of worn homespun trousers and a pair of too-large boots, the boy postured like some kind of important man. "You think I'm stayin' here to end up in some *buckra's* shackles again? I already been caught once and taken back. This time nobody's going to take me back alive! I'm gettin' out of here soon as night come again."

Studying him, Gideon tried to keep in mind the kind of life the youth had most likely led up till now. In spite of the boy's defiance and churlishness, after what he'd learned from Asa about a slave's existence, he couldn't help but feel sorry for him.

"You'd be foolish to take out on your own," he said. "Your best chance is to stay with the rest of us."

The boy twisted his mouth in a sneer. "Like you and that old man could be of any help."

Gideon's patience was beginning to wear thin now. He gave a shrug. "Suit yourself, then. But if it went hard on you before, maybe you ought to consider what getting caught will be like the second time. You'd best think about it before doing anything foolish."

"I don't answer to you," the boy shot back and walked away.

Gideon watched him for a moment, then took Mac with him and went to try and reassure the little ones—and the grownups as well.

It was a long, stressful day. Gideon couldn't count the number of times he had wished for Asa's calming presence. The man had a way about him that most likely could convey peace in the middle of a raging battlefield. After spending an entire day in the woods in the midst of frightened runaways and hungry, fretful children, wondering how long this would go on and what might lie ahead, he was feeling a bit frazzled himself.

When the man who had first warned them off the road finally made his appearance around dusk, it was a huge relief. But some of that relief quickly fled as he heard what came next.

"There are too many of you to stay in one place, but I've found two stations in the vicinity where you can wait until the optimal time to get back on the road again."

As he went on, Gideon noted that he spoke like a highly educated man and had the clean and well-kept hands of a gentleman. He couldn't help but wonder who he was and why he was willing to risk his own safety by helping a group of fugitive slaves.

"Once we're sure the slave hunters have left the area, we'll see that you're reunited and stock up your provisions so you can get on your way again. In the meantime I'm going to take you to where you'll be staying tonight—and possibly several nights."

A thought struck Gideon as he helped the people into the back of the wagon. He hoped this delay wasn't going to prevent them from reaching their destination by too long a time. His mother was getting married in November, and as upset as she probably still was about his leaving Riverhaven to travel north with these folks, she was going to be a lot more aggravated if he didn't make it home in time to see her married to Doc Sebastian.

He absolutely *had* to get back for Mamm's wedding day!

28

NIGHT OF RAIN AND FEAR

I will fear no evil.

PSALM 23:4

Midnight had gathered in. The wind was up, driving a rainstorm, and in his house on the hill, a brooding Jeremiah Gant paced the floor.

He couldn't be sure because he'd been only semiconscious and, according to Doc Sebastian, merely a few hours away from death, but he thought the night he arrived in Riverhaven nearly a year ago must have been very much a night like this.

He remembered nothing about that night, nothing at all, except that he must have opened his eyes long enough to see what appeared to be the face of an angel looking down on him with concern. He remembered that face and nothing more.

Rachel.

On nights like this, had he been a drinking man, he would have indulged himself by now. But the drink had never been his vice. He had seen it destroy too many of his people to follow that same pathway.

Not that he would admit his state of mind to a living soul, but this was a night when loneliness seemed to seize him by the throat and hold him captive. He found himself wishing his dog, Mac, was here. And Asa. Tonight he was missing them both in the worst way.

He had to smile, albeit grimly, at the irony. For years he had convinced himself that he was content to be a solitary man—that he needed no one, that indeed he was better off with no one. He prized his freedom, after all. Freedom was the very thing that had brought him to this country. Without ties to bind him, he could go where he chose, stay as long as he wanted, and not have the burden some men did of a family or loved ones awaiting his return.

He was not a man, he told himself, to be needed, not a man to be restricted by having others dependent on him. To the contrary he was a man who needed freedom to survive as other men needed food.

For years he had managed to believe that delusion, live comfortably with it, even relish it. If whispers of discontent occasionally circled round his mind like birds of prey seeking purchase, he ignored them. He had his boat, his work, and the river. He needed nothing else.

And then he came to Riverhaven.

He stopped at the window, looked out but could see nothing. It was as if the entire night were veiled in a wind-blown curtain of black rain. He lifted his shoulders and stretched his neck, trying to ease the day-long tension that was quickly escalating to a thundering headache.

But it was the ache in his heart that threatened to undo him.

His smug enjoyment of the solitary life had been lost in the dust, dispelled by his love for a winsome, gentle woman with dark eyes and a breath-stealing smile. A woman who had taught him for the first time that love was about much more than desire or *wanting*, that it was far bigger and went much deeper than he could have ever dreamed, that perhaps it was as much about the things of heaven as earthbound feelings. A woman who made him want what was right and good for her, even if it meant an agony of loneliness for himself.

She was the woman he couldn't have.

But the fact that she was forbidden to him didn't mean she didn't fill his thoughts and his prayers and his heart every hour of the day. Nor did it help to drive away his fear for her—the fear that something of the evil that had insinuated itself into the valley of Riverhaven would somehow touch her and wrap its deadly tentacles of malevolence and destruction around her.

There had been a time when he didn't believe in evil, at least not in the literal sense that he'd eventually discovered in the Scriptures. He had first recognized the reality of evil when he encountered the institution of slavery and saw for himself the existence of something so corrupt, so wicked and immoral that he found it impossible to believe that anything *less* than evil could account for what men were capable of wreaking upon each other. Later, when his search for under-standing—along with Asa's subtle leading—had finally brought him to the Word of God, he began to grasp the many guises evil could take to deceive and destroy.

After another moment, he crossed to the walnut desk he had made for himself some months past and sat down. Resting his head in his hands, he tried to pray. Even now, after years of turning his life over to his Creator, he sometimes found it difficult to plumb the words from his heart that would convey his deepest longings, his fears, or his gratitude.

For too long a time he had prided himself on his independence, counting on no man nor means other than himself. Whether he succeeded or failed in any pursuit, he credited or blamed only him-self.

Giving his life—everything he was—over to another, even to the God of the universe, at times had been excruciatingly difficult for him. Sometimes frustrating, sometimes a seemingly impossible turning of himself inside out, his submission had not come like a wave crashing onto land to be absorbed once and for all, but instead had come like a tide washing in and out upon a rocky shore, over and over again. Tonight, however, his fear for Rachel as well as for

her family and the good Plain People who had befriended him—
outsider though he was—overwhelmed his innate tendency toward
self-reliance, and he found himself quick to confess his neediness
and his weakness and ask for help.

Someone *must* find who and what was responsible for the violence
being perpetrated upon the Amish. No hope existed for stopping this
wave of ugliness and devastation until its origin could be found.

*"Use me, Lord God, if You will. Use whatever strength is left to me
to destroy this darkness that pursues the good people of Riverhaven. They
won't fight for themselves, they won't go seeking their enemy to combat
him, they won't even defend their own lives. Show me the face this evil
wears and give me the wits and the means to drive it from our midst.*

*"I expect I need to ask for patience, as well, Lord, for something tells
me this will be no quick and easy offensive. And, please, while You're
working and while I'm watching and waiting and searching, surround
Rachel and her loved ones, her neighbors and friends—surround all
these good people with Your presence and Your protection and Your
power..."*

A gust of wind slammed against the outside walls just then, rattling the windows of the rambling old farmhouse and sending a
chill cascading down his spine.

The house seemed to echo throughout with the wailing of the
wind in a mocking reminder of just how alone he really was.

Rachel couldn't sleep. She had tried for over two frustrating hours,
but the wind was fierce, with the sky emptying its clouds in loud,
crashing torrents.

Thunder and lightning didn't bother her so much, but wind always
made her restless. Nearly an hour ago, she had finally given up and
gone to the kitchen. After lighting the kerosene lantern on the table,
she fetched her Bible and sat down to read.

Tonight she was feeling the emptiness of the house. She had never been fearful about living alone, once she'd grown accustomed to Eli being gone. But over the past few months—and especially now after what had happened to poor Phoebe—she often felt jittery at night.

Of course, Fannie stayed over often, and she was always glad for her company, but she realized her sister couldn't stay *every* night. Tonight, with the wind moaning and a furious rainstorm taking place, she found herself jumping at every little noise.

One of the things she missed most about being married was the companionship she and Eli had shared. Their times together were usually quiet and relaxed. They could spend many an hour without saying much—she would read while Eli worked at his whittling or studied the Scriptures. It had always seemed enough, just being together.

She sometimes wondered what it might have been like for her and Jeremiah, had they been allowed to marry.

Best not to let her thoughts drift down that road, hopeless as it was...

Yet her mind seemed intent on clinging to thoughts of him, perhaps because the night he had showed up here at her house last November had been so like *this* night. It had been stormy that night too, with a high wind and a driving rain. She doubted that she would ever forget the first time she had seen him, leaning heavily on Asa, bleeding badly, and looking more dead than alive, needing help in the worst way.

At first she'd refused to let them in, but Asa had looked so desperate and seemed so kind—and Jeremiah, well, he appeared to be no threat, barely alive as he was.

Nothing had been the same since that night. And somehow she knew nothing would ever be the same again.

She drew a long, shaky breath, looked down at the Bible on the table in front of her, and began to read. Soon she found herself searching the Scriptures for those verses having to do with fear or, rather, courage in the *face* of fear.

"The Lord is with us: fear them not."

"The Lord is my light and my salvation; whom shall I fear? The Lord is the strength of my life; of whom shall I be afraid?"

"Fear thou not; for I am with thee."

"The Lord is my helper, and I will not fear what man shall do unto me."

On through the next hour Rachel read and prayed. She prayed for courage and steadiness, no matter what might lie ahead. She prayed for a wall of protection around her family and friends, around the entire Plain community—and around Jeremiah.

Finally her spirit grew calm and peace settled over her. She put her Bible away, extinguished the lantern, and went back to bed. And though she still keenly felt the echo of loneliness in her house and in her soul, after a time she fell asleep, with the reassurance of God's Word whispering to her heart, *"Fear thou not; for I am with thee."*

29

CARING FOR THE BISHOP

That healing gift He lends to them
Who use it in His name;
The power that filled His garment's hem
Is evermore the same…
That Good Physician liveth yet
Thy friend and guide to be;
The Healer by Gennasaret
Shall walk the rounds with thee.

JOHN GREENLEAF WHITTIER

David Sebastian left the house of Isaac Graber with no small measure of concern for his patient.

The bishop had him worried on a number of levels, not the least of which was his diabetes. The elderly Graber was a man of considerable girth who loved to eat. He insisted that he stuck faithfully to the diet David had advised him to follow and didn't overindulge.

David believed him. He was an Amish bishop, after all, not the sort of man given to dissembling.

Yet his weight had ballooned over the past months, and for some time now, David had suspected the additional pounds were to blame for the man's increasingly labored breathing and decline in activity. Frequently this was the kind of thing that perpetuated itself—a weight gain led to less activity, and decreased activity commonly led to a weight gain. The problem was compounded by the bishop's age. He was only a few days short of turning 82.

Added to his concern about Bishop Graber's physical problems was a growing uneasiness about the man's mental condition. The aging bishop was showing signs of waning mental faculties, perhaps even the onset of dementia. If true he could experience the decline of rational thought processes, a more severe form of memory loss than normally associated with the aging process, and an unpredictable, uncharacteristic—especially for the bishop—tendency toward confusion in decision making.

After he left the Graber home, David decided to drive into Riverhaven, thinking he might stop and have lunch with Gant. He couldn't discuss his suspicions about Bishop Graber, of course—not even with his closest friend. Not even with Susan for that matter. Not only would it be unprofessional, but it simply wouldn't be the Amish thing to do. He supposed he'd been "Amishized" enough by now that he would do things in keeping with the Plain way.

But lunch with his mercurial-witted Irish friend would, at least temporarily, help to take his thoughts off more troubling matters, such as the bishop's state of health and what it might mean if the man continued to fail. After all, if Isaac Graber were declining both physically and mentally, decisions would have to be made.

Bishop Graber was a widower of several years now. He lived in the *Dawdi Haus* alone, the "grandparent's house" connected to the home of Noah, his youngest son, and his family.

The Amish took care of their own. When a man was no longer young and became unable to farm, the homestead passed to the youngest son and the parents moved into a smaller house on the property, a house provided just for them.

Noah Graber, the bishop's son, was a busy farmer with eight children and a wife who undoubtedly worked from dawn to dark taking care of those children, her husband, and their home. But it went without saying that they would look after the patriarch of their family in a loving, caring fashion.

No, David's concern had nothing to do with the quality of care Bishop Graber would receive.

The question gnawing at him as he approached the crossroads and prepared to turn right onto the road that led to Riverhaven was actually one mired in his lack of knowledge as to how things were done in the "governing" processes of the Plain community.

What happened, for example, when a bishop or another member of the ministerial body responsible for the overseeing and spiritual guidance of an Amish district could no longer perform his duties?

Was Bishop Isaac Graber approaching that point?

David wasn't certain. He had to allow for the possibility that this was a temporary lapse, that the bishop would snap out of his present malaise and recover from the disturbing symptoms he'd been experiencing.

But as a doctor with years of experience, he knew that while at least a partial recovery might be possible, it wasn't *probable*. And as the bishop's personal physician, where did his own responsibility lie? What would happen if he reached the point that he no longer believed Isaac Graber was capable of fulfilling his position as bishop? Who would need to be told?

Or would Bishop Graber take the matter into his own hands and make the decision that was best for his people?

More to the point, if and when the time to act finally came, would the bishop be *able* to make the right decision?

As it happened Gant was out of the shop when David stopped by. Terry Sawyer explained that his employer had driven to Marietta that morning to "tend to some business" and most likely wouldn't return until later in the afternoon.

"Well, since I'm this close," David said, "I might just pay that new daughter of yours a visit and see how she's coming along. Think your wife would mind if I dropped in?"

"'Course not," said Sawyer. "Ellie would be right glad to see you, I'm sure."

So a few minutes later, David stood at the window of the Sawyer's sitting room holding a rosy-cheeked, cooing baby girl who looked remarkably like her momma.

"I'd say she's thriving, Mrs. Sawyer. I do believe she's grown since I was here last week."

Ellie Sawyer smiled and came to stand next to them. "I'm so glad to hear you say that, Doctor. She's such a good baby too. She scarcely ever cries, and she seems perfectly content most of the time."

"Ah, then you've got a little charmer, all right. I expect her daddy thinks she's pretty special too."

David was surprised to see a shadow cross the young mother's face. It was quickly gone, but he didn't think he'd imagined it— especially when she hesitated before replying to his remark.

"Yes, Terry's...very proud of her."

David passed little Naomi Fay back to her. Trying for a casual tone, he said, "So—how long have you and Mr. Sawyer been married?"

"Going on three years now," she said, cuddling the baby close.

Ellie Sawyer spoke with a soft drawl, her voice so quiet David had to stoop slightly to hear her.

She was a small woman, quite petite and delicate in appearance, a pretty little thing with light blonde hair and large blue eyes. Although she gave the impression of fragility because of her diminutive size and fine features, David somehow sensed that she might be stronger than she looked.

"Well," he said, "we hope you'll like it here well enough that you'll decide to stay."

"Oh, I doubt that's likely," she said. "Terry is already getting restless.

He's anxious to move on to Indiana. He's always found it hard to stay in one place very long."

David didn't much like the sound of that, not for a man with a wife and a new baby. "You have family out there, do you?"

She nodded. "Terry has an uncle who's going to let us have a piece of land to farm. It won't be very big, and we'll have to build us a house, but maybe we can finally put down roots."

David thought he detected a wistful note in her voice. "It's always good to have a place of your own."

"I expect so," she replied, her tone vague as she shifted the baby from one shoulder to the other. "We've already moved around a good bit, so I hope once we get to Indiana we can settle in and stay there."

"Have you decided when you'll be leaving?"

She glanced away. "We don't really have the money just yet. Terry will have to work awhile longer before we can go, and I don't want to start out on a trip like that until the baby is a bit bigger."

"That's good thinking, Mrs. Sawyer. It would be best to wait, for the sake of the baby if for no other reason."

Again her expression darkened. "Terry, he's talking of going on ahead of us, getting things ready and such." She hesitated, then added, "He's thinking that by the time he comes back for us, Naomi will be more ready to travel, and so will I."

So *that* was what had her worried. It was only natural that she wouldn't like the idea of being stuck here alone in a two-room flat with no family but a new baby.

"Perhaps he'll change his mind," David said, meaning to reassure her. Worry was no good for her or the baby.

The look she turned on him plainly indicated that she had little hope of that happening, but she merely said, "Perhaps," and dropped the subject.

Watching her David suspected that she was more concerned about their situation than she was letting on, but it wasn't his place to dig any deeper.

Before leaving he did inquire as to anything they might need, but when she assured him that "thanks to Captain Gant" they were doing all right, he said his goodbyes and left without further discussion.

As he drove away, David couldn't quite get Ellie Sawyer and her circumstances out of his mind. The young woman was seemingly trapped in a situation that was none of her own doing. Apparently her husband was, in her own words, getting restless. She'd also indicated that in only three years they had already "moved around" quite a lot. That didn't necessarily bode well for the future.

They had a newborn baby, no real provisions of their own, and apparently their only funds were whatever Sawyer had managed to earn working for Gant. In such a short time, that couldn't be much.

As long as they were here, Gant would see to it that they didn't lack for anything. David had also slipped his friend some money to help out, as well as foregoing any medical fees owed to him. But once they left Riverhaven, they would be on their own, at least while they were on the road.

There was no mistaking Ellie Sawyer's reluctance to move on just yet, but clearly she was also resistant to the idea of staying behind without her husband. He couldn't help but empathize with her dilemma.

He sighed and slowed the buggy a little. Susan said he drove too fast, and he supposed he did out of habit. He was so often racing to an emergency that driving fast was simply the norm for him.

Susan had also suggested that he fretted too much about his patients. She seemed to worry that he'd eventually make himself ill. The thing was he had always found it difficult to detach himself from concern for a patient. He supposed it was just his nature.

In any event he didn't expect he'd be changing, not after all these years. He would probably always carry more burden than he ought to for those he treated, a thought that again brought Bishop Graber to mind.

He tried to guard against anticipating the worst, but just in case it should become necessary, how would he handle the situation with the ailing bishop?

There were only three men he could approach with such a request without violating the Amish tenet for privacy. He could seek the confidence of one of the two ministers, Abe Gingerich and Malachi Esche, or the lone deacon who served among the ministerial brethren—Samuel Beiler.

He dismissed Samuel Beiler from his mind right away. He had known Beiler for several years, had delivered two of his sons, and treated his late wife during her illness. He'd found the Amish deacon to be a seemingly cold man with an unmistakable disdain for anyone outside the Plain People's community. Even with David, his own family physician, he had rejected any overture of friendliness.

Besides, he had known—no, he'd *suspected*—certain things about Beiler that to this day stirred in him a dark uneasiness. He wouldn't be comfortable speaking to him about the bishop or anyone else.

Abe Gingerich was one of their two ministers and a good man. So was Malachi Esche.

He knew immediately that he would be most at ease speaking with Malachi. He disliked the idea of burdening the man, who was undoubtedly still grieving the loss of his wife, Phoebe. But perhaps when and if the need arose to alert someone to the bishop's failing health, a sufficient length of time would have passed that Malachi might have moved beyond the grieving process.

For now he thought the best he could do would be to monitor the bishop's condition and say nothing. He could also hope it would ultimately be unnecessary for him to consult anyone else, that either the bishop himself or a family member would take care of that part of things. After all, he found it hard to believe that no one else had noticed the changes in Bishop Graber. Surely at least a member of the family or perhaps one of the ministerial brethren had seen signs of the bishop's failing health and mental illness.

His mind circled back to Ellie Sawyer and her husband. He did think he might mention his concern for the couple to Gant. After all, it seemed only fair that his friend be alert to the fact that his part-time employee might not be around too long.

Clearly Sawyer's wife suspected that might be the case.

30

WORDS FROM A FRIEND

Did you know that I waited and listened and prayed,
And was cheered by your simplest word?

AUTHOR UNKNOWN

When Gant heard that Doc had been in town looking for him earlier in the day, on impulse he decided to pay him a visit that same evening.

Gant wondered if anything in particular had brought him to the shop. Even if that wasn't the case, he had a question or two of his own he wanted to raise with his friend. Besides, they hadn't talked alone in quite some time. They were due for a visit.

He hoped he might catch a glimpse of Rachel if she happened to be outside as he went by, so he slowed Flann to an ambling walk. But when there was no sign of her, he signaled the big gelding to resume his earlier pace as they went on down the road.

In front of Doc's house, Gant stayed in the saddle a moment, his gaze scanning the property. Thanks to Doc Sebastian's generous offer, this was where he had stayed during the final weeks of his recovery after being shot last winter.

It was a small house, owned and sometimes used by Doc Sebastian—mostly in the winter—to be closer to his Amish patients when the weather was bad or when he had an expectant mother nearby about to deliver. But after beginning the process to turn Amish and becoming engaged to Susan Kanagy, the doctor had sold his home place, a farm between Riverhaven and Marietta, and took up residence here, at the far edge of the Plain People's community.

Over the past couple of months, he'd had an extension added for office space. Gant had done some of the work, Gideon part of it, as well. Of course, Doc and Susan planned to live at her farm after their marriage, but he would still need at least a small office, and with some more work and redecorating, this place should serve him well.

Because he had been a physician to the Amish for several years, once he made his vows for conversion and married Susan, he would still be practicing medicine—but only among the Amish. The bishop had stipulated there would be no outside "doctoring" to others. Gant saw this as one more example of too much control on the part of the Amish leadership, but even though Doc admitted that he didn't like this turn of events, it came as no surprise—he'd expected his practice would be limited after his conversion.

In fact, Doc being the man he was, had already been contacting other physicians and medical colleges in an attempt to attract another doctor to the area.

Gant had liked staying here during his recovery. He'd enjoyed getting to know some of the Amish neighbors, and he'd appreciated the quiet, natural beauty of the countryside.

Over time, however, he'd become aware that the seeming peace of his surroundings was a deceptive one, for the Riverhaven Amish had been plagued with an ongoing series of vandalism, pranks, and thefts.

Eventually the harassment escalated to an attack on Rachel's little sister, Fannie. The girl had been tormented by a group of boys she believed to be *Englisch*. They had teased her, shoved her, and actually kicked her about until she fell unconscious in the snow.

Fannie recovered, but not Phoebe Esch, the latest victim of the horrors wreaked upon these good people. No doubt Phoebe's death had left the entire community wondering what might come next.

Suddenly the screened door at the front of the house swung open, and Doc stepped outside.

"Well. Are you going to sit out there admiring my house the rest of the day, or are you coming in?" Doc chided him.

Gant grinned, his spirits brightening somewhat at the other's good-natured dig. He had no doubt but what he could look forward to more of the same for the rest of the evening.

❖

It was still early in October, but the evening was cold—cold enough that Gant's bad leg had begun to ache even more than usual by evening.

Inside Doc had a nice fire going. "Ah," said Gant, going to stand in front of the fireplace. "That feels good."

Doc returned from the kitchen with two mugs of warm apple cider. He handed a cup to Gant. "Or would you rather have coffee?" he asked.

Gant shook his head. "Not at all. Susan make this?"

"She and Rachel. Fannie led me to believe that she also helped."

Gant smiled. "No doubt."

"All the women have been buzzing around, busy as can be, what with the harvest and the extra work it brings for them. Every time I make a call, I come away with a jar of apple butter or a gallon of sweet cider. Remind me, and I'll send some of their handiwork home with you."

"That's an offer I'll not turn down."

Doc sat down in front of the fire, but Gant waited a few minutes more, letting the heat seep through him before taking a chair.

"The leg doesn't like the cold, I expect," Doc said.

Grant pulled a face. "It's not even that cold out. I hadn't thought it would be this sensitive."

"It'll be worse as you get older."

"Ah. Something else to look forward to."

"Heard anything from Gideon and Asa?"

"I had a note from one of the stations they'd stopped at recently. They were both good, and so far there hasn't been much in the way of trouble."

"Susan worries, not only about their safety, but she frets about Gideon getting back in time for the wedding. I do hope he makes it. She'll be crushed if he doesn't."

"Well, once they get to Canton, they'll be relieved by someone else, and they can head back. They should make it home in plenty of time."

"Good." Doc took a sip of his cider.

Watching him Gant felt fairly certain the man had something on his mind besides the wedding. "Something wrong?" he said.

Doc paused, his expression still thoughtful. "Not exactly, but there's something I think you should be aware of."

He went on then to explain the conversation he'd had with Ellie Sawyer and the concern she'd expressed about her husband possibly moving on without her for a time.

Gant thought about that and discovered that he wasn't all that surprised. "I've seen the restlessness in him. He's a fella who can't sit still more than a few minutes at a time, and he's forever talking about 'when they get to Indiana.' No, I can't say it would be any great shock to hear that he's leaving before they can actually afford for him to go. Too bad, though. I don't mind helping out his wife in his absence, and she'll get help from other folks around town once they hear she needs it—but it's not fair to her. Not at all. Seems to me the right thing would be for him to wait until she and the baby are fit to go with him."

Doc nodded his agreement. "Suppose it would do any good if one of us was to talk with him?"

"We could try, I suppose, but I have my doubts. He's a roaming sort, I suspect, and when a man has the wanderlust, there's not much chance of holding him back."

"Why do I think you're speaking from experience?"

Gant shrugged. "I'll not deny it. I know what it's like, at least I used to."

They sat in a comfortable silence for a time before Doc stretched both arms out in front of him as if to ease the tension from his back. "So—shall we have a game?"

The two spent many an evening trying to best each other at checkers. Both fiercely competitive, they seldom passed up a chance to play. But at the moment, Gant had another matter on his mind. "Maybe later. There's something I want to ask you about first."

Doc set his cup on the table beside him. "All right."

Gant searched for just the right words. After all, Doc was well on his way to being an Amish man himself, and there seemed to be all number of matters the Plain People refused to discuss. He had no desire to offend his closest friend, but this thing with Samuel Beiler had been simmering in him ever since the day the man had come into his shop.

"If you don't want to answer this, it's all right. I don't mean to put you on the spot, but what I'm wanting to know is would an Amish man give what might be considered a somewhat costly gift—not just a small and impersonal one—to an Amish woman if they're not married or at least engaged?" He paused. "More to the point, would she *accept* such a gift?"

Doc frowned studying him. "Does this have something to do with you and Rachel?"

"Just tell me what you think based on your knowledge of the Amish."

Doc eyed him with a speculative look. "Well. I suppose it might depend on the circumstances, but I'd say it's highly unlikely on both parts. Even if he should make the gesture, I'm fairly certain she would refuse. Amish relationships, even their courting customs, are guided by secrecy and very strict standards. A couple won't even discuss their romantic interests with their own parents. And as far as special gifts are concerned—it simply isn't done, except from a man to his wife or perhaps between engaged couples. I'd have to ask Susan to be sure I'm right, but even with an engaged couple, I doubt there would be an exchange of anything but a token gift, perhaps a small something in remembrance of one or the other's birthday."

He stopped and then added, "Does that answer your question?"

Gant quickly processed Doc's explanation before replying. "Aye, it confirms my own assumption."

"As I said I'd have to get Susan's opinion to be sure, but I believe I'm right."

"No, best not to say anything to Susan."

"So it *does* have to do with you and Rachel."

"Rachel perhaps. Nothing to do with me."

Doc lifted an eyebrow. "Another man besides you is giving Rachel a significant gift? *Who?*"

Gant looked at him, wondering just how much he should say. Still, he trusted David Sebastian more than any other man besides Asa. And he needed to get this off his chest before it ate a hole in his heart.

"Might I ask you to say nothing to Susan?"

Doc seemed to consider that. "We don't keep secrets from each other—"

Gant nodded to show he understood.

"But if it's that important to you, I'll keep your confidence, so long as she can't be hurt by not knowing."

"This has nothing to do with Susan, my hand on it. Only Rachel."

He stopped, waiting for his friend's reply.

"All right, then."

"It's about Samuel Beiler."

Doc's expression darkened. "What about him?"

"He came into the shop the other day and placed an order for a sideboard for Rachel. For her birthday."

Doc's mouth thinned to a hard line, his eyes narrowing as he regarded Gant. "I find that a bit strange."

Gant sat forward. "So did I. More peculiar still, I had the distinct feeling that he didn't think I'd agree to do it."

"But if that's the case, why would he place an order with you?"

Gant expelled a long breath. "This may sound stranger still, but my sense was that he was deliberately trying to goad me, or at least he meant to make it clear that he and Rachel...are a couple. He seemed genuinely surprised when I agreed to make the sideboard."

Doc frowned. "I'd not be telling you anything you don't already know if I said Beiler *wishes* he and Rachel were a couple. We've talked about that before."

"Aye, we have," Gant said nodding. "Rachel herself has told me enough to let me know Beiler's been fairly...insistent in his attempts to court her."

"Then you also know she's not interested."

"Not up until now."

"You can't think she's changed her mind. That doesn't sound like Rachel at all. From watching her when Beiler is around, my impression has been that she doesn't even *like* the man."

"But if she's still refusing his attentions, why would Beiler go to such lengths? If nothing has changed between them, then he has to know she wouldn't accept a gift of that nature from him."

"I don't know the answer to that, but I don't believe for a moment Rachel has suddenly changed her feelings for him. Perhaps your notion is right—perhaps he simply wants you to *think* she's changed her mind so you'll stay completely away from her. But if that's the case..."

Gant could almost see Doc's mind working as his words drifted off. "If that's the case," Gant repeated softly, "the only explanation for it is that Beiler somehow knows I have feelings for Rachel, perhaps even knows I'd hoped to be converted to Amish myself so we could be married. But how would he know that?"

He waited, but when the other made no reply, he continued. "No one knew about Rachel and me except *Rachel*—and you and Bishop Graber. Now I hardly think Rachel would have filled Beiler in on the two of us, and I think I know you well enough to know you wouldn't have said anything to anyone. So then, given what you've told me about the Amish not discussing their relationships among their own, not even with family members, how could Beiler know anything about my feelings for Rachel? Why would he be suspicious of me? Surely the bishop wouldn't have said anything to him."

"No, I hardly think so," David said, trying to sound more convinced than he felt.

Given the suspicions that lately had been gnawing at him, it took a concentrated effort to keep an impassive expression, but he thought perhaps he'd pulled it off rather well when Gant said nothing more about the bishop.

"Well, *something* triggered Beiler's actions. He doesn't seem the type of man who'd act on impulse or a whim," Gant pointed out.

David's mind raced even as he formulated a reply to Gant's statement. "I suspect it's just what you thought, that he was bent on making you believe he and Rachel are a couple. As to why he felt the need—" he lifted his shoulders in a helpless shrug, "I've no idea. Sounds somewhat perverse to me. So—you're actually going to make the sideboard?"

"I am." Gant's smile was anything but pleasant. "But you wouldn't want to know what I'll be thinking while I ply my carving knife."

"No," Doc said dryly, "I expect I wouldn't."

"You're convinced that he hasn't won Rachel over, though?"

"I assure you," Doc said, "I can't even imagine a situation where that might happen." And he couldn't. He desperately wished he needn't be furtive with his friend. It had already occurred to him that if Isaac Graber were no longer bishop, there might still be some hope for Gant and Rachel. He wished he could offer Gant that hope, but he simply *couldn't* violate his professional ethics, nor could he in good conscience go against the Amish convention of privacy—not even for his closest friend.

He was relieved to hear Gant change the subject. "Well, I've bent your ear enough for one night. I do thank you for letting me talk this through. Now I'm ready to give you a proper thrashing at the checkerboard." He held up his cup. "If you have plenty, I wouldn't mind a bit more."

Given David's churning thoughts, he didn't doubt but what Gant *would* thrash him.

Throughout the rest of the evening, he did his best to concentrate on the game, but his concerns about the bishop—and now this matter with Samuel Beiler's behavior—cluttered his mind with even more questions than had been there before.

As they finished up and Gant prepared to leave, David decided to pose a question outright, a seemingly innocuous one he hoped. He had witnessed for himself his friend's pain, both physical and emotional, and felt pressed to speak to the reason behind at least a part of that pain.

"About Rachel," he said, choosing his words with care. "You haven't given up on her, have you?"

Gant was obviously surprised by the question but answered forthrightly, "If you mean do I still have any real hope things will work out for us, well, no. Why would I?"

"You can't be sure of that. Things happen."

Gant shot him a look that was pure skepticism.

"If something were to change," David went on, "something unforeseeable right now—you'd still want to marry her, wouldn't you? Your feelings haven't changed—have they?"

Gant glanced away, turning toward the door as he shrugged into his coat. "No, my feelings haven't changed," he said. "And they won't. I'd marry her in a shake if I could."

He turned to face David again. "But I *have* begun to wonder if I'm doing the right thing—for Rachel and for myself—by staying here. It's hard, you know. Being this close to her but never being able to see her, at least not alone. I can't even be a friend to her, not really. It's just...*hard.*"

"I know," David said quietly. "I went through a time—years actually—of loving Susan from a distance but not being able to do anything about it. I haven't forgotten the frustration and the anger."

Something quickened in Gant's expression. "Yes, that's it—anger—the unfairness of it all! Sometimes I get so angry I think I'll strangle on it. It shouldn't be like this! We're right for each other—I *know* we are." He raked a hand through his hair. "Sometimes I think I'll have to leave just to save my sanity. And maybe that would be best for Rachel too. She still has feelings for me, I can tell. Maybe if I'd just go away..."

He let his words drift off, his thought unfinished.

Gant wasn't the type of man to be consoled, not a man to warm to platitudes. But on impulse David reached to touch his arm, then dropped his hand away. "Don't," he said. "Don't leave. Not yet."

Gant looked at him. "The only thing that keeps me here is her. That and the fact that I told her once I wouldn't leave, that I wasn't going anywhere. Truth is I don't know if I *could* leave. But sometimes I think I *should.*"

"Listen to me," David said, feeling compelled to speak out. "God has His ways of changing things—even lives. He can turn things around in a heartbeat, in a moment. We can't predict from one day to the next what He might do."

Gant's eyes narrowed. "What are you trying to say, Doc?"

"Only this—if you love her, don't leave. Wait."

David didn't know where the words came from. He wasn't an articulate man, never had been. Most of his thoughts he kept to himself. But suddenly it was as if a stream of words came pouring out of him, words he hadn't planned to say, words he hadn't even thought of before this moment.

"You've built a life here, man. People like you. They respect you. You have friends, a business, your work with the runaways—you have reasons to stay besides Rachel. Give this time. Trust God to bring about His will for you and for Rachel. If it's right for you to be together, somehow He'll make it happen. But even if you can never be together, you have a home here, if you want it. Don't go doing anything rash. *Wait.*"

It was the strangest feeling, the exhaustion that overtook him as soon as he'd said his piece. It was as if somehow the entire day had been leading up to this moment, and now that the moment had passed, he found himself completely depleted.

He became aware that Gant was watching him closely. He could feel himself flush slightly from the scrutiny, yet knew he'd said only what he must.

It was an awkward moment, finally eased by a typical touch of levity from Gant. "You can be a little strange sometimes, Doc," said Gant.

"Yes, so I've been told."

"No doubt. Well then, I'll think about what you've said tonight."

"I hope you will."

"Oh, I will," Gant said opening the door. "You see, I've noticed that, even when you seem a bit wild-eyed, you're often right in what you have to say."

With that Gant stepped outside and, with a wave of his hand, started down the path to take his leave.

⇒31⇐

WHISPER OF SECRETS

And men loved darkness rather than light.

JOHN 3:19

L ong after Gant left the house, David's thoughts refused to give him any peace. He finally fixed himself a cup of coffee and, moving his chair a little closer to the fire, sat staring into the gently lapping flames, letting his mind roam free.

More than anything else of an unpleasant nature that had come to his attention this day—including his own concerns for Bishop Graber and the difficult situation young Ellie Sawyer would seem to be facing—Gant's encounter with Samuel Beiler troubled him most.

When he was wrestling with his thoughts about the bishop earlier today, he'd felt the same distaste that too often accompanied any mention of Beiler. But Gant's account of the Amish deacon's visit to his shop and the reason for it had induced even stronger feelings.

He had long suspected Beiler of a behavior that, as a doctor and as a man, he abhorred. It was no secret to David, especially in his capacity as a physician to the Amish, that there were among the Plain community a few men—*very* few he believed—who routinely mistreated their wives and their children—some to the point of beating them. Such actions were never spoken of but kept veiled in a dark cloud of secrecy.

Because the Amish were such an isolated people, handling their own matters of conduct among themselves rather than bringing in the *Englisch* authorities, it was a behavior fairly easy to conceal. However, it could not always be kept hidden from their physician. Defying the importance that Plain People placed on privacy, on two separate occasions David had actually confronted husbands about this disgusting treatment of their wives and children. In both cases he had seen for himself the physical evidence of abuse and simply could not keep his silence.

In one instance he believed his interference had shamed the husband to the point that he discontinued the beatings. In the other case, however, the man was so furious with David he would no longer allow him to treat any member of his family.

He had absolutely no evidence that Samuel Beiler might be the sort of man who would beat his wife. But in the years that he had treated Martha Beiler and their children, he had seen signs in her that something was amiss. He'd heard it said about Martha that she was the "perfect" Amish wife, an example the younger wives should aspire to. Maybe so, but David had seen the way she looked at her husband on occasion as well as the way she shrank from close contact, and while she might have been a perfect wife, he had his suspicions that their marriage might not be so perfect.

Delivering their two youngest sons had been a devilishly frustrating task, made even more trying by Beiler's insistence on being in the birth room and the glowering frown he wore the entire time. Clearly Martha had not wanted him there, and although David probably wouldn't have resented the presence of most husbands during a delivery, the reality was that most husbands, including Amish ones, typically removed themselves, leaving the process entirely to David and sometimes a midwife.

He wondered, too, about Beiler's relationship with his boys. His impression of the younger two were that they behaved like inanimate wooden figures when their father was anywhere nearby. As for the older one, who must be sixteen or so by now and in his *rumspringa,* well, David had to wonder if he might be a case of the apple not falling far from the tree. From what he had seen of the boy, he was a surly sort. Rumor also had it that he was a wild one and had a temper to be reckoned with.

In any event he had always been relieved that Susan's Rachel seemed to want no part of Beiler's attentions. He liked Rachel and respected her. He would have hated to see her involved with Beiler if he actually were the type of man David suspected he might be.

As for what Beiler might be up to with Gant and the business of ordering a gift for Rachel, well, it reeked of a certain territorialism that, if it didn't anger Rachel, would almost certainly embarrass her.

He could only hope it wouldn't come to that. Perhaps Beiler would realize before things went much further how utterly foolish it would be for him to try to stake a claim on a woman who didn't want him.

This whole business with Beiler, Gant, and Rachel sparked the uneasy thought of a spider that blindsides its prey—capturing by stealth and a web of deception what might be difficult, if not impossible, to secure in an open confrontation.

He shuddered and abruptly pushed to his feet. All this sitting around, fretting about this and that, one thing and another, simply proved that Susan was right. He worried too much about his patients and everything else. He needed to learn to think less and relax more.

He would start tonight by going to bed instead of upsetting himself any further. God willing, a good night's sleep would make a difference in his outlook on things.

If nothing else it might go far to alleviate the throbbing headache that had begun to form earlier in the evening.

32

A PROBLEM SOLVED

He did not wring his hands, as do
Those witless men who dare
To try to rear the changeling Hope
In the cave of black Despair.

OSCAR WILDE

Gant planned to wait a week before confronting Terry Sawyer about the possibility of his leaving Riverhaven, but as it happened, Sawyer approached him first, before he had a chance to say anything.

On Friday morning, before the shop opened for business, Sawyer came to the back room where Gant was mixing some paint. "Captain?" he said, standing a few feet away with his hands behind his back. "Could you spare me a minute or two?"

Gant turned to look at him and, seeing the expression on the man's face, capped the paint container before replying. "I can," he said. He was fairly sure he knew what was coming and was glad he'd waited. He had hoped Sawyer would approach him first, before he had to bring up the subject.

The younger man seemed fidgety, shifting from one foot to the other a few times before getting to the point. "Ellie and I have been talking," he said, not quite meeting Gant's eyes, "and we've decided I should go on ahead to Indiana without waiting any longer."

Gant wiped the paint stick and put it on the table. "You did, eh? You and Ellie decided that?"

"Yes, sir. For several reasons it seems the wise thing to do."

Gant stood watching him until Sawyer finally met his gaze. "Why is that, I wonder?"

"Sir?"

"Why do you believe it's best that you leave now rather than waiting?"

"Oh—well, for one thing winter will be on us before long, and I need to get a house at least partly underway before the weather turns. My uncle Norman, he says that Indiana winters can be hard."

"So can an Ohio winter, lad, and you'll be leaving your wife and baby to face it alone." Gant knew he sounded curt, but truth was he didn't feel all that kindly toward young Sawyer at the moment.

Sawyer looked down at the floor. "I know. But it'll be better for Ellie and Naomi Fay to stay here for now."

"So—when were you planning on leaving?"

"Well, sir, if you can do without me, I'd like to get on my way in a couple of days. The sooner I leave, the sooner I can get things settled for us and come back for Ellie and the baby—before the worst of winter sets in."

Was he right? *Would* it be foolish to wait any longer and risk traveling in bad weather?

"You can't wait at least until Gideon gets back? You've seen for yourself that I need someone to help me out in the shop."

At least the lad had the decency to look uncomfortable.

"I know that, sir, and I'm sorry—I really am. You've been awful good to us, and I hate leaving you in a spot. But, Captain, I can't help but think this is the best way for my family.

"And if you're thinking I'd be leaving them for others to take care of," he hurried to add, "that wouldn't be the case. We've put by every cent we could save, and I figure with my wages due today, we'll be all right for a while. Once I get there, my uncle says he'll stake me for a time so I can send enough money back to Ellie to do her till I come and get her and the baby."

Gant waved off his words. "It's not your family's keep I'm concerned about," he said. "I'm no expert on women, but it seems to me it would be a hard thing entirely for a new mother to be stranded in a strange town with a baby and no husband. What if there's some kind of an emergency, lad? What if one of them gets sick or there's an accident and you're out there in another state? Have you given any thought to that?"

Sawyer visibly bristled. "'Course I have, Captain. I know this won't be easy for Ellie, and I know things could happen. But I still think it will be better for them this way than to try and travel right now."

"You're missing my point, man!" Gant instantly regretted the gruffness of his tone, but if nothing else, Sawyer needed to see all sides of what he was proposing to do. His actions didn't affect him alone. "Why do you have to go *now*? Why can't this wait?"

Clearly he'd offended the other. Sawyer's face turned crimson, and his chin shot up in a jerk. "I thought I'd already explained that, sir. If we wait until after the chance for bad weather is past, that'll mean staying here another five months or so! We're wanting to get on with our lives, Captain."

Wanting to get on with *his* life, maybe, but Gant wasn't so sure Ellie Sawyer wouldn't have preferred to slow things down a little.

But he knew he'd be wasting his breath to say anything more. Sawyer's face had turned hard-rock stubborn with his last words.

"All right, then," he said giving a shrug. "You can collect the wages due you at the end of the day."

Sawyer's expression brightened. "You're sure, sir? That would really be all right with you?"

Exasperated with him by now, Gant just wanted this conversation over with before he said something he'd regret. "If you mean am I sure you're doing the right thing for your family—no, I'm not sure at all. But you have to do what you think you must, and I can see you won't be swayed. For now we both need to get to work."

He turned then and, without another word, started for the door to the shop.

This hadn't gone the way he'd hoped it might. His idea had been to try to reason with Sawyer, to make him see that this couldn't be a comfortable situation in which to leave that young wife of his. He had hoped for an amicable discussion that might bring about a change in the younger man's plans.

Apparently Ellie Sawyer had been surprisingly candid in her words to Doc Sebastian about her husband's "wanderlust," his difficulty in staying in one place for any length of time, and his desire to leave Riverhaven for Indiana as soon as possible. Still, Gant had thought—wrongly so as it turned out—that he might be able to convince him to wait, that ultimately Sawyer would put his wife and baby first, before his own wishes.

Grudgingly he admitted to himself that probably the man had convinced himself he was doing just that. And maybe he was. Who was *he* to judge another man's decision on what was best for his wife and child?

After all, it wasn't as if he'd had any experience or was ever *likely* to have any experience in that area.

Two days after Terry Sawyer left Riverhaven, Gant reluctantly went to see Mrs. Sawyer—reluctantly because he didn't quite know what to expect or what to say to her.

If he had anticipated nervous weeping, Ellie Sawyer proved him wrong. She let him in with a smile—a little forced, he thought, but at least she didn't seem tearful. She held the baby propped against her shoulder, patting her back while they exchanged a few words of greeting.

She asked him to sit down, but Gant declined, still uncomfortable with his reason for calling. "I have to get back to the shop," he said by way of excuse. "I just wanted to come by and see how you're doing."

She nuzzled her cheek against the top of the baby's head and then went to stand close to the window. "Terry left you without any help at all. I'm so sorry for the trouble, Captain."

He shrugged off her apology. "It's not that big of a problem, Mrs. Sawyer."

"*Ellie*," she put in. "Please."

"Anyway," he said, "if things start to get too hectic, I just put up the *Closed* sign and take a walk until I unwind a bit. Folks around here are fairly patient, for the most part."

"Everyone I've met has been very kind," she said. "I wouldn't have minded staying here indefinitely, but Terry really wants to farm his own place and be close to his uncle."

Again Gant was struck by Ellie Sawyer's youthful appearance. Standing there by the window, the afternoon sun splashing gold on her flaxen hair, she could have easily passed as a schoolgirl.

Except for the baby in her arms—a reminder to Gant of why he'd come.

"Mrs. Sawyer—"

"*Ellie*," she reminded him.

He smiled a little. "Ellie—I just wanted to make sure you and the baby are doing all right, and I wanted to tell you too, that if you need anything, anything at all, you send word to me."

She returned his smile, continuing to pat little Naomi Fay, who made soft baby noises against her shoulder. "Thank you so much, Captain. You're very kind. But we'll do fine, I'm sure. In fact Mrs. Haining just this morning offered me a situation that she assures me will work to her advantage as well as mine."

"Oh?"

"She keeps quite busy here, as I'm sure you know, what with letting out rooms and running the restaurant as well."

Gant nodded.

"I'm going to be helping her in the kitchen and perhaps even waiting on tables when things are really busy. For doing that she's offered a small wage—and our room and board free."

"Well, that's good news! Really good. For *both* of you. Mara Beth has needed help around here for months, but she just hasn't been able to find anyone."

"Even better, I'll be able to keep Naomi Fay with me. Mrs. Haining says I can fix her a nice place in the back of the kitchen, so she'll be right there, close to me the whole time I'm working. Doesn't that sound just perfect?"

"It surely does…Ellie. And you'll like working with Mara Beth. She's a fine woman. She'll do right by you."

"Oh, I know she will! And she just dotes on Naomi Fay. She seems to enjoy her so much. It's a shame she hasn't any children of her own."

"Well, I'd have to say this sounds made to order for both of you. I should be going, but don't forget what I said. If you need anything, you've only to let me know."

"Thank you, Captain. I'm sure we'll do just fine, but I hope you'll stop by to see us now and then. And I do hope Terry's leaving doesn't make things too difficult for you."

Gant gave a wave on his way to the door. "It will all work out. I'm sure Gideon and Asa will be back before long, and I'll have plenty of help then."

Gant left the boardinghouse, his heart considerably lighter than it had been earlier. Ellie Sawyer had been on his mind almost constantly since her husband left town. He had wondered and fretted over just how much he could help her without crossing the border of propriety or wounding her pride. Now it seemed that Mara Beth Haining had stepped into the gap and taken care of things in a way he never could.

Mara Beth's plan would enable Ellie Sawyer to be largely

self-sufficient. He would still keep an eye on her and the baby, of course. No doubt, as a young wife and mother, she would still have her times of loneliness until her husband returned for her, but keeping busy would at least help to relieve those times.

Here at last was a problem solved.

If only some of the other troubles that continued to weigh him down could be worked out half as efficiently.

On that note he reminded himself not to take this, or anything else, for granted. It had been his experience that the very time when things seemed to be going surprisingly well often turned out to be the very time when something was almost sure to go wrong.

He sighed, sincerely hoping this wasn't one of those times.

33

LEAVING FOR HOME

So long as there are homes to which men turn
At close of day;
So long as there are homes where children are,
Where women stay—
If love and loyalty and faith be found
Across those sills—
A stricken nation can recover from
Its gravest ills.

GRACE NOLL CROWELL

The night was heavy with clouds and fog, a damp, cold night permeated with wood smoke when they chanced to pass a farm along the way.

With all their passengers safely turned over to the next conductor at Canton—all but the belligerent Micah, who had taken off on his own while they'd still been hiding in the woods—Gideon and Asa were on their way home.

"Are we going to make it, Asa?"

Asa lifted an eyebrow and turned to look at him. "You always this impatient, young Gideon?"

"Only when my mother's getting married and I'm this far from home."

Asa nodded. "I suppose that's reason enough. Didn't I tell you we'd be there in time for the wedding?"

"You did, but that was before we got stuck outside of Canton."

"Well, we're on our way now."

"But I don't see how we can possibly make it back in time for the wedding at this rate."

Asa shook his head. "I wouldn't have taken you for such a worrier."

They rode along in silence for a few more minutes until Gideon had another thought. "I don't suppose you'd be willing to unhitch one of the horses and let me ride it the rest of the way. I could probably cut the time in half."

Asa seemed to consider that. But not for long. He gave another shake of his head. "I can't do that. The captain would be fit to be tied. I'm responsible for you."

"No one is responsible for me except myself," Gideon bit out. "I'm not a child."

Asa scratched his head. "I have to wonder how many times you've reminded me of that fact on this trip." He sighed. "I know you're not a child. But this is your first time working with passengers. Now you tell me if I'm wrong, but I have a suspicion you've never been out of Riverhaven before, at least not far."

"I went to Columbus once."

One side of Asa's mouth twitched. "At least you're honest."

"I can find my way back easy enough. I could take that map you've got in back. You probably don't need it."

When Asa didn't answer, Gideon pressed. "I'm a good rider. I've been riding a horse practically since I could walk."

Asa shot a skeptical look at him.

"Well, I wasn't *much* older than that. Come on, Asa. It's not like you need both horses to pull an empty wagon."

Asa made no reply, so Gideon tried again. "All I need is the map and the horse. I'll be fine."

Even as he tried to persuade him, however, he could tell Asa wasn't warming to the idea. And Gideon had learned during their time together on the road that when Asa made up his mind about something, there wasn't much point in trying to talk him around to a different way.

Still, he decided not to give up. He'd give him time to think about it for a spell. Maybe he'd come around on his own.

Gideon was just about to nod off when two men on horseback crashed out of the trees just ahead, startling the horses and blocking their way. Roused by the sudden stop of the wagon and the frightened horses, he caught a sharp breath. "Uh-oh! What's this?"

"Don't know," Asa said, his voice low, "but I don't like the looks of it. Thank the good Lord we already delivered the passengers. Stay alert, though."

Behind them a low growl started in Mac's throat, but Asa hushed him.

"Asa—look!"

Another man could be seen now. Shuffling behind the two, this one was on foot and roped to one of the horses. His hands and feet were shackled, his neck trapped in an iron collar. His shirt was torn to little more than rags.

"It's Micah!" Gideon rasped. "I tried to warn him! I told him he should stay with the others."

There was no more time for words. The men drew up their horses, waiting as Gideon and Asa approached and slowed the wagon.

Mac stood totally upright, his ears pricked, his tail fanned, and the noise in his throat, though low, still a threatening grumble. Gideon reached behind him and caught hold of the dog's collar and held on. "Stay, Mac. Stay," he warned.

As they drew to a halt, the slave, Micah, turned toward them, his eyes sparking with recognition. Though the boy still seemed to pulse with anger and resentment, Gideon thought he also detected a glint of fear.

"I've seen these two before," Asa said in a low whisper. "Low as they come."

Both men on horseback were filthy. One was burly with a matted beard and hands the size of dinner plates. He carried a shotgun, held at the ready. The other, holding up a lantern, had a narrow-faced, weasel look about him. Long, greasy gray hair fell ragged and uncombed around his face, spilling out from a broad-brimmed hat covered with dust. His expression was one of raw meanness. Gideon knew the noticeable absence of a gun didn't necessarily mean he didn't have one.

Something in the eyes of these men signaled a warning that spelled danger.

⇥⇤

There had been no time to react. Now, facing these two, Asa felt a numbing chill of certainty that they meant nothing but trouble for himself and Gideon. He had narrowly escaped them once before, three years ago down around Uhrichsville. He and the captain had been on horseback, with a runaway and his son riding double right behind them. The captain had spotted them just in time, and they'd managed to pull off the road and into the woods until they passed by.

These were the same two slave hunters, he was sure of it. The captain had called them "blackbirders." They would capture anyone with black skin—freed men with papers like himself, women and children, young or old. The law meant absolutely nothing to them. They wouldn't think twice of picking off a man who had been free his entire life and hauling him down to the nearest auction block.

They were vile and contemptible men, men to avoid at all costs. And now they were here, in front of them.

Somehow, some way, he had to keep the boy beside him from doing something foolish and getting hurt—and at the same time, help the hotheaded Micah get away from them.

But how?

"Well now, boys," said the thin man with the long gray hair. "Where might the two of you be headed?"

Though it galled Asa all through, he kept his head down in a deferential pose as he replied. "Just on our way back home, suh, to where we lives."

"And where would *home* be?"

"Just on the other side of Uhrichsville, suh."

"What's *your* name?" The man jabbed a finger in Gideon's direction.

"Me?"

As if young Gideon had instantly caught on to what Asa was up to—what they had to do—*must* do—he adopted the guise of a not-overly-bright youth. Even his voice changed. "Why, I'm Gideon Kanagy. And this here," he said pointing to Asa, "is my daddy's overseer. We're just on our way back from delivering some produce from our harvest up to Canton."

The stocky man with the shotgun sneered. "You ever heard tell of a slave bein' an overseer, Herb?"

"Never did, Rusty."

"Oh, Asa ain't no slave, mister," Gideon hurried to say. "He's a free man."

"A free man, eh?" the one called *Rusty* said. "You got papers, Mr. *Free Man*?"

"Papers—oh, yes, suh. I surely do."

"Well, get down off that wagon and show 'em to me!"

The thickset man darted a look at his partner—*Herb*.

Asa stalled for a moment, pretending to search his pockets, though he already knew they had no real interest in his papers.

"I said *down!* Both of you!"

The bearded man leveled the shotgun at Asa, who grinned and waved his papers over his head as he clambered down out of the wagon.

⇢⇠

Keeping the man with the gun in view out of the corner of his eye, Gideon took his time climbing down from the wagon. The instant he touched ground, he pretended to stumble and go to his knees, groping the ground with both hands as if to steady himself.

He came up with a large, jagged rock in each hand. Whipping around toward the man with the gun, he hurled the biggest one straight for the man's head, immediately following it with a throw directly in front of the horse just to spook him.

The man bellowed and grabbed his head with his free hand. The horse reared and threw him to the ground, hard enough to knock the gun free. Then the animal stormed away, pounding the road as he made his escape.

Asa dived out of the gun's range, scooping up a rock of his own and hurling it toward the same man, now on the ground.

In that instant Gideon saw Asa charge forward and grab the shotgun, sling it up under his arm, and target the man on the ground with it.

Meanwhile the gray-haired "Herb" slid down from his horse, righted himself, and turned toward Gideon, who this time launched a rock at *him*. He missed, but in that instant Mac leaped from the wagon and charged the man, snarling and barking like he'd gone mad. With one punishing lunge of his solidly muscled body, he hit the man full-force, knocking him to the ground. The man hit the road with a thud and lay groaning.

Asa shot a look at them and shouted, *"Hold, Mac! Hold!"*

Planting both meaty front paws on his quarry's sunken chest, Mac held.

The thin man's horse, however, clearly spooked by the chaos, shrieked and reared. Gideon took one look at the horse's wild eyes and knew it would bolt any second—taking Micah, still shackled and tied behind the animal, with it. The boy would be dragged, resulting in serious injury or even death.

He *had* to stop that horse from running.

Acting purely on impulse, he planted himself in the road, directly in the path of the horse but with his back to it. With one arm at his side and the other hand behind him, he began to take small, slow steps forward, all the while speaking softly and kindly, much as he might have to a child.

When he realized the horse had quieted and was cautiously following him, he pulled a deep breath and slowed his steps even more, then stopped. Taking a deep breath, he offered his hand, palm down, to the animal and let it sniff him. Only then did he carefully grasp the horse's halter.

Waiting until he trusted the animal to stand still, he freed Micah from the rope that held him captive to the horse, then went to the wagon for more rope so he could tether the horse to the trunk of a tree.

Asa still had the shotgun leveled at the man on the ground—who was dazed but conscious—so Gideon went first to tie the fellow up. Then he freed Mac from his hold on "Herb" and tied his hands and feet behind him.

Asa went from one to the other in search of the key to Micah's chains. When neither would say a word, he set Mac on first one, then the other. It took only a moment with Mac baring his teeth in the thin man's face to convince him to talk.

Asa unlocked Micah's shackles with such a smooth, deft hand that Gideon figured he must have had some experience in that area before. A sudden image of Asa, himself in shackles, flashed through his mind but was quickly gone.

Gideon simply could not imagine Asa—surely one of the most

noble and most gentle men he had ever known—shackled and chained. The very thought was somehow obscene.

Micah's voice yanked him back to his surroundings. "Mr. Gideon?"

He turned to face him. "Micah?"

"I just—I'll be on my way now. But I wanted to say thank you. I should have—" he stopped. Although the boy seemed to be near to strangling on the words he spoke, the look in his eyes was one Gideon had not seen there before. He was searching Gideon's gaze as if in…what? Apology?

For some reason Gideon couldn't quite stop a smile. Somehow he thought he knew what the boy was trying to say and even understood why it was hard for him to say it. "I know." He paused. "You can go back with us, if you want."

Micah shook his head. "There's nowhere safe back there—not for me."

Asa, who had gone to the wagon and returned, closed the distance between them. "Unfortunately you're right, young man. Your safest road is to the North. Here's a stop you might make." He handed Micah a piece of paper. "You can wait there for the next conductor to come through, so you don't have to go alone. You tell him you're the friend of a friend. That's all he'll need to hear. You can trust this man."

After giving him the piece of paper, Asa then handed over a blanket and a shirt from his own satchel. "And next time—don't be so impatient."

"No, I won't be. Thank you. Thank you both."

After Micah took off at a run through the woods, Asa clapped a hand on Gideon's shoulder. "Ready to go home now?"

Gideon gestured toward the two men, trussed on the ground, spewing oaths and glaring at him and Asa while Mac remained poised between them, as if standing guard. "What do we do about them?" he said.

Asa turned to look. "What do you think we should do?"

Gideon took one more look before turning to Asa. "Nothing," he said. "Absolutely nothing."

"I agree. Someone will come along and find them. Eventually."

Gideon went to the horse he'd tied and set it free, calling after it, "You deserve better than those two. Go find your friend!"

As they headed toward the wagon, Asa said, "You still want to ride one of the horses from the wagon so you can make better time?"

Gideon thought about it. "I don't think so. If you say we'll be back in time for the wedding, that's good enough for me. I'd rather not make the trip alone."

Asa smiled and kept on walking, with Mac trotting on ahead.

34

WHERE GRACE ABIDES

*From the fullness of his grace we have all received
one blessing after another.*

John 1:16 (NIV)

Soon after David Sebastian made his vows to the Amish church and his conversion was complete, the banns were published for his and Susan's wedding.

Busy as he was, the days usually passed quickly for him. Lately, however, they seemed to drag—no doubt because he was so eager to see the end of the single life.

In less than two weeks, he would once again be a married man, and it couldn't happen soon enough to suit him! Even so, he had a nagging suspicion that the days leading up to the wedding were going to virtually crawl.

He had his patients, his work, and his friends, of course. In truth he was usually too busy to feel lonely. But mornings always seemed too quiet and nights too long without a special someone to share them with.

That *someone* was, of course, Susan.

He couldn't remember the first time he finally realized that he was in love with Amos Kanagy's pretty widow. Perhaps he had subconsciously denied it for a long time before forcing himself to face the truth. Even then, the situation had seemed impossible, what with

Susan being Amish. Though he'd been a physician—and a friend—to the Plain People of Riverhaven for years, at the time he'd still been an "outsider." Because the Amish did not marry outside their church, any chance of a future with Susan had seemed altogether hopeless.

And yet just see what God had done. His own heart, long sympathetic to and in agreement with the ways of the Amish, had moved toward becoming one of them in every way. He had made that life-changing move, and now he and Susan were to be married. To find love the second time and at his age—what an incredible gift. What a blessing. What grace!

On this typical November evening, cold and raw with the threat of rain before morning, he was just about to lock up his office for the day and fix himself some supper. One thing he would most definitely not miss was his own cooking. Out of necessity, he'd learned to fend for himself, but he was a poor excuse of a cook, and he knew it. He also disliked eating alone, though there again he'd grown used to it.

Susan, on the other hand, was a wonderful cook. He liked to tease her that her cooking was what convinced him to marry her. In truth, just to sit at a table with her, watch her every movement, and spend time with her—well, every moment with her was a gift to him, and that was no exaggeration. He might be middle-aged, but he was crazy in love and didn't care who knew it.

He sighed, wishing he could be with her right now.

Well, why couldn't he?

They were engaged, after all, and about to be wed. Even the young courting couples among the Amish were allowed to be alone together at this point in their relationship, so why shouldn't he and Susan?

Never mind supper. He'd much rather have some time with his bride-to-be than eat a cold meal. He would freshen up a bit and take a ride up the road.

He was about to extinguish the lamp when someone knocked

on the door. He let out a long breath. Usually he didn't mind a late patient or two in the evening, but now that he'd set his heart on seeing Susan, he was impatient to leave.

But it wasn't his way to ignore a patient, so he crossed to the door and opened it. He was surprised to find Noah Graber, the bishop's son, standing there, his buggy parked at the end of the walkway.

"Noah? What's wrong?"

"Could I talk to you a minute, Doc?"

"Of course. Come in."

Hat in hand, the bishop's son stood in the middle of David's office, looking ill at ease. David had treated Noah's wife and some of his children, but never Noah himself, a splendid example of a brawny, healthy Amish farmer. Most likely he was feeling entirely out of his element.

"Dat asked me to come speak to you, Doc. He's not feeling so *gut* today."

Apparently Noah Graber didn't remember that David had had to learn the Amish *Deitsch* before converting because he started right in speaking English.

"Do you want me to stop at the house this evening?" David asked.

"*Nee.* I think he's all right—just under the weather. Thing is, though, Dat wanted to let you know that he's sent for another bishop—Bishop Schrock—to take his place at your wedding. He's not sure he'll be up to it himself."

David studied the younger man. "What's going on, Noah?"

A dejected expression crossed the other's face. "Dat isn't himself anymore, Doc. He don't feel good most of the time, and he don't always think so good either. It's like he gets mixed up a lot. Why, sometimes he thinks it's night when it's first thing in the morning. He said just last night that he can't keep up with things anymore, said maybe he might not be able to be bishop much longer."

A bolt of surprise shot through David. "Your father said that?"

Noah nodded. "He did. Truth is, Doc, we're pretty worried about him." He paused. "You were at the house a couple of weeks back. How did you find him then?"

David chose his words carefully. "Much as you've described. Your father isn't well physically—his diabetes is partly to blame, and he *is* getting up in years. I'd say there's been a decline in his mental faculties as well. I was actually going to speak with you about my concerns, but I'm glad your father brought it up first. I believe it's a good sign that he recognizes he has a problem. That should make it easier for me to talk with him about some things."

Noah's face clouded even more. "He's not going to die, is he, Doc?"

"I'm going to do everything I can to help him," David said, "and there are some things you and your wife can do to help too. I'll stop by and talk with you about this one day soon. In the meantime try to see that he follows the diet I gave him a few months ago. That's important. And keep a close eye on him. I know it's difficult, busy as you are, but maybe your wife and some of the children can help. I don't know that it's a good idea for him to go too far away from home if he's by himself."

Noah nodded. "I appreciate the way you take care of him, Doc. And I'm real sorry he won't be able to preach at your wedding. But he knows this Bishop Schrock, and he says he's sure he'll come down and do a nice job for you."

"Don't you be worrying about the wedding, Noah. Everything will work out. You just see to your father."

"Appreciate it, Doc."

David watched him until he pulled away in his buggy, then turned to go back inside. He wasted no time in leaving for Susan's. Now that Isaac Graber had spoken out about it himself, he felt more free to tell her about the bishop's condition—in confidence, of course.

Besides, since this affected their wedding, she had a right to know that a different bishop would be replacing him. Right now he mustn't allow himself to think too much about the implications this might have for the People. Later there would be time enough to consider things in more depth.

For now it was important to keep his thoughts focused on Susan and their upcoming marriage. He couldn't allow his concern for all the problems that seemed to be coming at the People these days to take anything away from Susan and the happiness they had found in each other.

Even so, there was no denying the sadness he felt for the ailing Isaac Graber, a man he had known and treated for several years. He had not always agreed with the bishop, but he had always respected him.

That was the way of things in life, though, wasn't it? Certainly as a physician he'd seen it often enough: God gave health and happiness, but beyond human understanding was the reality that He also allowed pain and sorrow.

David had come to believe that the soundest way to live a life pleasing to the Lord and at the same time live a life of serenity and peace was to abide in a state of thankfulness for all things.

Granted that was easier said than done. But one thing he had learned and tried to live by: God never runs out of grace. In every season of life, in every heart that knows Him, loves Him, and seeks to serve Him, God's grace abides.

35

THINGS BEST LEFT UNSPOKEN

Trust is a tenuous thread,
But one on which respect and love can safely cling.

ANONYMOUS

The knock on the door startled Susan. She never used to be nervous after dark, but these days she was ever so cautious. Moreover, she knew for sure and for certain that she was not the only one among the People who no longer felt safe, even in her own home.

Nothing was the same as it had once been. Although they tried as best they could to maintain their simple life of faith and hard work, there was no denying that the trouble and dark times that had come upon them had taken their toll. Daily she had to guard against allowing fear to become a hindrance to living as she believed the Lord God would have her live.

Fannie and her pup were at Rachel's tonight, so the house was unusually quiet. She had lamps burning in the kitchen and in the front room, but when the knock sounded again, she still hesitated before opening the door.

"Susan—it's David."

A rush of relief went over her at the sound of David's voice. Quickly she unlocked the door to let him in.

"David! What in the world—is something wrong?"

He was all smiles as he stepped past her into the front room. "Do I look as if anything's wrong?"

"Well—no, but what are you doing here?"

"Truth? I was overcome with a need to see you."

"There *is* something wrong—"

He pulled her close. "Come to think of it, I might be just a little mad. Love does that to a man, you know."

Susan stared at him. "David—"

He kissed her soundly, silencing her questions. "I thought we'd go for a buggy ride," he said. "I just yesterday picked up my new Amish buggy. I think we should try it out, don't you?"

"But it's cold out—"

"Not terribly. Besides, I have two perfectly good blankets in the buggy. We'll be warm enough." He paused. "You'd rather not?"

"Why—no, it's not that. I suppose a buggy ride would be nice."

He rubbed his hands together. "Good! Get your coat, then."

"Yes…all right."

He saw her hesitation. "Susan? It's really quite all right, you know. It's appropriate for an engaged couple to take a buggy ride by themselves now and then, don't you think?"

Still she hesitated. He was acting awfully peculiar. What in the world had come over him? David was usually so…sensible.

"After all," he went on, "my conversion is final. I've made my vows. Our banns have been published. We're being married in less than two weeks. All that considered, is there any reason we shouldn't spend some time alone together?"

Come to think of it, Susan couldn't summon a single reason, so she went to get her coat.

Outside he settled her snugly in the buggy, tucking one of the blankets around her before coming round to his side.

"I've missed you," he said, as he got in and sat down.

"You just saw me two days ago, David."

"But not yet today. That's why I've missed you." He leaned toward her and kissed her on the cheek.

"David! Remember you're Amish now. We don't show affection in public."

He looked around, his expression almost comic. "Where is this 'public,' Susan? There's not a soul to be seen."

"Still, we need to be discreet."

"Let's save being discreet for when there are people around. That's not the case at the moment." He leaned to kiss her cheek again, then picked up the reins, clicked his tongue at the horse, and started off.

Wasn't he strange tonight?

⋆⋆

"Like the buggy?" David asked her.

Susan looked it over. "It's very nice. So you'll use this for making your house calls as well?"

He nodded. "Probably won't have a choice. The bishop would most likely frown on my *Englisch* buggy."

"Oh—yes, I'm sure he would. I hadn't thought of that."

"Speaking of the bishop, I've something to tell you."

He went on then to fill her in on his visit from Noah Graber and the conversation that had transpired, including the bishop's own assessment that he might not be able to fulfill his duties indefinitely. After he'd finished, he glanced over to find her shaking her head, obviously disturbed.

"I'm sorry," he said. "I'm sure you'd rather have our own bishop at the wedding. On the other hand, I'm relieved that Bishop Graber recognizes that he has a problem and seems willing to face it."

"Of course, I'm disappointed," Susan said turning to him. "I almost feel as though I've known Bishop Graber forever. Why, he was the bishop when Amos and I got married. But I'm more concerned about *him*—about what's happening to him. Will he be all right eventually, David?"

He delayed any answer, trying to think what to say while not saying too much. This was Susan, and he trusted her completely, but that wasn't the real issue. The bishop was his patient, and that fact alone merited his confidence and privacy.

Suddenly Susan put her hand on his arm. "I'm sorry, David. I forgot. You really aren't supposed to talk about a patient, are you?"

He shook his head. "No, and thank you for understanding that, dear. But I can tell you this much, just between the two of us. I'm deeply concerned about Bishop Graber. I've dealt with other patients who have similar symptoms, and as I said, I'm concerned. No, I wouldn't count on him showing much improvement." He paused. "I'd best not say anything more."

"That's all right, David. I understand," she said, still clinging to his arm. "And I wouldn't want you to be any other way than you are, really."

He darted a glance at her, and the soft expression of love on her face very nearly undid him. He wasn't able to manage anything more than a rumble at the back of his throat.

"I suppose I should be getting you home," he finally said, already hating the thought of saying goodnight and realizing all over again how slowly the next few days were sure to pass—especially when she drew a little closer and leaned her shoulder into his.

They rode along in silence for a time. Susan's voice was hesitant when she finally spoke again. "David?"

"Hmm?"

"I can't help but think about what Bishop Graber said, that he might not be able to serve as bishop much longer."

David nodded.

"Are you going to tell Captain Gant?"

He shot her a look. "You know I can't do that."

"So I can't speak to Rachel about it either?"

"No, Susan. I know what you're thinking—a new bishop could ultimately mean a difference for them, but we can't repeat what the bishop said." He waited, then added, "And I daresay we probably shouldn't even think on it ourselves. What will happen will happen. There's always a chance the bishop might take a turn for the better—"

"But you don't really believe he will," she pointed out.

"No, I don't. But only God knows what's going to happen there, and it's not for us to speculate. Besides, Gant is smart enough to realize that something is amiss when he sees a different bishop at our wedding. And so is Rachel."

"Oh, I know," she said softly, "but it's hard not to wonder..."

She let her words drift off unfinished, and another silence hung between them for a few moments. This time it was David who spoke first. "If it should come to that—if the bishop *does* have to be replaced—how is this done? What's the process?"

"Why, a bishop is chosen by lot, just as ministers and deacons are. For a bishop—at least in our Order—only ministers and deacons are eligible."

David thought about that. "So that means it most likely would be Abe Gingerich or Malachi or...Samuel Beiler."

Susan didn't look at him when she replied. "Well, Samuel *might* be considered too young. On the other hand, he's held in high regard among most of the People, and he's been a deacon for quite some time." She stopped, and her voice dropped even lower. "He's been a good deacon, so he would probably be included in the casting of the lot."

David didn't voice what he was thinking, but he didn't like to even imagine Samuel Beiler as bishop—for a number of reasons.

It struck him then that, one way or the other, Bishop Isaac Graber's illness would definitely have serious consequences for the Plain People...*his* people.

And certainly for Rachel and Gant.

Keeping his expression as passive as he could, he turned to Susan. "We need to really pray about this, Susan."

She searched his face, and then, as if she had read his thoughts, slowly nodded. "Yes," she murmured, "I know."

36

THOUGHTS BEFORE
A WEDDING

When days are filled with pure delight,
When paths are plain and skies are bright,
Walking by faith and not by sight,
May they in Thee be one.

WILLIAM VAUGHAN JENKINS

The next morning David drove off in his new buggy to perform one of the many pleasant tasks associated with his wedding—that of "calling" or inviting those who would be welcome at the wedding reception. Anyone could attend the ceremony itself, but a personal invitation was required for the reception.

He had already heard from his son, Aaron, that he and his family wouldn't be attending the ceremony because his wife was expecting a new baby any day. David was disappointed, but Susan had agreed that they should make a trip to Baltimore for a visit soon after their wedding.

During this morning he would attend to offering invitations to his and Susan's mutual friends. His first stop was in Riverhaven at Gant's carpentry shop. As a non-Amish friend, Gant couldn't be an actual part of the ceremony, but David wanted him there and hoped he wouldn't have to insist. The stubborn Irishman could be unpredictable at times.

The front part of the shop was empty when he went inside, so he called out.

After a moment Gant appeared in the doorway that opened into the back room. David noted that he looked a bit worse for wear, somewhat distracted as well. His hair was a shade lighter from the sawdust sprinkled through, and his carpenter's apron was heavily splotched with oil and various shades of wood stain.

He came the rest of the way into the shop, wiping his hands on a cloth. "What are you doing up and about so early, Doc?"

"I'm always up and about early. Quite a bit earlier than you, most likely."

"Thought you didn't allow your patients to take sick before noon."

"Ha! If only. Anyway—I've come to invite you to a wedding."

"About time. Anyone I know?"

"Could be. How about the luckiest man in the county and the prettiest Amish widow to be found anywhere?"

Gant grinned. "Oh, *that* wedding. Sure, I'll be there."

Surprised, David looked at him. "Well, that was easier than I expected."

"Wouldn't miss it for anything, Doc, as long as they'll let me in."

"Actually anyone can come to the wedding—" David started to explain.

"Even a disreputable Irishman?"

"Even one of those. You'll have to clean up a bit, of course."

"Consider it done. I won't embarrass you, my hand on it."

Gant's expression sobered then. "Seriously, Doc—it really won't be a problem? Even with the bishop?"

David was careful to keep his expression impassive. "Oh, for goodness' sake, man. No, it won't be a problem! I want you there, and so does Susan." He paused. "And I'm sure Rachel and Fannie do too."

Gant's eyes met his, but he said nothing.

"Anyway, you won't be the only *Englischer* there," David said briskly. "Now make a note—the wedding is on the ninth, nine o'clock sharp."

"In the *morning?*"

David laughed. "In the morning."

Gant pulled a face. "That's not even civilized."

"I won't argue the point, but you have to remember that Amish weddings take a few hours."

"A few *hours?*"

Again David chuckled. "Afraid so. You can amuse yourself by trying to figure out what all the German preaching is about."

Gant groaned. "Doc, are you absolutely sure you want to go through with this?"

"I've never been more certain of anything in my life," he said, starting for the door. "I need to get going. I promised to help Susan paint the porch and the outhouses yet this afternoon."

Gant shook his head. "This is sad. Really sad."

"A labor of love, my friend," David shot back, doffing his hat as he opened the door. "And what's more, I also get to help kill the chickens for the wedding feast."

Gant stood just outside the shop, watching Doc pull away in his Amish buggy, still shiny and clean. He couldn't help but wonder just how much things might be about to change between him and his friend.

He was an unlikely friend, at that, this British physician who had once saved his life. Almost from the beginning, there had been little sign of the age-old enmity between the Gael and the Brit. The friendship that had sprung up between them—surprising them both—had seemingly been built on mutual respect and acceptance of each other's differences.

Gant wondered why that should be the case in individuals but not between nations.

He sighed, not having the energy—and certainly not the time—to speculate on any deeper matters today than filling some of his orders and finishing his wedding gift for Doc and Susan. In fact, he'd been working on the gift when Doc came into the shop. He'd about tripped over himself in his rush to cover it and hurry into the front before Doc could make his way to the back room.

He would have all he could do to get their gift finished before the wedding. Gideon's departure with Asa and then the loss of Terry Sawyer had complicated his life—at least the business side of it—considerably. He would surely be glad to see Gideon back in the shop—soon, he hoped, for his sake and for Susan's as well. Understandably she wanted her boy home for the wedding.

His thoughts about the wedding gift for Doc and Susan reminded him of the other "special gift" he'd been working on, the one ordered by Samuel Beiler for Rachel's birthday.

The taste in his mouth turned sour at the thought. Everything in him rebelled at the idea of Beiler having the right to give Rachel *anything*, much less a gift fashioned by Gant's own hands. He wished now he had flatly refused the man's request to build a sideboard for Rachel.

Whatever had possessed him to call Beiler's bluff? At least that was how it had felt at the time. Had it been pride, spite, or plain old Irish stubbornness?

Beiler had been so smug when he told Gant what he wanted, had actually seemed to savor Gant's initial awkwardness. Why hadn't he just swallowed his pride and dismissed the man without even considering the idea? But, no, he simply couldn't resist the temptation to best the Amish deacon by taking up what he assumed to be a deliberate challenge. He'd had to one-up him just to see the surprise on the other's face.

Now he was committed to providing something that no doubt

would endear Beiler to Rachel, when what he really wished to do was give the man a swift kick out of her life.

Thoroughly disgusted with himself, he blew out a long breath and went back inside. With all the work he had to do, there was no time to waste standing around making wishes.

Indeed, if wishes were fishes, every fool would cast nets.

Rachel was putting the final touches on the birdhouse she was making for Mamma and Dr. David's wedding gift. Reminding herself not to be prideful about her work, she nevertheless couldn't stop a smile at the sight of the white walls, the little blue porch, the intricate roof with its tiny wooden shingles, and the heart-shaped openings she'd cut out for windows.

If she did say so herself, it looked like a proper gift for a newly wed couple.

She wanted it to be special. It seemed to reflect her happiness for her mother and Dr. David, as she'd taken to calling him, echoing Fannie's name for the man who would soon become their stepfather. Mamma virtually glowed with happiness these days, and Dr. David was almost funny—in an ever so sweet way—every time he looked at Mamma with his heart in his eyes.

They were so right for each other! All their friends and neighbors said the same. It seemed that everyone wished them nothing but the best. But why wouldn't they? Mamma was always doing for others, always helping in whatever way she could, even lending encouragement and practical advice to the younger women who sought her wisdom. She was well-loved by the People.

And Dr. David—well, there was no measuring his goodness to the Plain People. For years he had sacrificed his time and energy and medical skills for the Amish of Riverhaven. He had been a loyal friend and a blessing to them all long before he and Mamma decided to marry.

The wedding was to be held at Mamma's house, where she and Dr. David would make their home. It would be a big event. No doubt almost all the People would attend as well as some of their *Englischer* friends. Rachel and Fannie had already promised, along with Sally Gingerich and Emma Knepp, to help clean the house from top to bottom a few days before the ceremony.

They would all feel dear Phoebe's absence during this time. Mamma had already shed more than a few tears when she spoke of how much she missed Phoebe and how she wished her friend could have been with them to share these blessed days.

Rachel missed her too but found some comfort in the awareness that, as much as Phoebe would have rejoiced with them during this happy time, she was now rejoicing in heaven. Any pain or fear she had experienced during the awful thing that had happened to her would have been washed away by now. She would be whole and well and at peace.

She and Mamma often talked about that these days. Mamma was reading Phoebe's Bible, giving special attention, she'd told Rachel, to the passages her friend had underlined—passages dealing with God's grace and the salvation available to them all through that grace.

Rachel could tell her mother was still questioning what Phoebe— and Rachel herself—had come to believe about the assurance of God's salvation, but she could sense that Mamma was gradually thinking and praying things through on her own. She was convinced that, more than all the discussions they'd had over the past few months about this very subject, those underlined Scripture verses had spoken the truth to her mother.

As she carefully set the birdhouse on a shelf to dry, she wondered, not for the first time, if Jeremiah would come to the wedding.

She was almost certain Dr. David would have invited him, good friends as they were. What would it be like to see him in her mother's house, among the People, a friend to many of them by now, though not one of them?

She had no doubt it would be difficult. It was always difficult to be near him while needing to avoid any real closeness. Yet she longed to see him, especially on such an important day.

There had been a time when Rachel dreamed of a wedding of their own, but the bishop's refusal to allow Jeremiah's conversion had shattered that dream, breaking her heart in the process. And yet somehow the two of them had remained friends. Even though they seldom saw each other, and even though they were forbidden to marry, something had bound them together. Still today there was a bond between them that time and distance had been unable to sever.

She still loved him. And unless she was gravely mistaken, what she saw in his eyes when he looked at her—that was love as well. Even so, she had fought against praying that the Lord God would change the bishop's mind. In truth she was often tempted to beg for that mercy, but instead she prayed for Jeremiah's best, for his wholeness and his happiness. She prayed that love would find him and that he would one day have a home and family of his own.

For herself—these days she prayed for peace, for the acceptance of God's will and the grace to live within it.

Somehow, now that she believed with all her heart that God had given her—*freely given her*—His love and His salvation, it simply didn't seem right to ask for more.

37

TOGETHER IN ONE PLACE

Think where man's glory most begins and ends,
And say my glory was I had such friends.

W. B. YEATS

In the early morning of her wedding day, Susan was surprised to realize that she wasn't nearly as *naerfich* as she had expected to be.

Oh, her stomach was tumbling, but that tended to happen on any special occasion. She would have thought that on this day, of all days, she would be a bundle of nerves, but in truth what she was most anxious about was the fact that Gideon hadn't made it home for the wedding.

She had so hoped he would be here. What mattered most, though, was that he stay safe, and according to the last note Captain Gant had received, both her son and Asa were all right.

Somehow she mustn't let her disappointment over Gideon's absence spoil the day for her and David. All she could do was pray for his safety and rely on the reassurance David had given her more than once that Gideon couldn't be in better hands than those of Captain Gant's friend, Asa. And as David also continued to remind her, her son was a man now, not a boy. He didn't need a "protector."

Maybe not, but she would feel better when she saw him standing before her again, well and healthy.

She started on a quick walk through the house, stopping in

her bedroom to admire again the wedding gift Captain Gant had dropped off the night before—an intricately carved memento chest of fine wood. The captain had etched "David and Susan Sebastian, November 9, 1856" on the lid. What a wonderful and beautiful gift! Bless him. The captain had acted awkward when he handed it to her until he finally seemed to realize that she was truly awed by his lovely, thoughtful gift.

As she continued on, she tried to be especially quiet. Rachel had spent the night, and she and Fannie were still sleeping. The house looked ever so *gut*. So many friends had come during the past few days to help her clean and scrub and polish in preparation for the ceremony. Rachel had offered her house for the wedding, but Susan really wanted to be married here, in the home where she had lived and raised her children over the years. Besides, they would have more room here—and they would probably need it all.

She shed a few tears as she roamed through the house, finally stopping in the kitchen. Thoughts of the years when the children were small and all the happy days they'd shared together within these walls came rushing in on her. How blessed she had been! Amos had been such a good and thoughtful husband. Her children were strong and healthy, each one of them, and they had done all they could after their father's death to help her maintain the farm. To this day even Fannie pitched in, young as she was, to assume a full measure of chores and, at the same time, delight Susan with her lively spirit and loving heart.

God had given her a wonderful life and had now added to it by allowing her to experience a second season of love with a fine and honorable man. She didn't deserve any of the gifts poured out upon her. No doubt Phoebe would have reminded her—as would Rachel these days—that God's grace and generous blessings were always free and undeserved, that *their* part was to accept His gifts and thank Him, not only with words from their lips but by the way they lived as well.

Her meeting with her memories came to an abrupt end when someone knocked on the kitchen door. She jumped, her heart pumping furiously as she went to peek out the back window. She saw a wagon pulled around at the rear of the house, but it was still too dark to tell who, if anyone, was in it.

Holding her breath, her hands shaking, she went to the door. At the same moment, the knocking sounded again. "Who's there?"

"It's me, Mamm."

Gideon!

Susan flung the door open with such force the very walls seemed to shake.

Her son stood there, grinning from ear to ear. His face was smudged with dust, his clothes rumpled, his eyes tired. But didn't he look wonderful-*gut!*

She was vaguely aware of the wagon pulling away even as Gideon stepped inside and opened his arms to her.

"Told you I'd be back in time for the wedding," he said.

Weeping and laughing at the same time, Susan hugged her boy until both of them had to draw back to catch a breath.

"You're all right?"

"I'm fine, Mamm. All in one piece. So is Asa. He dropped me off before going on to Riverhaven."

"You look awfully tired, son."

He laughed at her. "Don't fuss, Mamm. I really *am* fine. I was thinking you might still have some of my Plain clothes on hand," he said. "As you can see, I need to clean up a bit before the wedding."

"Of course, I still have your clothes," she choked out. "I was hoping you'd want them again eventually."

He put up a hand. "Now, Mamm, it's just for today, mind," he said quietly. "I figure your wedding day ought to be special, as happy as any day can be."

Susan reached up to grasp his shoulders. "And it is, son! *Now* it is."

→←

In one of the bedrooms on the second floor, David and Susan sat on two straight-backed chairs, receiving their prewedding counsel and encouragement from Bishop Shrock.

Every now and then, David couldn't help but glance at Susan, and every time he did, he nearly lost his breath. And why wouldn't he? She was breathtakingly lovely in her robin's-egg blue dress and crisp white apron. He caught her eye once and winked, enjoying her startled look and the faint blush that crept up her delicate features.

And then it was time to go downstairs and be seated. After the People sang a portion of the "Lob Lied" from the *Ausbund*—the Amish hymnal—Samuel Beiler, their only deacon, solemnly delivered the first sermon of the ceremony in German.

David did his best to put aside his personal reservations about Beiler, which was easier to do than he would have thought as he struggled to follow the German. His new second language was still a challenge for him, particularly when spoken at length. He had to pay close attention to understand each word in context.

Before they knelt in silent prayer, his gaze swept over the wedding guests. Susan's entire family, including Gideon, was there. So too were her friends and neighbors—Malachi Esch and his sons, Abe Gingerich and his family, and many others. A number of David's patients were also in attendance.

He glanced back to Gideon, somewhat amused by the way Susan's son couldn't seem to tear his gaze away from the Knepp girl. *Interesting.*

The house was full to bursting. It looked as though almost the entire community of the Plain People had turned out today. Susan had to be pleased at the sight of so many gathered together to share their wedding day with them.

And there was Gant, looking uncommonly formal in a dark

suit and tie, sitting in the back with their other *Englisch* friends and neighbors. His Irish friend's eyes seemed locked on the back of Rachel's head, except for an instant when his gaze met David's and he shot him a quick, roguish grin.

When they knelt in silent prayer for several minutes after the deacon's sermon, David realized his eyes were moist. Quite simply he was overwhelmed with feelings—with love for Susan, appreciation for her family and all their friends, with fervent gratitude to his Lord and Savior for this day of days.

"Thy blessing is upon thy people..."

Bishop Shrock preached the main sermon, after which he motioned to David and Susan to join him in front to hear their replies to the questions he posed and pronounce them husband and wife.

It was a blessed moment—a holy moment—and both the bride and the groom welcomed it with tears in their eyes.

→ ←

Gant had never attended a wedding like this. There were no flowers and no decorations other than the plain and simple loveliness of the bride's home—and the bride herself. No music was performed besides the unaccompanied hymn singing—not even a fiddle. His Irish countrymen would have been scandalized entirely.

And yet it was perfect—a perfect wedding for two very special people. He smiled, then caught himself feeling a little wistful at the sight of Susan tearing up and Doc's noticeably red-rimmed eyes. Even from the back of the room, he could sense his friend's emotion as the ceremony ended.

Come to think of it, he needed to wipe his own eyes. Now *that* had never happened at any other wedding he could think of.

Aye, it was a perfect day, and he was glad for them. But one question had been gnawing at him from the moment he became aware of Bishop Graber's absence. A different bishop officiating at this particular wedding was a real puzzle. He would have thought Doc and Susan would have been intent on having their own bishop present for their wedding. He couldn't believe they would have agreed to a last-minute switch unless there had been some sort of emergency. He made a mental note to ask Doc about it later on.

He realized then that the ceremony had ended. He stood and, with the other guests, moved outside to the rear lawn, where tables and benches had been set up, ready for the wedding meal.

Because it was November, the day was cool and had a sharp bite to it. But the sun was a golden sphere in the bright autumn sky, and no one seemed to notice the chill.

Gant went to offer his congratulations to the bride and groom, trying not to mind the sight of Samuel Beiler hovering about Rachel, his sternly fixed features now gone almost soft with attention to her. He was perversely pleased to see the way she avoided Beiler's closeness. In fact she seemed to keep her gaze deliberately averted from his, and he didn't think he imagined the way she backed off every time Beiler attempted to close the distance between them.

Clearly, though, the Amish deacon couldn't take a hint. Beiler seemed determined to shadow her every step, causing Gant to grind his teeth to the point of an aching jaw.

Platters and trays and buckets of food were carried from the house and set upon the tables, which soon looked fit to topple. Never in his life had Gant seen so much food in one place! The sight of such bounty tempted him to join the others for what looked to be nothing less than a veritable feast, but he simply wasn't comfortable doing so. He still keenly felt the sting of being an *outsider* in their midst.

He glanced at David and Susan, saw them surrounded by well-wishers, saw Rachel still being tracked by Beiler, and started to walk away, leaning heavily on his cane.

At the edge of the lawn, he was stopped by Fannie Kanagy rushing up to him and tugging at his sleeve.

"You aren't leaving, are you, Captain Gant?"

"I'm afraid I must, Miss Fannie. I have much work to do yet today."

"You can't go *now*!" she insisted. "You don't want the People to think you're *rilpsich,* do you?"

"And what would that mean—*rilpsich*?"

She frowned at him. "It means *rude,*" she said pointedly. "You're supposed to stay and eat."

Gant made an encompassing gesture with his arm. "Look at all these people, Miss Fannie. No one will even know I'm gone."

"*I'll* know," said a quiet voice behind him.

→ EPILOGUE ←

A TASTE OF HOPE

Be of good courage, and he shall strengthen your heart,
All ye that hope in the LORD.

PSALM 31:24

I'll know…"

Gant whipped around to find Rachel standing behind him.

She met his eyes, then glanced at her sister. "Fannie, I want to speak with Captain Gant, please. Would you go and see if there's any help needed in the kitchen before you eat?"

Fannie looked from one to the other, shrugged her shoulders, then ran to the house.

"Rachel…"

Gant stared at her, dizzy with her nearness. Caught totally off guard by her approach, her words, the way she was looking at him, he felt frozen, unable to speak or to move.

"Please stay, Jeremiah. Mamma and Dr. David would want you to share their wedding meal with us." She paused, her gaze never leaving his face. "And so do I."

Gant struggled to collect at least a thread of composure. "I—thought it would be best if I were to leave," he said.

She actually smiled, as if she sensed his confusion, his awkwardness. "You don't really want a lecture from Dr. David, do you?"

Gant studied her, finally managing to breathe again. "I can handle Doc. He's all bluff, you know."

He hesitated, fumbling for something civilized to say, inane as it might be. "It was a really nice wedding. I'm sure you had a lot to do with that."

"Not really," she said. "Amish weddings don't take a lot of planning. I've heard that *Englisch* ceremonies are more—involved."

Gant pulled a face. "Some of them are a bunch of foolishness, to my way of thinking."

She laughed, and he couldn't stop a smile. It was just so good to have her standing close to him, talking to him, hearing her laugh. Somehow it almost seemed…right.

Even though he knew it was anything *but* right.

"They'll be happy," Gant said. "Doc and your mother."

Her smile brightened still more. "Oh, I know they will! They're so—good for each other. They've known each other for years, after all. Mamma said last night that she was marrying her best friend." She stopped. "Well, there was Phoebe, of course…"

Gant nodded. "I know what you mean. You must miss Phoebe too. You were close friends, after all."

"I *do* miss her. A lot." She raised her eyes to his then. "I miss you too, Jeremiah. We were friends as well."

"We're still friends, Rachel," Gant managed.

She studied him, her eyes raking his face as if in search of something hidden. "Are we?"

On impulse he reached toward her, meaning to take her hand, but stopped. "Yes, Rachel. We are."

"I thought—there's something I think you should know." She paused. Her next words spilled out quickly and randomly, like glass marbles falling from a jar. "The bishop—Bishop Graber—may have to retire soon."

Gant stared at her, his throat suddenly going dry. "What— *why?*"

"He's ill. I only learned about it last night. I shouldn't say anything, but since you were at the wedding today and saw that he wasn't there, I knew you'd wonder…"

Gant nodded, his mind racing. "This other fellow—"

"Bishop Shrock," she put in.

"Aye. Will he take Bishop Graber's place?"

"No. He just came today to fill in. Bishop Graber didn't feel well enough to participate. If it becomes necessary, the next bishop will be chosen from among our own men."

"Rachel—"

She went on as if she hadn't heard him. "If Bishop Graber does have to retire, a new bishop will be chosen by lot. There are three men in our community who would be eligible—our ministers, Abe Gingerich and Malachi Esch, and our deacon…Samuel Beiler."

Gant pulled in a ragged breath but said nothing. All he could do was look at her. He felt as if he were falling into her heart. He knew as well as she did what this might mean. A chance at least.

Depending on the man.

He could almost taste the hope struggling to rise within him, yet he knew it could also spell the *end* of any hope.

Depending on the man.

He was aware that his hands had begun to tremble. In truth his entire body felt shaky, as if he might simply break and fall to pieces.

Instead he knotted his hands into fists and clenched his jaw, forcing himself to a steadiness that he knew might betray him at any moment.

"You won't say anything—to anyone else?" Rachel asked.

Gant shook his head. "No. Not to anyone. But Rachel—"

She looked at him, then shook her head and put a finger to her lips. "We mustn't talk any more about it. There's nothing to do but pray."

"*How* do you pray about something like this, Rachel? Tell me. Tell me *how*—and I'll pray too," he said, finding the words awkward to voice but sincere. "What do you ask for?"

As he watched, her features settled into a gentle look of serenity. "You ask for God's choice, Jeremiah. God's choice…and the grace to accept His decision."

Her expression changed then, brightening, even turning lively. She lifted a hand as if in invitation. "And now I'm asking you again—come and share the wedding meal with us. Please. As a friend among friends."

Gant hesitated, drinking in for one more moment the goodness and loveliness of her face, the hint of a promise in her eyes, before stepping out to follow her.

Did you miss book one in The Riverhaven Years...

RACHEL'S SECRET *by BJ Hoff*

Bestselling author BJ Hoff promises to delight you with her compelling new series, *The Riverhaven Years*. With the first book, *Rachel's Secret*, Hoff introduces a new community of unforgettable characters and adds the elements you have come to expect from her novels: a tender love story, the faith journeys of people we grow to know and love, and enough suspense to keep the pages turning quickly.

When the wounded Irish American riverboat captain, Jeremiah Gant, bursts into the rural Amish setting of Riverhaven, he brings chaos and conflict to the community—especially for young widow, Rachel Brenneman. The unwelcome "outsider" needs a safe place to recuperate before continuing his secret role as an Underground Railroad conductor. Neither he nor Rachel is prepared for the forbidden love that threatens to endanger a man's mission, a woman's heart, and a way of life for an entire people.

Discussion Questions

1. Early in the story, Gant refers to the rules of the Amish ministerial brethren as "manipulation." He seems to believe these rules have been established to prevent the Plain People from being infected by the "worldly influence" of the English (the non-Amish). What's your understanding of these regulations? Do you agree with Gant? Are they a means of manipulation, or what is the primary purpose behind them?

2. When Gant tells Rachel of the bishop's refusal to allow him to convert—thereby making it impossible for them to marry—she seems to accept the decision as the final word on the subject and tells Gant she can't go against the bishop. Could you do that? If your church required that you give up any hope of marrying the person you love or that you disassociate yourself from a loved one, even a family member, would you be able to obey, or would you be more inclined to give up your church?

3. Rachel and her mother, Susan, approach the assurance of salvation from different perspectives, which prompts the question from Rachel: "Do you really think it's so wrong to have questions about God's will for us? Don't you think He would *want* us to understand His teachings?" How would *you* answer that question?

4. What do you believe was the purpose behind Gant's special gift to Rachel's younger sister, Fannie?

5. Why did Gant and Asa seem surprised to see Gideon doing the supper dishes? What's the typical division of labor between Amish men and Amish women? How do you feel about this? Are tasks clearly marked in your household as to who does what? Does the system work well for you and your family?

6. What do you believe to be Gant's motivation for helping runaway slaves through the Underground Railroad? What prompts him to risk his own freedom to help others gain *their* freedom?

7. Incidents of harassment, persecution, and oppression have followed the Amish across time and place throughout the years. What do you believe accounts for such mistreatment? Can you relate their experience to other religions or ethnic groups?

8. How does Gant feel about the Riverhaven Amish? What does he see in them and their community that he secretly longs for in his own life?

9. What was your initial impression of Terry Sawyer, the newcomer to Riverhaven? Did your opinion change with the progression of the story? If so, why?

10. We often find experiences out of our "comfort zone" difficult to endure. Little about the flight North held any "comfort" for the runaway slaves. Obviously their primary concern and the source of their courage had to do with freedom. What would motivate you to submit to some of the harrowing events, dangers, and discomforts faced by the refugee slaves who were so desperate to make their way to the North?

11. What is the first sign to some of the Plain People—including Rachel and her mother—that something might be wrong with the bishop? Dr. Sebastian is also concerned, but what's the reason for their hesitancy to discuss the possible problem?

12. As much as Gant and Rachel love each other and want to be together, their prayers for each other take a different turn and begin to go in an unexpected direction. What do you believe accounts for this?

Enjoy cooking the Amish way...

THE HOMESTYLE AMISH KITCHEN COOKBOOK
by Georgia Varozza

Just about everyone is fascinated by the Amish—their simple, family-centered lifestyle, colorful quilts, and hearty, homemade meals. Straight from the heart of Amish country, this celebration of hearth and home will delight readers with the pleasures of the family table as they take a peek at the Amish way of life—a life filled with the self-reliance and peace of mind that many of us long for.

Readers will appreciate the tasty, easy-to-prepare recipes such as Scrapple, Graham "Nuts" Cereal, Potato Rivvel Soup, Amish Dressing, and Snitz Pie. At the same time they'll learn a bit about the Amish, savor interesting tidbits from the "Amish Kitchen Wisdom" sections, find out just how much food it takes to feed the large number of folks attending preaching services, barn raisings, weddings, and work frolics, and much more.

The Homestyle Amish Kitchen Cookbook is filled with good, old-fashioned family meal ideas to help bring the simple life home!

Shoo-Fly Pie

2 8-inch unbaked pie crusts

Syrup:
1 cup molasses
½ cup brown sugar
2 eggs, beaten
1 cup hot water
1 tsp. baking soda,
dissolved in hot water

Crumb Topping:
2 cups flour
¾ cup brown sugar
⅓ cup butter
½ tsp. cinnamon

Mix syrup ingredients thoroughly together. Divide mixture in half and pour into the two unbaked pie shells. Thoroughly mix together the ingredients for the crumb topping. Divide and sprinkle crumb topping onto the two pies.

Bake at 450° for 10 minutes and then reduce heat to 350° and continue baking until done, about another 30 minutes.

Enjoy!